YOU CAN TELL ME

ALSO BY MELINDA LEIGH

Echo Road

Bree Taggert Novels

Cross Her Heart

See Her Die

Drown Her Sorrows

Right Behind Her

"Her Second Death" (A Prequel Short Story)

Dead Against Her

Lie to Her

Catch Her Death

On Her Watch

Track Her Down

Beyond Her Reach

Kill for Her

Morgan Dane Novels

Say You're Sorry

Her Last Goodbye

Bones Don't Lie

What I've Done

Secrets Never Die

Save Your Breath

Scarlet Falls Novels

Hour of Need

Minutes to Kill

Seconds to Live

She Can Series

She Can Run

She Can Tell

She Can Scream

She Can Hide

"He Can Fall" (A Short Story)

She Can Kill

Midnight Novels

Midnight Exposure

Midnight Sacrifice

Midnight Betrayal

Midnight Obsession

The Rogue Series Novellas

Gone to Her Grave (Rogue River)

Walking on Her Grave (Rogue River)

Tracks of Her Tears (Rogue Winter)

Burned by Her Devotion (Rogue Vows)

Twisted Truth (Rogue Justice)

The Widow's Island Novella Series

A Bone to Pick

Whisper of Bones

A Broken Bone

Buried Bones

The Wrong Bones

YOU CAN TELL ME

MELINDA LEIGH

Montlake

Published by Montlake, Seattle

www.apub.com

EU product safety contact:
Amazon Media EU S. à r.l.
38, avenue John F. Kennedy, L-1855 Luxembourg
amazonpublishing-gpsr@amazon.com

ISBN-13: 9781662516993 (hardcover)
ISBN-13: 9781662517006 (paperback)
ISBN-13: 9781662517013 (digital)

Cover design by Shasti O'Leary Soudant
Cover image: © Jarno Saren / ArcAngel Images

Printed in the United States of America
First edition

For Logan.
I'm amazed by how much I can love someone I just met.
Welcome to the world.

Chapter One

Three years ago

Olivia jolted, her heartbeat quickening, sweat dampening her T-shirt.

What was that?

A glance at the clock on her nightstand told her hours had passed. It felt as if she'd just closed her eyes, but she must have fallen asleep. She scanned the darkness of her bedroom. Her gaze passed over her dresser and chair. Had she heard something real, or had it been a dream?

She concentrated, listening hard to the sounds of her house, but she heard nothing unusual. A thunk and hum signaled the heater switching on. Hot air blew out of the floor vent and moved the sheers that hung over her windows.

The alarm hadn't sounded. She reached for her phone. It was far too early to rise for the day. She double-checked the security system app on her phone. The house was secure. She needed to go back to sleep.

She shifted her legs under the covers, closed her eyes, and tried to get comfortable.

Something whooshed. Her eyes snapped open. A large shape rushed toward her. A heavy body landed on top of her, pinning her to the mattress. The weight and size of her attacker felt male. She flailed and tried to push him off, but her arms and legs were trapped as he straddled her.

She was cocooned in her comforter like a swaddled baby. Her throat constricted. She couldn't scream.

Panic sprinted through her bloodstream as she stared up at the dark assailant looming over her. His face seemed distorted, his features brighter and flatter than normal ones. He was wearing a mask.

With a bolt of gut-twisting horror, she recognized the character as Michael Myers from the movie *Halloween*.

A flash of terror shot up her spine. She inhaled, preparing to force a scream out of her tight throat.

He slapped her across the face. Pain, bright and sharp, sang through her cheekbone but faded in seconds as her adrenaline surged. The scream died in her chest.

He waved a knife in front of her face, then pressed a gloved finger to the mask's rubber lips. *"Shhh."*

Olivia stilled. Given their positions, she couldn't move anyway, and it was unlikely a neighbor would be able to hear her scream, not with her insulated windows closed.

Pretend to cooperate. Wait for an opportunity.

Her instinct was to flail, but he'd disabled both her flight and her fight responses. Her pulse echoed in her ears, each beat of her heart ramming against her breastbone. Her breaths came faster, until she was nearly hyperventilating.

What was he going to do?

After shrugging off his small backpack, he tossed it onto the bed next to her, then unzipped it. He set down the knife and shifted his weight from knee to knee while jerking her hands out from under the covers one at a time. He held both her wrists in one of his hands. She tried to pull away, but her wrists were thin and his grip secure. He pulled something from his bag, and fresh fear raced through her. She swallowed the metallic taste as he wrapped duct tape securely around both of her wrists. Once her hands were bound, he slapped a piece of tape across her mouth as well.

Tears ran from her eyes. Her nose clogged. She couldn't draw in enough air through only her nose. She grew lightheaded. Could she suffocate with her mouth covered? Her vision dimmed. Spots appeared in front of her eyes.

She needed to control her breathing. Lincoln's voice echoed in her mind. *Inhale, two, three, four. Hold, two, three, four. Exhale, two, three, four.* After three breath cycles, her vision cleared.

The intruder climbed off the bed and yanked the blankets off her body. Under her flannel pajama bottoms and sweatshirt, Olivia shivered, fighting the panic that threatened to debilitate her. Whatever he was going to do, she needed to be ready to react. If he was going to rape her, he'd need to take his hands off her to unfasten his pants. But he made no movement in that direction. Instead, he bound her ankles with duct tape.

Olivia's muscles went rigid. If he was going to kill her, he would have done it already, right?

While she was battling panic, he appeared calm. His movements were efficient and smooth, calculated, as if he were simply performing a chore. He didn't hurry, and he didn't appear to be excited.

Maybe he just wanted to rob the house. He acted almost professional. Hope blossomed inside her. She didn't care what he took as long as he left.

Please.

He showed her the knife again and whispered, "Don't move."

She froze. Standing next to the bed, he picked up her cell phone and the fob to her security system she had set on her nightstand. He slid both items into his pockets, then zipped his backpack and put it on.

Take what you want and go.

Olivia held completely still and tried not to make any noise—an effort to make him forget she was even there. She would give him no reason to harm her.

But he turned to face her again. His eyes were hidden behind the dark holes in the mask. She felt rather than saw his scrutiny. A whimper sounded deep in her throat.

No.

Please.

He leaned over, grabbed her by the arms, and hauled her to a sitting position on the side of the bed. The truth rushed over Olivia like ice water. He wasn't there for her things.

He was there for her.

Chapter Two

Today

Zoe March leaned over her microphone. She loved the end of a season. She'd worked for months to lay out a true crime case for her audience. Now she would get to see how they perceived the evidence she'd uncovered and presented. "On the first seven episodes of this season of *You Won't Believe This*, we've conducted our own investigation into the disappearance of Jonelle Collins eleven years ago. We've spoken with her friends and family, none of whom believe that Jonelle simply walked away from her life because she was despondent over her divorce. She'd built a successful career and devoted her life to her two children. According to her ex-husband, he and Jonelle had an unusually amicable relationship focused on coparenting. He doesn't believe Jonelle would have left her children. The police, however, found no evidence of foul play and declined to investigate further."

She spent a few minutes summing up some of the more interesting details of the case. "To those of you who've listened to all seven episodes, what do you think? Did Jonelle vanish willingly? Was she the victim of a stranger or serial killer, as her mother believes? Or is someone who was close to Jonelle lying?" Zoe sat back and switched her tone from mysterious to inquisitive. "Now, we want to hear from our listeners. What do you believe?"

Seated next to Zoe, her producer, Wendy Simon, flipped a switch and tapped a piece of paper with a name written on it.

Zoe nodded. "Let's take caller number one, Patrice from Albany. Hi, Patrice. What do *you* believe happened to Jonelle Collins?"

An older woman's voice sounded in Zoe's headphones. "I think her husband is lying. I don't know anyone who is best friends with their ex. He killed her for the money."

"Is there something specific that makes you believe this?" Zoe reinforced her show's branding by repeating the word *believe*, a recent suggestion from Wendy. To Zoe, the repetition felt awkward, but she'd give it a try.

"His statements just aren't believable," Patrice said.

"Are you married, Patrice?" Zoe asked. Personal connections made the show more interesting. People wanted conflict. They might claim to watch documentaries, but research showed they loved reality TV more.

"I've been married to the love of my life for forty-two years," Patrice answered. "Here's the thing. Jonelle and Travis were married for twelve years. Marriages are built on emotion, and it's rare that both spouses agree that they want to dissolve a long-term relationship. One person always gets their feelings hurt. If my husband ever left me, I'd be devastated."

"So, your theory is based on your personal experience with a good marriage?"

"Yes," Patrice said. "Jonelle's husband moved on to another woman awfully fast. I think he killed her so he wouldn't have to pay alimony or child support. Plus, he eventually collected on her life insurance. Win-win for him."

"Do you think both parties can ever agree that their marriage isn't working?" Zoe asked.

"I guess it's possible, but I've never seen it."

"You've raised some interesting points, Patrice. Thanks for calling in." Zoe ended the call. "Does anyone else agree with Patrice?"

Wendy wrote another name.

Zoe continued. "Greg from Glens Falls, tell us what you believe."

A man answered, "I agree with Patrice. When couples split up, one of them is always resentful. But I think Jonelle was the one who cheated, and that's why Travis killed her."

"Why do you think that?" Zoe asked.

"First off, he refused your request for an interview, but he did a bunch of other interviews. Why not talk to you? I think he was only willing to discuss preapproved, softball topics. He didn't want to face someone who would ask hard questions. He didn't want to be challenged."

Zoe was flattered. She'd been a reporter in the past, back when hard-copy newspapers were delivered to doorsteps every morning—before generating clicks became more important than reporting the truth. She liked to think she brought an element of hard-hitting journalism to her true crime podcast, but sometimes she felt like her show was devolving into clickbait territory. People wanted gossip. They reveled in scandals. There had to be a way to grow her audience without resorting to sensationalism. "So you think he was jealous?"

"Oh, yeah. Plus, I know if my wife cheated on me, broke up our family, and I had to pay alimony because of it, I'd be pissed." And there it was: the personal connection. No one existed in an emotional vacuum. It was unusual that human beings could be completely objective. Everyone carried their own insecurities based on *their* life history. Rare was the individual who could truly put themselves into another person's perspective. Callers' opinions on the cases were almost always a reflection of their own experiences.

Zoe knew this because her own personal situation was fucked. But she found it so much easier to critique other people than deal with her own life issues.

She let a few seconds of silence punctuate Greg's statement. "Are you married, Greg?"

"Yeah." His answer was too clipped.

"And you love your wife?" she asked.

"Of course I love my wife." Anger resonated in his words, but then his tone softened. "And she loves me." She heard the doubt behind the conviction.

Zoe lowered her voice. "And you'd naturally feel hurt, angry, and betrayed if she cheated on you."

"Naturally."

"But you'd never kill her because of it, would you?"

"Of course not! I never said I would!"

"But you said you think Jonelle's husband killed her because he was jealous over an affair and angry that she cheated, and he might have to pay alimony. Yet we have no proof Jonelle was cheating. In fact, it was her husband who moved on to another woman." Zoe almost felt guilty for what she would say next. Then again, Greg was putting out nasty, suspicious undercurrents. "Is your wife cheating on you, Greg?"

Greg snapped. "Fuck you!" The line went dead.

Zoe spoke to her listeners. "I guess Greg doesn't want to answer difficult questions either."

Wendy gave her a thumbs-up and an excited grin. She loved the reality-show vibe, but the exchange left a sour taste in Zoe's mouth. How would listeners view her discussion with Greg? She didn't like provoking callers during live shows. When she taped episodes ahead, she could listen to her words, edit mistakes, ensure she said exactly what she meant. Live shows brought additional stress in permanency. Once something was out there in the digital void, there was no getting it back.

Yet she had to admit Wendy made some good suggestions. This season of the podcast was the most successful yet. Listener analytics showed increases in subscribers and an improvement in engagement. People were tuning in, and the show was holding their attention. The number of callers had doubled compared to last season.

Zoe glanced at the recording time. She liked to keep each episode to sixty minutes or less. Over the past ten years, attention spans had contracted like Shrinky Dinks in the oven. "We can take one more caller." She still had to do the season wrap-up and the teaser for her upcoming special.

Wendy tapped another name handwritten on her notepad.

Zoe said, "Abel from Auburn, you're on the air."

"Hi, Zoe. Longtime listener. First-time caller."

His voice lifted goose bumps on Zoe's arms. He wasn't exactly whispering, but his tone was soft, almost suggestive. Something about it was familiar, as if her subconscious recognized him. Was Abel someone she knew?

She swallowed. "What do you believe, Abel?"

Abel continued to speak in his strange whisper. "I think someone killed Jonelle and hid the body to make it appear as if she'd left. Maybe her remains will be pulled out of a lake someday."

The hairs on the back of Zoe's neck rose. She shook off the sense of foreboding. "What makes you believe this, Abel?"

"Because betrayal is human nature, isn't it?" he asked. "People sin, and they've done so since biblical times."

"Who do you think betrayed Jonelle?"

"Someone close to her. After all, murder is a most personal act." His whisper took on a mocking tone. "You should know that better than anyone."

She didn't want to ask the natural follow-up question: *How so?* There was no way she'd take the conversation in an even more personal direction. She wanted to hang up and accept another call. But her listeners would want her to respect her caller. Plus, Wendy was rolling her hand, her expression encouraging. Zoe decided to assume he meant she should know because of her podcast.

Zoe redirected the discussion back to the caller. "Have you been betrayed, Abel?"

"In the worst way."

"By someone close to you?" Zoe's voice cracked.

"If it isn't someone close to you, someone you trust, then it wouldn't be a betrayal, would it? A stranger can't betray you." Abel's voice sank into a true whisper. "Everyone has their Cain."

Suddenly chilled, Zoe rubbed her biceps. The caller's voice definitely sounded familiar in some way she couldn't pinpoint. She didn't know anyone called Abel. The name was distinct. She wouldn't forget meeting an Abel.

Maybe that isn't his real name.

"Was it your brother?" Zoe's belly knotted as she drew on the biblical reference. Inexplicable tension filled the sound booth.

"Yes, and no." Was he toying with her?

"Can you explain?" This was her show. She was in charge. Abel was the one in the hot seat, so to speak. Yet it did not feel that way.

"I don't have to. You already know."

Her mouth went dry. Sweat broke out under her arms.

No! It couldn't be.

Zoe ended the call abruptly, smacking the button like she was swatting a spider. She stared at the microphone, her heartbeat accelerating in her chest as if every beat were a footstep and she were running away.

Wendy mouthed, "What the fuck?"

Zoe ignored her.

But Wendy wasn't so easily put off. She nudged Zoe with an elbow and motioned for her to keep going. She mouthed, "We're live."

Shaking, Zoe glanced at her notes and wiped her damp palms on her thighs. She could barely think. Thankfully, she'd closed her show dozens of times. Her subconscious kicked in. Yet she was incapable of slowing her words. They rushed from her mouth. "And that's all the time we have this week. I hope you enjoyed our investigation into the murder of Jonelle Collins. Join us next week for the first part of our exclusive special interview with true crime writer Olivia Cruz, who was the victim of a bizarre and horrific kidnapping three years ago, as Olivia talks for the first time about her terrifying ordeal. Also, follow us on social media and look for our announcement on the case we're delving into for next season. This is Zoe March, signing off on *You Won't Believe This*."

Wendy ended the live recording. "What the fuck was that, Zoe?"

"I don't know. He freaked me out." She pressed a hand to the base of her throat, where anxiety threatened to choke her.

"He *was* creepy. Which is exactly why you should have kept him going for a few more minutes. The tension he brought to the show was incredible. You could have milked that. Listeners were probably holding their breath."

"Maybe." But nausea flattened Zoe like a steamroller. The air felt stifling, and the small sound booth seemed to shrink. She needed to change the conversation. She needed a distraction. "Let's finish prepping for tomorrow's interview." She bolted for the door, as if Abel had physically been in the room.

"OK."

Zoe went into her office. Wendy followed. They spent the next two hours reviewing and editing the list of questions. But Zoe couldn't get Abel out of her mind. She could still hear his voice, crawling through her like an earworm, as if he were stalking her thoughts.

"Make sure you press her on the specifics. Listeners want the dirty details."

Zoe hated that saying. "We're not a tabloid."

"But we need to generate rapt attention, which leads to subscribers, which lead to sponsors."

"We do. Olivia's story will do that without us reducing ourselves to paparazzi." Zoe would glean what she could from her guest—who was also a friend—while being respectful and professional. The interview would be hard enough on Olivia without Zoe making it worse.

"I think you're overestimating the attention span of the general public. They like a juicy scandal more than the facts." Wendy wasn't as concerned with respecting guests—or rooting out the truth. She wanted to monetize everything.

"I appreciate the need to be profitable, believe me," Zoe said. "But I won't choose money over integrity."

Her podcast commenter whispered in her imagination.

You already know.

She couldn't escape Abel's words.

"I think we're done," Zoe said. She had to get out of that room. Air. She needed air.

"OK," Wendy agreed. "Every word doesn't have to be perfect on the first take. The interview isn't live. We can edit."

Zoe's phone vibrated on the desktop. Dylan's picture flashed. Zoe sent the call to voicemail.

"You don't want to get that?" Wendy raised a brow.

"I'll call him on the way home."

After casting her a disapproving glance, Wendy headed to her own office. Zoe texted Olivia to meet her a little early, so they could discuss the questions without her producer's input. Then Zoe stood, collecting her purse, laptop, and notes, then shoved everything into her backpack. She slung the bag over one shoulder and rounded her desk toward the door. Her phone buzzed with a text. She glanced at the screen. *Unknown number.*

Probably spam.

But her fingers trembled as they hovered over the messages app. She took a shaky breath and tapped the screen. Every organ in her body went cold as ice. Her knees buckled. She slapped a palm on her desktop to steady herself.

No.

"Hold on," Wendy called. "I'll walk out with you."

But Zoe could only stare at the message on her phone screen as fear wrapped around her chest, coiling, tightening until she could barely draw a breath.

Chapter Three

Olivia Cruz adjusted the handles of the coffee mugs on her kitchen shelf so each of her perfectly spaced mugs pointed in exactly the same direction.

The squeak of sneaker treads announced the return of her boyfriend, Lincoln Sharp, from his morning run—though there was nothing about Lincoln that looked boyish. His eyes roamed constantly. A former police detective turned private investigator, he had a gaze that matched his name—always assessing, always suspicious.

He tugged off his black-brimmed cap. As he toed off his sneakers, he ran a hand over his salt-and-pepper hair, as if his buzz cut were long enough to get mussed. He had the lean, hard build of a runner and was fitter than most people half his age. "I have a laser level if you want to make them exactly even."

She turned back to her open cabinet. She didn't need Lincoln's comment to know exactly what her perfectly positioned mugs were—precise rows of tiny soldiers she used to battle the demons she couldn't vanquish. She'd had enough therapy to know she controlled her environment when her memories made her feel powerless. With a deliberate movement, she closed the cabinet. She turned to face him and changed the subject. "How was your run?"

"Fine." He crossed the kitchen to stand next to her and switch on the electric kettle. He reached past her, opened the cabinet, and selected a mug. After setting it on the counter, he added a green tea bag and looped the tag around the handle once. "Want to join me in a cold plunge?"

Olivia shuddered. "No, thank you. I don't know how you bear it."

He shrugged. "It's good for inflammation."

"Still a hard pass for me." Olivia was mostly disciplined about diet and exercise, but she was never going to willingly submerge her body in ice-cold water regardless of its anti-inflammatory properties. She shivered again at the thought.

"Why don't you let me go with you today?"

Olivia stiffened at the suggestion, not because the idea was abhorrent—no, the opposite. She'd love to take him with her. But it was far too easy to rely on Lincoln to ease her anxiety. She wouldn't allow herself to become over-reliant. The more she let him be her protector, the more she would want it.

As it was, she struggled with being alone in her house at night. Prior to her abduction, she'd loved her little bungalow and had felt very safe in it. She'd moved to Scarlet Falls in upstate New York when she'd inherited the property from an aunt, at the same time she'd changed careers. The house was nothing like the modern loft she'd previously rented, but the little house had grown on her as she'd renovated and painted, made it her own—made it her home. Yet she no longer felt secure in it. Her kidnapper hadn't taken her life, but he'd stolen a piece of her, and she was determined to take it back.

She forced her shoulders to relax. "I need to do this myself."

He contemplated her for a few seconds, the deepening of the crow's-feet at the corners of his eyes somehow making him even more attractive. "I appreciate that, but the offer stands."

"You have a full schedule. Aren't you and Lance tied up all day with your case?"

"Yes, but you come first. If you need me, I'll cancel." His tone suggested he regretted making plans with his younger partner, Lance Kruger.

Olivia's heart warmed. So tempting. *No!* She mentally rolled her eyes. *Do not give in to his charm.* "Lance needs you to watch his back. I won't be alone, and I shouldn't need a security escort for a simple drive into the countryside."

Lincoln's gaze never wavered. "To the place where you were held captive."

Her heartbeat stumbled, and she broke eye contact. "It's been three years . . ."

"I don't think that's something you just *get over*."

She raised her chin and met his gaze again. "If I never step beyond my comfort zone, I will *never* get over it."

"I shouldn't have made plans for today." He'd been with her for the first two terrible anniversaries. But his current investigation had heated up over the past week, and he needed to stay on it or risk losing momentum.

"I told you to." Olivia usually wrote about crimes inflicted on other people. She sympathized with victims and their families, but as an outsider, she could be objective, one step removed from the emotions, able to visualize them, but always at an arm's length. Today, she would be on the other side of the interview, recounting her own experience as a victim for a friend's true crime podcast—*You Won't Believe This*. She hoped that going public with all the details—forcing herself to recount the trauma in a logical, clinical, and public fashion—would somehow purge it from her soul. No more secrets. No more holding back. No more wondering if the person she was talking to knew her truth. It would all be out there. "I need to do this—without you. I *need* to be independent. It's something I have to prove to myself, that I can function—that he didn't take something from me that I'll never get back. I can't explain it any better than that."

He wrapped his arms around her and kissed her head. "I get it, and it makes sense." He had more faith in her than she did. For a few seconds, she leaned into him, absorbing his body heat, as if she could borrow some of his confidence. But no, she needed to find it for herself. Some things had to be acquired the hard way.

"I haven't been able to write since." And there was her long-term fear.

He frowned down at her. "If you need money . . ."

"It's not just about the money." Her book sales hadn't stopped, but they had leveled off, which was normal. "I won't starve, and I inherited this house, but that's not the whole issue. I'm a writer. It's more than what I do. It's who I am, who I've been my entire adult life. Even before that. I was the editor of my high school newspaper. I don't remember a time when I wasn't looking for the truth and writing about it."

"You're more than any job."

She pressed away. "Thank you, but I'm not ready to give it up just yet." She wouldn't let her kidnapper take away her career too. Though the fact that her abduction had been orchestrated by her literary agent as a PR stunt didn't help. Olivia hadn't even looked for another agent yet.

"So you'll work it out, but even if you can't, I'm here for you, for whatever you need."

"Thank you."

His eyes remained worried when he turned back to his steeping tea. He opened the fridge and gathered the ingredients for his morning green protein shake.

Her phone beeped from its charging stand. She grabbed it and unlocked the screen. Zoe had sent her a message the night before. Olivia kept her phone on the do-not-disturb setting at night to minimize disruptions to her already restless sleep. She opened the text. MEET AT 10. NEED TO TALK.

Olivia glanced at the time. "She wants to meet a half hour early. I'd better go."

A memory seared her brain. *Running barefoot over rough ground, tree limbs slicing her skin, her lungs tight. Not enough air.* The flashback lasted just a few seconds but left her palms clammy and sweating.

Stuffing greens into the blender, Lincoln eyed her. "Are you OK?"

"Fine," she lied. Then she wiped her palms on her jeans, crossed the room, and kissed him.

He kissed her back. He glanced down at her brown suede ankle boots and shook his head. "You're wearing those into the woods? They're heels."

"It's a low heel. Very practical." *For her.* Olivia admired the soft chocolate-colored suede boots for a moment. The kitten heel *was* low, and she'd bought a crossbody bag to match. "And I won't be traipsing through the woods in them. I'm bringing my hiking boots."

He shook his head again but said nothing more. He owned one pair of dress shoes and wore either running shoes or boots on a daily basis.

Olivia checked the charge on her power bank and tossed it into her purse, along with her electronic tablet. Then she grabbed her extra jacket, the hiking boots, and her backpack. Before she'd turned to true crime writing eight years before, she'd been an investigative journalist. She always packed a change of clothes, water, snacks, and a phone battery charger. She also kept an emergency road kit and basic tool bag in her car at all times. Leads on a story could change in a heartbeat. She'd always liked to be ready to go wherever the trail led. Her true crime writing usually focused on old crimes. Research tended to be slower paced and planned—more predictable and less in the moment. But the habit had stuck.

Being kidnapped and nearly killed had only intensified her need for vigilance and preparation.

She slung her bag over one shoulder and left the house without a backward glance. She set her backpack in the rear of the Prius, next to her gym bag. Then she slid behind the wheel and drove. With every mile that rolled beneath her tires, she felt her heartbeat climb. By the time the lake came into view, she could feel her pulse thrumming through her body. No sign of Zoe's Jeep. Olivia pulled to the side of the road. Her stomach twisted, and she regretted the small container of yogurt she'd managed to get down for breakfast.

He's in prison. There's nothing to fear.

She checked the time on her phone. A minute after ten. Where was Zoe?

Olivia stepped out of the vehicle and stared out over the water. September in upstate New York was usually pleasant, but the breeze warned of an incoming chill. A heavy, clouded sky reflected on the surface of the water, turning it a murky gray. The lake was U-shaped, and the road ran along the bottom of the *U*. On the other side, a peninsula jutted into the lake. The wind gusted, whipping the water into choppy, angry whitecaps. She shivered. The last time she'd seen the lake, she'd almost drowned in it. Three years had passed since her abduction, since she'd nearly died being held captive on that point of land. Would she ever be able to fully put the trauma behind her?

She paced, checked the time, and paced some more. No Zoe. Olivia pulled out her phone and checked the text. Zoe hadn't suggested an alternative meeting location. Zoe was as punctual as a Swiss watch. When she was fifteen minutes late, Olivia sent her friend a quick message: WHR R U? No response. She waited another five minutes, then called Zoe's number. No answer. Olivia left a short voice message. "Call me. I'm worried."

The sound of an engine carried on the chilly wind. Relieved, Olivia looked beyond her Prius, parked on the shoulder of the country road. An SUV approached. She was expecting both Zoe and Zoe's producer, Wendy Simon, whom Olivia had never met, since Zoe had hired Wendy recently. But when the SUV parked behind the Prius, it held only a single occupant. The woman who stepped out was tall, with a long auburn ponytail. Not Zoe.

"Olivia?" the woman called out as she walked closer, zipping her puffy jacket to her chin. "I'm Wendy Simon."

Olivia accepted a quick handshake. "Where's Zoe?"

"She should be here." Wendy glanced over her shoulder, but no vehicles approached.

The small, unnamed lake was in Middle of Nowhere, Upstate New York. Not much traffic passed through this area. It could be hours before they saw a vehicle.

Wendy pivoted to face the water. The peninsula on the other side just looked like woods. The only sign of the original camp was a rough dock. "The property used to be a survivalist camp?"

"Yes," Olivia said, not elaborating.

"It's changed ownership?" Wendy asked.

Olivia nodded.

"We can start without Zoe," Wendy suggested. "I have the sound equipment with me."

"I'd rather wait." Olivia and Zoe had discussed beginning at the road, where Olivia would recount the abduction from her home in the middle of the night. Then they'd proceed to the camp itself, where Olivia had been kept in a root cellar. She would walk Zoe—and her listeners—through the rest of her ordeal—suffocating asthma attacks, multiple escape attempts, being chased through the woods, and almost drowning in the lake—before Lincoln had found her. Olivia had obtained permission to visit the property from the current owners, a charity group that had purchased the land with the intention of repurposing it into a summer camp for kids from underserved communities. She wondered if they'd torn down the buildings. Would it look the same? Would it *feel* the same?

A shudder rocked her bones. She shoved her hands into her pockets and clenched them into fists.

Wendy squinted at her. "Is there some reason you don't want to talk to me?"

I don't know you? That sounded defensive, even if true. She'd been counting on her friendship and familiarity with Zoe to ease the way through the interview. They'd weathered the changes in journalism—and job losses—together. They'd supported each other on their respective career paths. Zoe understood things about Olivia no one else would. They had history. But Olivia didn't want to explain.

She said, "I only want to do this once." Which was also true.

She hadn't told her story since she'd given her statements to the police three years ago. Her abductor had negotiated a plea deal and was currently in prison. There'd been no trial. Going over the entire ordeal one final time felt like the best way for Olivia to purge any remaining demons. With all the details out there, she should have no more secrets. In her previous investigative journalist career, when a story caught her attention, it held it. Telling that story was the only way she could get it out of her head. She hoped her personal trauma could be expelled the same way. She had no doubt she'd always carry the trauma with her, but the burden could hopefully be eased if shared.

But Wendy didn't take the not-so-subtle hint. "How does it feel to be here on the three-year anniversary?"

Olivia didn't answer. The producer's attitude felt prickly, like cactus barbs. Olivia stepped away. "I'm going to call Zoe." *Again.*

For the second time, her call went directly to voicemail. "Zoe, this is Olivia. Where are you? Call me, OK? I'm getting worried." She lowered the phone. "I don't like this."

Wendy shrugged. "Zoe and I worked late last night after the show, prepping for today. Maybe she overslept."

Ever-punctual Zoe was more than a half hour late, and she knew how important today was to Olivia. She knew Olivia would be on edge. Zoe and Olivia had worked tight deadlines together. Zoe was not the type of person who overslept when she had an important meeting.

"I'm going to call Dylan," Olivia said. Zoe had married Dylan Sanders almost ten years before.

"*I'd* like to call Dylan," Wendy muttered under her breath. "That man is *fiiine.*" She fanned herself.

Olivia shot her a look. She didn't know Wendy. Was she usually this inappropriate? Olivia had expected more professional behavior from

Zoe's producer. Feeling uncomfortable, she stepped away before dialing Zoe's husband.

He picked up the phone on the first ring. "Hello," he said in a rushed voice.

"Hey, Dylan. This is Olivia. I'm looking for Zoe. She was supposed to meet me this morning."

"She didn't come home last night." Dylan sounded worried. "I can't talk. I'm on hold with the police."

"Are you reporting her missing?"

"Yes." His voice was clipped. The line went dead.

Clutching her phone, Olivia turned back to Wendy. "Dylan doesn't know where she is."

"What time did she leave the house?" Wendy asked.

"Zoe didn't come home last night."

Wendy's eyes widened. "Are they having marital problems?"

"Not that I know of."

The producer shrugged. "It wouldn't surprise me. He's a lot younger than she is."

"What are you suggesting?"

"I don't know. Maybe he has someone on the side. Zoe *does* work a lot."

Olivia didn't respond. Speculating with little to no information was counterproductive. It felt intrusive, like gossip, a betrayal of her friend's privacy. "What time did you finish up last night?"

"Around midnight."

Olivia pictured the parking lot of their studio. It would have been empty at that hour. Zoe would have parked near the door, but still . . . "Did you see her leave the office?"

A hair blew across Wendy's eyes, and she anchored it behind her ear. "We walked out together."

"You're sure her Jeep started?" Olivia asked. Zoe's SUV was old.

Wendy nodded. "I saw her leave. I got a text from a man I've been dating. I answered him from behind the wheel. Zoe drove out of the lot before I did."

"And she didn't say she was going anywhere else?"

"No. I assumed she was going home." Wendy's mouth opened, then closed.

"What?"

"Nothing. She was just a little weird after the show. There was this caller that freaked her out."

"In what way?"

"Nothing specific," Wendy said. "He was just creepy. We get those sometimes."

Olivia made a mental note to listen to the show. "Nothing else happened?"

"No."

But something had happened to Zoe on the way home. Had her Jeep broken down? There weren't any areas between the office and her house where she would have been out of cell service. If she'd gotten a flat, she would have changed the tire. If she'd had engine trouble that she couldn't fix, she would have called Dylan, a tow truck, or an Uber. Maybe her phone had run out of charge. Engine trouble combined with a dead phone battery was possible.

She considered Wendy's marital issues comment. If Zoe had been mad enough to check into a motel, her credit card would show the charge. Dylan could check their accounts. Though Zoe could have stayed with a friend, Olivia supposed.

Her mind churned with investigative steps. She'd reviewed missing persons cases in the past. "I'm going to start looking for her."

"You don't want to do the interview?" Wendy asked.

"I want to find Zoe."

"She was fine at midnight." Wendy frowned.

"Dylan is concerned enough to call the police and report her missing." As was Olivia. As she'd expect Wendy to be.

But Wendy shrugged. "She's an adult. If she doesn't want to go home, then she doesn't have to. Maybe give her more time before you start looking for her?"

"No. The warmer the trail, the better." Olivia turned toward her Prius.

"Zoe will turn up," Wendy called.

Olivia slid behind the wheel and shut the door. Through the windshield, she studied Wendy for a few seconds. She didn't move. Her face was locked in the same irritated frown. Olivia had no proof that Zoe and Wendy had left the office at midnight. What if Wendy was lying? Zoe rented space in a Scarlet Falls office park for her small sound studio. Did they have surveillance cameras in the parking lot?

Olivia did a U-turn. As she drove away, she glanced in the rearview mirror. Zoe's business partner jerked open her vehicle door, as if exasperated. Why wasn't she more concerned?

A little voice inside Olivia said, *Wendy was the last person to see Zoe.*

Chapter Four

Fueled by worry, Olivia drove back toward Scarlet Falls at maximum speed. She detoured to Zoe's office, cruised past the lot, then took the most likely route Zoe would have used to go home. While the Prius hummed along, Olivia scanned the sides of the road. But she saw no sign of Zoe's Jeep. There were no vehicles on the shoulder. No SUV nose-down in the roadside ditch.

Olivia continued to the apartment complex where Zoe and Dylan lived on the outskirts of Scarlet Falls. The *K* was missing on the sign for Hawk Meadow Apartments. A half dozen two-story buildings surrounded a rectangular parking lot. Brick facades were faded. Paint peeled from the wood trim. Weeds grew through cracks in the asphalt and between the square slabs of the concrete walkways. Though it was daylight now, she knew the exterior lighting was spotty and inadequate. Could Zoe have been carjacked? Olivia circled the lot and was surprised to spot two cameras mounted on light poles. Given the complex's run-down nature, she hadn't expected them to have any security at all.

After making a mental note to contact maintenance, Olivia parked in a guest spot and crossed the asphalt to Zoe's numbered and empty space, but there was nothing on the ground. Nothing that Zoe might have dropped if she were accosted as she got out of her Jeep.

Cases were only that easy on TV.

Olivia strode to the apartment door on the first floor. Her knuckles had barely left the metal when the door swung open, revealing a disheveled Dylan.

He waved her inside. "I thought you were the police." He wore jeans and an untucked button-up blue shirt with a dark-red stain on the front. At forty, he was eight years younger than Zoe. Yet, lately, his face was looking . . . hard? As if he'd lost weight or—impossibly—shed more body fat from his extremely lean frame. Lines fanned from the corners of his eyes, and his shoulder-length dark hair looked uncombed. "They're sending someone."

"Good." Olivia stepped inside. As usual, she shuddered as the cluttered space closed in on her. Papers, mail, remotes, game controllers, dirty dishes, and used glasses covered tables and shelves. Water rings and crumbs showed on any spot of bare furniture. There wasn't a coaster in sight. Zoe might be punctual, but she was not tidy. "Have you tried pinging Zoe's cell?"

"Yes. No response." He closed the door. "I tried to locate it on our Find My app too. Her phone isn't showing up at all." He exhaled hard. "What does that mean?"

"Maybe her battery ran out." Olivia tried to be optimistic. There was no point in panicking Dylan. "Did you look for her last known position?"

"I don't know how to do that. You know I'm not a tech guy. I'm finally getting the hang of editing short videos and Reels." Dylan was a personal trainer. He'd recently launched a fitness influencer campaign. He posted exercise and diet advice with the goal to use social media to sell workout equipment, clothing, protein drinks, and subscriptions to virtual workouts.

Olivia shrugged out of her jacket and turned toward the coat-tree. Outerwear occupied every hook. She draped her jacket over her arm. "Her Jeep doesn't have emergency or locator services?"

"No. It's too old," Dylan said. "I've tried to get her to buy a new car, but you know how she is about that Jeep."

"I do."

Zoe had owned the same ancient Jeep Cherokee—she'd nicknamed it "Bestie"—as long as Olivia had known her.

"Would you help me find her?" Dylan asked.

"Of course. When did you see her last?"

"Yesterday. She came home for dinner, then went back to the office." Dylan paused. His breath hitched. "I tried to call her around midnight, but she didn't pick up. So I went to bed. I didn't realize she didn't come home until I woke up this morning. I called Shannon, in case she heard from her." Shannon, Zoe, and Olivia attended the same yoga classes. Sometimes they had lunch or coffee afterward.

Olivia made a mental note to talk to her. "She didn't?"

"No." He hadn't called Olivia, though, and Wendy didn't say he'd called her either.

"Did you know she was meeting me for an interview this morning?" Olivia asked.

Dylan shook his head. "I remember her mentioning it, but I didn't remember that it was today. I just knew she was working today." He turned toward the coat-tree behind the door and reached for a jacket. "I should go look for her."

"Where?" Olivia asked.

"I guess I'll start driving all the roads between here and her office. I don't know what else to do." He shrugged into the jacket.

"I already checked Stars Road on the way over here. But you need to talk to the police before you go anywhere," Olivia reminded him.

"Right." He leaned on the wall.

Olivia's gaze dropped to the red stain on the front of his shirt.

Dylan followed her gaze with his own. He flushed. "Red wine. I just grabbed the closest clothes when I woke up and saw that Zoe wasn't here."

So, he'd been drinking last night. Olivia wandered toward the kitchen, which was just a few steps away. Spices, bottles of cooking oil, and bags of snacks covered the countertops. Burned liquid caked the electric stove. Two empty bottles of pinot noir sat on top of the recycling container. Zoe enjoyed wine, but since she'd planned to go back to work, she wouldn't have indulged. Had Dylan finished two bottles all by himself? That would explain why he hadn't woken all night.

As if following her train of thought, he looked away, blushing again. A muscle in his jaw flexed, as if he was going to explain, but a hard knock on the door jolted him. He strode across the carpet and looked through the peephole. "It's the police." He sounded relieved and opened the door, admitting two uniformed patrol officers. The lead cop was older, with a slight paunch, graying hair, and a strong aura of competence. The younger cop was a young blond woman with a thin face and piercing brown eyes.

The older partner led the way inside, removing his hat as he crossed the threshold. "I'm Officer Billings and this is Officer Hasty." He pulled business cards from his pocket and handed one to Olivia and one to Dylan.

Officer Billings studied Dylan, while Officer Hasty was assessing the apartment. Her critical cop gaze passed over everything, missing nothing. She leaned forward to study a wedding photo.

"Tell us what happened, Mr. March," Billings said.

"My name is Sanders. Zoe's name is March." He sounded annoyed. Because Zoe hadn't changed her name or because the cop had called him by his wife's last name?

Dylan launched into a quick rundown.

Billings nodded. "Has your wife ever stayed out all night before?"

"No." Dylan shook his head emphatically. "Not unless it was planned ahead of time."

Billings took Zoe's basic information: name, physical description, and location of her office. Then he studied Dylan's face as he asked, "Is it possible she just needed to get away?"

Dylan's brow furrowed. "If she wanted to go on a trip, she would have told me and booked one."

Billings pulled a small notebook and pen from his pocket. He clicked the pen with his thumb. "Does she do that often? Go on girls' trips or just take off for a few days?"

"No," Dylan said. "If she has to go somewhere, it's usually work related. She hosts a true crime podcast, unsolved murders or people who have been missing for a long time." He rolled a hand in the air. "That sort of thing. She interviews witnesses and family members, anyone involved with the case." He licked his lips, then added, "She would never just leave without telling me."

The hairs on the back of Olivia's neck quivered. Dylan's demeanor felt off.

"When was her last research trip?" Billings asked.

"A few months ago?" Dylan yanked his cell phone from his back pocket. "I can check my calendar." He scrolled. "May nineteenth through the twenty-second. She stayed in a B and B in Summerton, New York. That's a couple of hours west of here."

"What was she researching on that trip?"

Dylan shook his head. "A case she was considering for the show. I don't remember which one."

"Has she made any enemies?" Billings asked. "Has her show angered any victims or criminals?"

"No." Dylan shook his head. "Mostly she studies old cases. Ones from like, decades ago."

Billings turned his attention to Olivia. "And you are?"

"A friend of Zoe's." Olivia introduced herself. "She was supposed to meet me this morning. When she didn't show up, I called Dylan."

Hasty stared at Olivia for a few seconds, as if trying to place her.

Billings glanced between Dylan and Olivia, his expression suspicious. Did they think there was something going on between them? Indignation heated Olivia's cheeks, but she said nothing. Jumping to conclusions and overexplaining would only make her look guilty.

A shoe shuffled on the carpet. Olivia was almost startled to see Hasty in the kitchen. She hadn't seen the cop move, but Hasty was quietly sweeping through the rest of the apartment. Their eyes met. The cop's gaze was a one-way street, taking in all the information, giving away none.

"You tried to call her?" Billings asked.

"Several times. I also texted her. No response," Dylan said. "I tried to locate her phone too. Nothing. Maybe her battery ran out."

Billings nodded. "Or she turned it off." He squinted harder at Dylan. "Has she ever done that before? Turned off her phone?"

Dylan's Adam's apple bobbed as he swallowed hard. "No."

"Not even if she's working?" Billings's voice rose.

Dylan sniffed. "She usually keeps it on silent."

"What about in May, when she was on that research trip?" Billings's brow arched.

Dylan answered in a sharp tone. "We texted during the day and talked every night."

Billings let it go. He caught his partner's eye and shifted his gaze to Olivia, then the door.

Hasty's radio crackled. She listened for a second, then reached to her duty belt and turned down the volume. Walking toward Olivia, she said, "I'd like to speak with you outside."

On her way toward the door, Olivia heard Billings say, "Your wife is not required to report her presence to you. If she turned off her phone, maybe she doesn't want you to find her."

Olivia followed Hasty outside before Dylan responded. The clouds had passed, and the sun warmed the air. But Olivia was still chilled and slid her arms into her jacket.

Hasty studied Olivia for a second. "You're the reporter who was kidnapped a few years ago."

"Yes."

Hasty lifted her phone. "I looked you up. You're a big deal. You won two George Polk Awards. That's one of the most prestigious awards in journalism."

"Correct."

"I read the piece you did on suicide in law enforcement a while back. It was spot-on. Actually, so spot-on, it was hard to read." Hasty grimaced.

"It was hard to write."

Hasty's gaze was assessing. She jerked her chin toward the apartment door. "Does the place always look like that?"

"Yes. Zoe is not neat."

Hasty tilted her head. "Has she ever mentioned being afraid of her husband?"

"No."

"Do they fight often?"

"Not that I'm aware," Olivia said. "I mean, everyone argues." Except her and Lincoln. Occasionally, they had disagreements, like whether *A New Hope* or *The Empire Strikes Back* was the best Star Wars film.

Hasty's focus tightened on her face. "So they *did* fight?"

Olivia regretted her answer for a second. No. Finding Zoe was more important than a little embarrassment over marital spats. "She might have mentioned being irritated with him a time or two. Nothing more serious than that."

"Do you remember any specific incidents?"

"My boyfriend and I met them for dinner a few weeks ago. Dylan made them late. Zoe was irritated with him. Like I said, minor stuff."

"But you don't think she was afraid of him?" Hasty didn't use a notebook. Her attention remained uncomfortably riveted on Olivia. It felt as if she would remember every word of their conversation.

Olivia chose her words carefully. How well did she really know Dylan? "She's never mentioned it."

"How long have you been friends with her?"

"A little over fifteen years. We met when we were both journalists with the same newspaper." They'd had some adventures for sure.

The cop nodded. "And you both left to go into true crime?"

"Eventually, yes. The print newspaper is a thing of the past." Journalism had changed. Olivia wanted the freedom to pursue the stories she chose, and she would not measure her work by the number of clicks her articles generated.

"How often do you see each other?" Hasty asked.

"A few times a month?" Olivia guessed. "Sometimes more, sometimes less. It depends on our lives and careers. We don't talk or text every day, but our friendship is solid. I know if I needed help, Zoe would be there for me. When we worked together, she always had my back—and I had hers. Once, I was doing a piece on women being victimized at shelters. I went undercover as an unhoused person. Zoe followed me everywhere, also disguised. She refused to let me out of her sight. This went on for weeks until we discovered that it was one of the shelter personnel who was raping the women." A quick shudder passed through Olivia as she remembered. "Anyway, that's how I know Zoe wouldn't have missed our meeting today unless something happened to her. She knows how important today is for me. She would never let me down, not today."

Hasty raised a brow.

Olivia explained, "It's the three-year anniversary of my kidnapping."

"Oh." Hasty made a note. "So if she was having serious marital issues, she'd probably tell you?"

"If she wanted a sounding board or advice, yes," Olivia answered. "But she wouldn't complain just to complain."

The cop took in her careful answer. "How long have Zoe and Dylan been married?"

"Not quite ten years."

"In the wedding photo, she looks older than him."

Olivia bristled. "Yes, by eight years."

"Is the age gap a source of friction between them?" the cop asked.

"I don't know." But Olivia knew that Zoe was self-conscious, especially lately. She'd recently started dyeing her hair, and she seemed to be wearing more makeup. But the questions still made Olivia prickly. "If he was eight years her senior, would you even ask that?"

Hasty ignored her very valid point. "Does she have any money?"

"I don't know the details of her financial situation, but she doesn't live like she has money."

"Is her podcast successful?"

Olivia thought of Zoe's cramped apartment and old Jeep. "I think so, but I don't know how much money podcasts make. Her show's success is recent."

If Zoe had been making a hefty profit, she hadn't been spending it. Then again, Dylan also had a job. With two incomes, they should be able to afford a nicer apartment. Zoe had recently commented that Dylan's attempts to launch his fitness influencer business were costing more than they made. She said she understood that new ventures went through a start-up investment period. But Zoe had high hopes his business would start turning a profit soon. How much had she invested in his career or her own podcast? Had she used up her savings launching them both? If not, why did they live like they were broke? Could they be in debt?

"Is there anyone else who might have information about Zoe's whereabouts? Close friends, et cetera." Hasty circled a hand in the air.

"Her producer, Wendy Simon." Olivia relayed her earlier conversation with Wendy.

This time, Hasty pulled out a notebook and took down the name and a couple of bullet points that Olivia couldn't read upside down.

"Is there anyone else we should talk to?"

Olivia shook her head. "She doesn't have any family."

"None?"

"Her parents are dead. No siblings."

"She's never mentioned any extended family?" Hasty's voice was flat, but Olivia could sense her disbelief. "Not even an aunt or second cousin twice removed?"

"No." Olivia had never questioned Zoe's backstory, but now, answering the cop's question, the strangeness became apparent. Olivia had a large family. How many people didn't even have a stray aunt or distant cousin?

Hasty shoved her notebook into her pocket and gestured toward the door. Olivia went back inside. She stepped aside to give the cop room, but Hasty closed the door and remained outside.

Billings asked Dylan for a photo of Zoe. Dylan pulled out his phone and tapped on the screen. The cop wrote down a basic physical description and the address of Zoe's office. "Can you check your credit card and bank accounts for activity?"

Dylan tapped on his phone screen again. "Our joint bank account hasn't been touched. We have individual credit cards. I can't access Zoe's."

Billings's brows rose. "Does she have her own bank accounts as well?"

"Yes. We keep a joint account for bills and household expenses. Other than that, our finances are separate." Dylan's lips compressed, as if their separate accounts annoyed him.

"Do you know how much money your wife has in her account?"

"No."

"Not even an approximation? A hundred dollars? A million?" Billings asked.

"No." Dylan's voice went as flat at his mouth. He circled a hand in the air. "But I doubt it's much, considering where we live."

The cop didn't press the issue, but the corners of his eyes crinkled tighter. "Has Zoe's behavior changed over the past few days? Did she seem distracted, frightened, different at all?"

"No." Dylan crossed his arms in a defensive posture.

"Does she have an E-ZPass on her vehicle?" Billings asked.

Dylan shook his head. "I tried to get her to apply for one. It's free, and you save a lot on tolls. Seems like a no-brainer to me, but she wouldn't do it."

"Did she say why?"

"She's wary of anything that tracks your movements. She can be a little paranoid about being watched by the government."

"But she had a smartphone?" Billings asked.

"Yes," Dylan said. "I pointed out the ridiculousness of her argument. I mean, as long as she was carrying her phone, she could be tracked. But she wouldn't budge, which annoyed me, to be honest. She was always nagging me about saving money."

"Was money another issue you fought about frequently?" Billings asked.

Dylan paled, like a feral cat that had walked right into a humane trap only to have it slam shut before he'd even tasted the tuna. "Everyone argues about money."

When Billings didn't agree, Dylan went on the offensive. "What are you going to do to find my wife?"

Before Billings could answer, Hasty opened the door and walked in, her eyes cold. She stepped up to stand next to her partner, leaning forward, her posture the opposite of defensive. "The neighbor says you and your wife had a fight last night."

Dylan's weight shifted backward onto his heels. "I wouldn't call it a fight."

Hasty leaned in, pressing into Dylan's personal space. "What would you call it?"

"A minor argument." He tried to sound casual, but his voice was tight.

Hasty jerked a thumb at the wall. "It was loud enough that the neighbor overheard."

Sweat broke out on Dylan's upper lip. "This is a cheap apartment. The walls are thin."

Hasty's brows rose. She wasn't buying his explanation. "What did you *argue* about?"

"She worked too much. I was complaining about her putting her podcast first. I know I married a workaholic, but sometimes I just miss her. She left annoyed, not furious."

"Were you also *annoyed*?" Hasty asked.

"A little," he admitted.

Olivia's gaze automatically tracked to the recycling bin. *Annoyed enough to drink two bottles of wine?*

"Could she have been angry enough to stay out all night? Maybe she wanted to teach you a lesson," Hasty suggested.

Dylan cleared his throat. "When she didn't come home, I did briefly consider that I'd misread her." His posture jerked straight. "But she would never shut off her phone and refuse to take my calls because she had some residual anger from our argument. She'd want me to call. She'd want to talk about it."

Hasty didn't comment, but doubt clouded her eyes. "Have you had this *argument* before?"

"Yes," Dylan admitted.

Billings's gaze never left Dylan's face. "How angry were you when she left?"

Dylan's mouth went slack with shock. "What are you implying?"

Billings's focus didn't waver. "I'm not implying anything. I'm asking."

"I called you. Why would I do that if I had something to do with my wife disappearing?" Dylan's eyes shone with indignation.

Neither cop responded. They glanced at each other. Their matching expressions said they were not swayed by Dylan's logic. Arsonists liked to watch firefighters work. Murderers went to their victims' funerals. His argument didn't hold much weight.

He propped his hands on his hips. "My wife is missing. What are you going to do to find her?"

Billings gestured to the apartment around them. "Mind if we look around?"

Dylan waved a hand. "Feel free. I don't have anything to hide."

The cops split up. Hasty headed to the bedroom. Billings toured the living room, then went into the adjoining kitchen. He paused in front of the recycling bin, then opened the top drawers.

Dylan stepped sideways to stand next to Olivia. "I can't believe this. I call for help, and all I get is an accusation."

"They have to consider all the options," Olivia said. What she didn't say: Statistically, women are usually victimized by their significant other. She checked the time on the clock. No one had seen Zoe since midnight. It was now noon. Zoe had been missing for twelve hours, and the cops had made it clear that the first line of investigation they would pursue was Dylan.

Chapter Five

Olivia watched the door close behind the cops.

"Do you really think they're going to look for her? Because it sure feels like they already suspect me of something. I don't even know what." Dylan wasn't wrong.

"It's too early to assume what the police will do." Olivia turned to study his face. His eyes were full of apprehension. But what was he afraid of? That the cops wouldn't look for Zoe?

Or that they would?

Olivia shook off her own suspicions. She was letting the cops' attitude affect her judgment. She knew Zoe better than they did. She should follow her own instincts.

And what were her feelings about Dylan? One, she didn't know him all that well. Two, Zoe had never expressed any fear of her husband. She always seemed to love him, even if she was occasionally annoyed or exasperated, which seemed pretty normal for them. Three, as far as Olivia knew, Dylan was more financially dependent on Zoe than the other way around. Zoe had mentioned a time or two that her husband couldn't save a nickel on his own. Money seemed to disappear from his accounts like a coin from a magician's palm, which was a good reason for maintaining separate bank accounts. Dylan needed his wife.

"You said you'd help me." Dylan turned his nearly black eyes on Olivia. "What can we do?"

Do I want him working alongside me, knowing every step I make?

Olivia's answer was in her own question. "Do you and Zoe share a cell provider? If you do, then I need the login information to try and find her phone. Access to your cloud storage account could also be helpful."

Dylan walked to an end table, opened a drawer, and pulled out a pad of sticky notes. He jotted down a few lines and peeled off the top sheet. "Here, but if her phone battery is dead . . ."

"I have a friend who might be able to help with that," Olivia said vaguely as she took the paper. She was hoping she could discover the last time Zoe had used her phone. "Can I look through Zoe's things? Maybe she left a clue."

Dylan shifted his weight. "I don't know if she'd like that."

Olivia raised a single brow. "She's missing. You're worried enough to call the police. Do you want me to look for her or not?"

"I do." He gestured toward the bedroom door, then brushed back his thick hair. The light glinted on a few silver strands. He might be younger than Zoe, but he was aging too. He fought it hard, but no one could hold off time forever.

Olivia walked to the bedroom, where she thought it more likely that Zoe would keep something personal or valuable. Dylan followed her and leaned on the doorjamb.

The nightstands were covered with clutter. Olivia suppressed a shudder. "Which nightstand is Zoe's?"

"That one." Dylan pointed to the table closest to the door.

She crossed to it and scanned the objects crammed together on the surface: lamp, tissue box, earbuds, phone charger, notepad, pen, hand cream, coaster with coffee rings layered on top of one another. She picked up the notepad and flipped through it. The pages were blank. No impressions on the top sheet. She set it down and opened the single drawer to view Zoe's current knitting project, something quite large in soft blue wool. A sweater? Olivia closed the drawer and went to the dresser. The first drawer contained men's underwear and socks.

"Zoe's stuff is on the left side," Dylan said, his message clear.

Olivia's cheeks flushed as she closed the drawer and took a step to the left. Zoe's drawers were stuffed full of clothes to the point of barely sliding. Olivia ran her fingers around the edges, then checked the underside of each drawer. She moved the dresser a few inches forward and examined the back. Nothing.

"Do you think she hid something?" Dylan asked. "She didn't keep secrets from me." But his statement ended on a rising note, as if he wasn't certain.

"I have no idea." Olivia didn't want to insult or embarrass him. She needed his cooperation to find Zoe. "I'm trying to be objective and look at the case from an outsider's perspective."

"Oh." He sounded placated.

Olivia moved to the closet and opened both bifold doors. A purse tumbled off the top shelf and landed at her feet. For a few seconds, the sheer amount of clothing and accessories—both Zoe's and Dylan's—jammed into the small space staggered her. The closet was a can of coiled paper snakes. She waited for a few seconds, expecting more items to tumble out. Then she settled in to search Zoe's things. Purses were precariously piled on the top shelf. Olivia pulled each one down, opened it, and checked interior and exterior pouches. She moved to the hanging items, packed so tightly she could barely move anything, and slid her fingers into every pocket of every jacket. Stacked shoeboxes covered the floor. Olivia dropped to her knees and lifted each lid. Finding nothing, she sat back on her heels.

Dylan never moved from his position in the doorway, nor did he offer to help, which made Olivia's search feel even more intrusive. Did he suspect she didn't completely trust him?

"Anything?" he asked.

"Nothing that seems relevant." Olivia stared up at the packed closet. She hadn't even found a stray receipt, coin, or hair tie. She was ridiculously, almost ruthlessly, tidy and organized, but even her purses would undoubtedly contain a forgotten bobby pin or receipt. Zoe, on the other hand, was a slob. The absence of normal clutter among a mountain of it felt odd.

Olivia climbed to her feet. The bathroom was as small and overfilled as the rest of the apartment, but contained nothing that stood out as important or unusual. She left the room. She'd leave the more public rooms for Dylan to search.

She and Dylan returned to the living room. "Today is Sunday. Do you know what she did for the last couple of days?"

"Worked." He shrugged. "Her calendar is on her phone. If she's not recording, she's researching or writing copy. A one-hour podcast takes a lot more work hours to produce than most people would think."

Zoe might leave a trail of messiness everywhere she went, but she was meticulous about her show. If her phone was set to automatically back up data, Olivia might be able to access her calendar—and other information—through their cloud account. She almost said so, but then stopped. Her instincts screamed not to include Dylan, just in case he *was* involved. Statistically, he would be the prime suspect.

"I need to make some calls," she said.

"What should I do? Drive around and look for her?"

The police would do that, but she understood that he needed to feel useful.

"Sure. But also"—she made a gesture toward the living room—"go through the rest of the apartment very carefully. Every drawer. Between the cushions. Check all the places the police might have missed. Look for recent receipts, notes she might have jotted down, papers, that sort of thing."

Dylan glanced around, no doubt realizing searching the piles of chaos would take many hours.

"Do you know anything about other cases she might be working on?" Olivia asked.

Dylan shook his head. "She's always working on different ones. I can't keep up."

"Do you have a key to her office?"

"No," he snapped, mouth tightening with irritation. He crossed his arms, and his posture stiffened. "She was at the office, so she had her key with her."

And she'd never made one for him, Olivia noted, which he was angry about. Maybe their marriage *was* on the rocks. She wished Zoe had been more of a complainer. "OK, then. Make flyers. Use a recent photo. We're going to want at least a hundred copies, maybe two hundred. We can post them all over town." Was she giving him busywork to keep him out of her way?

Yep.

She added, "Make sure your phone ringer is on. If anyone calls, you don't want to miss it."

Dylan's face paled. His temper deflated, but she could sense it hadn't completely dissipated. "Are you thinking she was kidnapped, and someone might call demanding a ransom?"

The question caught Olivia by surprise. "Uh. No. I was thinking Zoe might call, or the police, maybe a hospital ER . . ."

"Oh." Realization dawned in his eyes. "If she was in an accident . . ."

"You could call local hospitals and see if she's been admitted, though I'm fairly sure the police will do that." They'd call the morgue too, but Olivia kept that to herself.

He swallowed. "I should have already called the hospital. Why didn't I think of that?"

"Because your wife has never gone missing before."

He nodded, his gaze at his feet. "OK. I'll make the calls, search the rest of the apartment, drive around, and put together a flyer. You'll get back to me later?"

"Yes." Olivia should comfort him in some way, a pat on the forearm or shoulder, but she didn't want to touch him, not with his short temper hovering just beneath the surface. Words would have to suffice. "We'll do everything we can to find her."

He nodded, but when Olivia left the apartment, he was still standing there, staring at his shoes.

Behind the wheel of her car, Olivia called Wendy, who didn't answer. She left a message. Then she texted Zoe's friend Shannon Green. She'd flown to Florida for her aunt's funeral that weekend. Olivia couldn't remember which day she was coming home.

Before she could put the car into gear, her phone vibrated from the cupholder. Her brother's name—Stephen—popped onto the screen. He'd been transferred to Japan for the last two years, where it was currently dark o'clock. She was too tired to do math. Olivia pressed "Answer" and the call connected via Bluetooth. "Hey."

"Liv?" Her brother's voice was rough, and he didn't bother to tease her.

"What's wrong?"

"It's Nicki. I've been trying to reach her, but she won't answer my texts or calls."

Stephen's twenty-five-year-old daughter lived in Scarlet Falls. "How long have you been trying?"

"Two days. Have you seen her or texted with her?"

"She was at family dinner Thursday night." Olivia's parents hosted dinner every week for anyone in the family who could make it. "I haven't texted with her since then." Her niece was seemingly allergic to making phone calls. "I'll run by her place now and call you back." She didn't bother trying to soothe her brother. Their sister's son had overdosed years before. Stephen would worry no matter what Olivia said. The whole family was extra sensitive.

She headed for her niece's place. Nicki didn't own a car. She lived near the university, within walking distance of shopping and restaurants.

Housing was plentiful but parking was a problem. Olivia circled two blocks before finding a spot. She parallel parked and then walked to her niece's front door—an old three-story house that had been divided into six apartments. She approached the front door behind a lanky young man with a backpack slung over one shoulder. He entered the code, pulled open the door, and held it for Olivia.

"Thank you." She stepped inside the vestibule before adding, "But you shouldn't let strangers into the building."

He grinned down at her from his significant height advantage. "You don't look very dangerous." He loped up the steps, leaving her in the foyer.

Olivia sighed. Being short could be so annoying, though she acknowledged that her nonthreatening physique occasionally worked in her favor. She took the steps to the third floor. She knocked on Nicki's door. When her niece didn't answer for a solid minute, anxiety began to coil in Olivia's belly. She banged a full fist on the door. When Nicki still didn't respond, Olivia opened her purse to find the key her niece had given her when she'd moved into the place the previous year. The sound of footsteps approaching unraveled the knot, and apprehension shifted into irritation.

The door opened. Her niece stared at her, blinking at the daylight pouring through a nearby window. "What?"

"What have you been doing?" Stress sharpened Olivia's voice, and she quickly toned it down. "Your dad has been trying to reach you."

"Sleeping." Nicki pivoted on one sheepskin bootie and walked to the breakfast bar. She snapped her phone off its magnetic charging base. "Oh."

"Oh?"

Without looking up, Nicki typed with both thumbs. "There. I answered him. It's cool."

Olivia closed her eyes for a single deep breath. Opening them, she focused on her niece. Unlike Olivia, Nicki was Cuban and Irish, but there was no sign of her mother's heritage in her features. She and Olivia had the same deep-brown eyes and hair, the same complexion. Nicki was Olivia's mini-me. Today, she wore flannel pajama bottoms and an oversize sweatshirt. Her dark hair was scooped into a messy bun on top of her head. A pillow crease divided her left cheek. Olivia had obviously woken her. "Your dad was worried."

"Is that why you're here?" Nicki rolled her eyes. "He's always worried."

Olivia said nothing. She let the guilt marinate. Nicki would try to rationalize her behavior, but she was maturing, moving from young adult to adult. Part of that transition was learning to see situations from other people's perspective.

Nicki huffed, but it was obviously a cover. She *knew* she'd caused her dad unnecessary stress. "I played in a video game tournament last night and forgot to check my phone. Unlike you and my dad, I'm not married to my devices."

Olivia ignored the quip and stayed on message. "He said he's been trying to reach you for two days."

"Huh. What day is it?" Nicki rubbed an eye with a knuckle.

"Sunday."

"Feels like a Monday."

"It's not." But Olivia agreed. It did, indeed, feel as crappy as a Monday.

Nicki worked from home as a social media marketer. Since she'd quit her job and started her own business, her hours didn't adhere to the usual business-day calendar. She opened a text and grimaced. "Technically, he's only been trying for a day and a half, but I lost track of time last night. I'm sorry."

"Don't apologize to me." Olivia nodded toward the phone. "*Call* him. I'm sure he wants to hear your voice. You know the family is paranoid." She didn't need to say why. Olivia's kidnapping had changed everything.

The realization swept over Nicki's face. "Yeah. You're right." She tapped on the screen, then took the phone into the bedroom.

Olivia scanned the apartment, a tiny one-bedroom barely bigger than a hotel room. A few dishes sat in the sink, and an uncountable number of fleece blankets were piled on the couch. Her niece liked to cocoon. A game controller, a laptop computer, and an empty sushi container occupied the coffee table. A tall stack of her latest book binge—a romantasy series with dragons on the covers—occupied the end table. Other than that, the space was tidy in a normal, lived-in way. Nicki kept her apartment clean enough, but she didn't obsess about it. Olivia couldn't judge people by her own unrealistic, possibly—definitely—compulsive standards.

Nicki emerged from her bedroom. "I'm going for coffee. Wanna come?"

"You have a coffee machine right there." Olivia pointed to the pod-style machine she'd bought her niece as a housewarming gift.

"I'm not in the mood for straight coffee. Plus, I want a breakfast sandwich."

"It's after two o'clock."

"Call it a brunch sandwich, then." Nicky traded her bootie slippers for big, black lug-soled boots.

"Aren't you going to get dressed?"

Nicki looked down at her pajamas and shrugged. "I could change, I guess." She called over her shoulder as she walked back into the bedroom, "Everyone doesn't have to be a fashionista, you know." She returned in less than a minute. She'd swapped her pajama bottoms for a pair of yoga pants. That was it.

Olivia pressed her lips together. She shouldn't comment on her niece's appearance. It was superficial and could damage her self-esteem, though Nicki had never exhibited confidence issues. Quite the opposite, actually. Nicki's attitude bordered on arrogant. But at least her niece was wearing actual clothes. Olivia couldn't comprehend why anyone would want to go out in public wearing pajamas. Her nieces and nephews couldn't understand why it mattered.

"What are you doing this afternoon?" Nicki filled a giant stainless steel tumbler with water, then collected her keys and phone from the nearby counter. "Isn't today your big interview?"

"Zoe didn't show."

"What?" Nicki stopped. She often went to yoga class with Olivia. That's where she'd met Zoe a few years before. Last summer, Nicki had started handling the social media marketing for Zoe's podcast. Zoe had been thrilled and impressed with the success of Nicki's campaign. "That doesn't sound like her."

"I know. No one has seen her," Olivia said. "Dylan reported her missing."

They left the apartment. Nicki locked her door. "Did you look for her phone's GPS location?"

"Dylan tried. The phone is either off or the battery is dead."

"What about the last known location?"

"Dylan gave me the password for their cell service account. He's not very tech savvy. I was going to go home and try that on my computer."

"Doesn't he have a laptop? You could have done that at his place."

"I told him I needed help," Olivia said in a vague tone.

"You lied."

Olivia winced and admitted, "Yeah."

"So you don't trust him," Nicki concluded.

"I didn't say that."

"You didn't have to."

"I just don't know him well enough to decide. When I get together with Zoe, he rarely comes along."

"That's fair."

Nicki studied Olivia's face for a second. "She hasn't been unavailable for long, but you have a bad feeling about it?"

When Olivia had been kidnapped, she'd only missed one appointment, but Lincoln had known immediately that she'd been in trouble. He hadn't wasted a second before starting to look for her. His determination had made the difference between Olivia's life and death. "Yes. Something is wrong. Anyone can miss a meeting, but Zoe would have called if she could."

"OK." Nicki unlocked her door, slipped back into her apartment, and grabbed her laptop from the coffee table. She tucked it under one arm. Back on the landing, she relocked the door and jogged down the steps. "We'll check her cell history at the coffee shop."

Olivia hustled to keep up with her niece's longer legs. Nicki was average height, but she was taller than Olivia. But then, most people over the age of twelve were taller than Olivia. She rarely wore shoes without a heel because she preferred to be perceived as an adult. "Didn't we just agree that I don't need help with the tech?"

"I'm bored, and I'm better with devices than you are. I can do it faster than you can. You'll save time."

Olivia couldn't argue with that. It often seemed as if her nieces and nephews had been born with a computer chip embedded in their brains, and Nicki had professional technical expertise.

Nicki flashed a grin over her shoulder. "You can buy me my breakfast."

"Brunch," Olivia corrected.

The sun emerged, warming the air.

"It'll be faster to walk." Nicki headed down the tree-lined street at a brisk clip.

Olivia hustled to keep up. Footsteps pounded the pavement behind her. She turned toward the sound. A shoulder slammed into her back, knocking her forward. Her crossbody purse strap jerked against her neck, the counter pull throwing her further off balance. She lost her footing, stumbling onto one knee, her heart slamming into her rib cage.

She extended a hand, reaching for a tree planted in the middle of the sidewalk, and lurched back onto her feet.

Olivia recovered her balance to focus on the man pulling at her purse strap. He was big, well over six feet, and broad shouldered. A bandanna was tied around his face but had slid a few millimeters on one side, exposing the top edge of a dark beard. Over the impromptu mask, hostile brown eyes glared at her. Though he was dressed like a college student in jeans, a hoodie, and sneakers, the crow's-feet around his eyes told her he was older.

"Give it," he snarled. "Or I'll hurt you."

Fear—and a flashback—paralyzed Olivia as her memory sucked her backward in time. Her muscles locked into place, refusing to respond to her brain's command to *run*. All she could see was a dark underground cellar. Unrelenting cold seeped into her bones, dampness tightening her throat, her airway narrowing to the size of a cocktail straw.

She couldn't breathe. Tiny starbursts exploded in her vision like mini fireworks. Her eyes locked open. She couldn't even blink. Time slowed, until the current attack melded with flashbacks of her kidnapping.

Can't breathe. Can't breathe can't breathe.

She blinked, her survival instinct dragging her back to the present.

A large fist drew back, aiming for her face.

Chapter Six

Olivia couldn't move. Couldn't think. Her feet were stuck to the sidewalk as if they were glued down.

"Hey!" Nicki yelled. "Get off her."

Nicki's shout snapped Olivia out of her flashback trance.

The man turned toward Nicki, a hand raised, poised to strike her.

"Oh, no you fucking won't." Olivia's instinct—and the self-defense techniques Lincoln had taught her—kicked in. Even if she'd wanted to hand over the purse, the way the man was yanking on it prevented her from slipping the strap over her head. Instead, she used the leverage to pull herself closer to him and stomped on his foot, her pointy kitten heel skewering the soft mesh toe of his sneaker.

"Fuck!" He yanked hard on the purse strap, jerking Olivia sideways, off his foot.

Nicki raised one leg and front-kicked his kneecap with her giant boot. He spun to absorb the blow on his thigh, grunting as the lug sole connected. His leg buckled. Cursing, he released Olivia's purse and turned toward Nicki.

Olivia's fear dissipated instantly, and rage flooded her.

If he lays one hand on Nicki, so help me . . .

"Don't you fucking touch her!" She pulled her purse strap over her head and swung it in a circle to gain momentum, like a knight winding up a mace. At the apex of her swing, she shifted her balance. With the forward flick of her wrist, she struck him upside the head with the bag. The electronic tablet and weighty power bank inside connected with the front of his skull with a solid *thunk*. He stumbled backward, his arms windmilling, falling onto his ass. A hand slapped down, the palm splayed on the concrete for balance. He didn't stay down for more than a second. Pushing off his hand, he scrambled to get his feet under him, his eyes narrowing with anger and determination. Olivia felt his focus—and hostility.

She pulled back her purse, ready to strike again, although she doubted the same move would work twice. She'd taken him by surprise the first time. He hadn't expected her to fight back. He wouldn't make that mistake again. He moved forward, his attention riveted on her with the fixation of a coyote stalking a rabbit. "You bitch."

As he strode toward her, Olivia walked backward, toward the foot traffic on the busier street half a block away. If she turned and ran, could she reach the crowd before he caught her? She contemplated throwing her purse in the opposite direction, hoping he'd go after *it* and not her or Nicki. There was nothing in the purse that was worth her life or Nicki's. But she'd have to throw it as far as possible to give them time to reach the safety of the main street.

Nicki stepped in and bashed him with her water bottle. The stainless steel rang on his temple like a gong. The reverberations rang in Olivia's bones. The man face-planted into the sidewalk and lay still. He moaned and turned his head.

Not dead.

Olivia moved toward him, the fury at seeing him turn on her niece making her want to kick him in the head a few times. But getting close enough for him to catch one of her feet was the wrong move.

"Let's get out of here." Nicki grabbed Olivia's arm and tugged her toward the main street. Ahead, she could see the steady stream of Sunday-afternoon foot traffic.

They raced down the sidewalk and into the next intersection, cutting between a half dozen cars crawling toward the traffic light. Olivia's heart sprinted in her chest, urging her to run faster. She kept her niece in front of her, ensuring that her own body was always between the attacker and Nicki. Drivers honked and hit their brakes. Olivia slapped a palm on a hood for balance as she maneuvered between a sedan and an SUV. Nicki reached the curb first. Olivia joined her, panting, lungs burning. Pedestrians moved around them. Now that they were on the other side of the intersection and within the relative safety of a crowd, Olivia paused and glanced backward. The sidewalk where they'd been accosted was empty. The man had vanished.

"He's gone," she said, bending forward and resting her hands on her thighs while she caught her breath. The adrenaline mainlining through her bloodstream ebbed. Its absence left her vaguely disoriented, nauseated, and lightheaded.

Two college-age women, a blonde and a brunette, rushed toward them. "Are you OK?"

The blonde waved her phone in the air. "I called for help."

Olivia could only nod and squeak out a breathless "Thanks."

A few minutes later, she heard the sound of an approaching siren, and a campus police vehicle pulled to the curb. An officer stepped out. "Someone reported an attempted mugging."

"Me! I did," the blonde said.

The word *mugging* didn't sound accurate, but Olivia said, "Yes, a man tried to steal my purse." She gave a quick description of the incident. "He was several inches over six feet tall, but his face was covered."

The young women and Nicki confirmed Olivia's account with their own.

"They beat the crap out of him," the brunette said, her voice filled with admiration.

The cop took notes. "But you didn't see his face because of the bandanna?"

"That's correct," Olivia said. "I'm pretty sure he had a beard, though."

His gaze swept over her. "If I were looking for a target on this street, you'd be it. You look like you have money. Show me where it happened." The cop followed them back to the spot. He turned in a circle and studied the surroundings: the sides of residential buildings. "No entrance facing this direction, so no cameras. Too far from the intersection for the traffic cam to have caught the incident." He frowned. "I'll file a report, but without a description, a photo, or video, I don't know how we'd find him. Half the kids on this street are wearing jeans and a hoodie. And even if we did find him, how would we prove it was him? You don't know what he looks like."

"He'll be the one with the big bruise on his head." The brunette touched her own temple, her voice slightly disgusted.

The cop ignored her and scratched his head. "Neither one of you is injured? He didn't get anything?"

"We're fine," Olivia said, knowing this was the end of it. "Thank you for taking the report."

The cop returned to his vehicle. The two young women disappeared into a store. Nicki started down the street.

Olivia jogged to catch up. "Where are you going?" *She can't still want to go to brunch . . .*

"The café." Nicki didn't break stride. "He's gone, and I'm still hungry."

Still on edge, Olivia stuck close as they walked the additional block to the café. Olivia chose a table outside and handed Nicki a credit card.

Nicki set her laptop on the table. Miraculously, she hadn't dropped it while fighting off their attacker and fleeing. "The usual?"

"Please." Olivia put her back to the building and faced the street, watching traffic in case he decided to look for her in a vehicle or on foot. She would not be caught by surprise again. But they were on the main street now. The sheer number of pedestrians would deter an additional attempt to rob her. Still, she kept the strap around her body and tucked the purse in her lap.

In an attempt to settle down, she turned her face to the sun, trying to enjoy its rays. She didn't want to sit and warm her face. She knew that using technology was the next step in finding Zoe, but Olivia was still antsy from the attempted mugging and subsequent adrenaline crash. She irrationally wanted to do something physical, even if that wasn't logical.

Nicki returned, handing Olivia her green tea and egg white soufflé. Nicki drew a long pull of her creamy, syrup-laden latte and unwrapped her bagel sandwich. Strips of bacon hung over the edges, and melted cheese dripped onto the wax paper. "I doubt that was a random mugging. There isn't much crime here, and the crowd is mostly students. That dude was way too old to be a student."

"If it wasn't random, then we were targeted."

"*You* were targeted." Nicki narrowed her eyes. "He followed you here."

"You could be right." A creepy sensation crawled through Olivia's belly. If she'd been followed, she hadn't even noticed. She needed to be more vigilant.

Shit—Dylan! Olivia pulled out her phone and dialed his number.

"Did you find something?" he asked without a greeting.

"No," Olivia said. "I just wanted to check in. Someone tried to snatch my bag."

"You think it has to do with Zoe?" he asked.

"I have no evidence of that, but check outside your apartment."

"OK." Footsteps sounded over the line. "I don't see any strange vehicles in the parking lot."

"Lock your doors and watch your back anyway, OK?"

"OK. You be careful too," he echoed before ending the call.

"Nothing on his end?" Nicki asked.

"He didn't see anyone, but I didn't see the guy who jumped me either. Why would someone follow me and not Dylan?"

"No offense to Zoe, but Dylan isn't exactly nuclear scientist material. He's so focused on himself, he wouldn't notice an elephant behind him."

"That isn't nice," Olivia reproached.

"Still true." Nicki sipped her latte.

"You've only met him a few times."

"Zoe hired me to help him plan the initial social media campaign for his fitness influencer business," Nicki deadpanned. "But he wouldn't listen to me. So I stopped. I didn't want to take Zoe's money for nothing. Also, I didn't want my name or company to be associated with Dylan's account."

"Why not?"

"His production quality is below par. The filters he uses to smooth out his wrinkles are too obvious. He's awkward on camera, and he was inconsistent with his messaging. To be a real social media influencer, you have to be able to talk in circles with complete confidence. You have to sound like you know what you're talking about even when your 'facts'"—Nicki used air quotes around the word—"are a bunch of made-up nonsense. You have to convince people of weird shit, like that tanning their testicles will increase their testosterone, or that drinking yak colostrum—which you sell as a powder for the low, low price of $29.99—is a magic fat burner. You'll say anything to get more followers, more shares, more clicks. You can be an idiot, but you have to *sound* smart. But Dylan?" Nicki played one of his videos on her phone. "See? Dude's clueless *and* sounds it."

She isn't wrong.

Nicki added, "Zoe also gave him a tight budget, and that irritated him too. He'd make occasional snarky comments about her commitment to his business."

Dylan's video *was* cringy. Still, Olivia wasn't willing to verbalize the insult. Instead, she changed the subject. "Let's get back to finding Zoe."

Nicki nodded. "Her cell account info?"

Olivia pulled the paper out of her pocket and handed it over. Nicki opened her laptop, then simultaneously slurped, dripped cheese, and typed.

Olivia stared at the stickers covering the top of the computer. She had no idea what any of them represented. "Maybe you should finish eating first."

"I got this," Nicki answered without a pause in her keystrokes. "Multitasking at its finest."

Olivia bit into her soufflé. Usually, she considered it a nice treat, but today she barely tasted it. Nicki's sandwich shed crumbs onto her keyboard. Olivia resisted the urge to brush them away.

"Got it." Nicki turned her laptop to face Olivia.

Already?

Olivia stared at the map. "That's where Zoe's phone is?"

"That's the last known location." Nicki finished her sandwich in one huge bite.

"How did you get that so quickly?"

"I reported the phone lost."

"How will that affect the police investigation of the phone's movements?"

"I dunno." Unconcerned, Nicki balled up her trash and tossed it into the receptacle near the table. She stood and picked up her latte. "Ready?"

"For what?"

"To go there." Nicki pointed with her drink to the computer screen. "Though I don't know why anyone would go to Kellsville, New York." She zoomed in on the dot, then opened another window and did an internet search. "According to the map, it's pretty rural. The population is 610."

"She could have been doing research. She works on multiple cases at a time." Olivia leaned over to peer at the map. Zoe's phone had indeed last been used in a little town about seventy-five miles west of Scarlet Falls. "Maybe we should leave it to the police."

Nicki frowned. "Someone chased us today. I want to know why. I'm going. Besides, you told me the police had to wait for warrants and stuff."

"They do." Olivia didn't like involving her niece. She'd rather go alone. "You don't have a car."

"I'll rent one or call an Uber." Nicki lifted a stubborn chin, then leaned in. "I know you're going, and I'm not letting you do it alone."

Exasperated, Olivia said, "I was going to wait for Lincoln to come with me." She'd texted him, but he hadn't responded. "You don't have plans tonight?"

"I do, but not until eight."

"A date? Someone special?"

"Not a date. We're having coffee." Nicki lifted her phone. "I've met him a couple of times, but only briefly. He's a friend of a friend. It's no biggie if I don't make it." She closed her laptop, tucked it beneath her arm, then gathered the rest of her things. "I know you. You are absolutely not going to wait for Sharp." She tapped a toe on the pavement. Her eyes narrowed with determination.

Olivia knew that look. Her niece had been born with more than her share of the family stubbornness gene. "What if that man comes after us again?"

Nicki laughed. "I think he's going to want to ice his face for a while first, and there's no way you won't spot a tail driving all the way out to Kellsville." She turned serious. "Now, are we going together or am I going alone?"

What choice do I have?

Olivia stood. "Together. But we're not going to *do* anything. We're just looking."

"Sure," Nicki said, turning away.

Was that an eye roll?

Olivia checked her messages. Wendy hadn't responded to her voicemail. She really wanted to search Zoe's office, but she couldn't break in. Right? Breaking in had to be a last resort, and she'd have to do it at night—after she found out if the building and parking lot had functioning security cameras. And she should probably wait until Lincoln was available to help. A covert, nighttime—illegal—activity felt too complicated for an amateur. Would the management company even release any footage to a random person who didn't work or rent space in the building? Probably best to wait until Wendy responded before making a decision on that line of investigation.

Which left the last known location of Zoe's phone as the only lead. She pulled out her phone and called Officer Billings. His voicemail picked up. Olivia left a message, letting him know they'd found the last known location of Zoe's phone.

She turned back to Nicki. "OK, then. You can come with me. As long as you promise not to take any action without permission."

This time, Nicki's eye roll was unmistakable.

"I mean it," Olivia said.

Nicki sighed. "Whatever."

"Then let's go to Kellsville."

Chapter Seven

Olivia followed the GPS directions for the next ninety minutes while Nicki interrogated her about Zoe's disappearance. By the time they were approaching the dot on the screen, it was nearly five o'clock. Zoe had been missing for seventeen hours. Neither Officer Billings nor Wendy had returned her calls, and Olivia knew firsthand what could happen in that length of time. She pushed back at the memories. They wouldn't help her find Zoe.

"I see no signs of life," Nicki commented from the passenger seat.

The landscape had grown more and more rural, lots of trees and fields. They hadn't seen a building for a while.

"How accurate is the last known location?" Olivia asked.

Nicki pointed to the car's screen. "Just because this is the last known location doesn't mean the phone is here now. It means the phone was last used here. As to the accuracy of the ping . . ." She shrugged. "It depends. In more populated areas, GPS in general is fairly accurate. Out here"—she waved a hand to indicate their surroundings—"who knows?"

"Right," Olivia said.

Nicki frowned at her phone, which was plugged into the car and commanding the GPS. "Cell service has been spotty for the last fifteen or twenty miles, so the area might be larger than we'd like."

Great.

Olivia watched the remaining distance countdown and slowed the vehicle. Nicki's GPS used a woman's voice with an Australian accent as it said, "You have reached your destination."

Olivia pulled over. They stepped out of the vehicle and stood on the shoulder of the road. There was nothing in sight but forest. She retrieved her hiking boots from the back of her vehicle and changed her footwear. "Shall we look?"

"With good connectivity, the GPS can be accurate within a couple of square yards, so let's give it a try." Nicki stared at her phone screen. "We should be organized about this."

"Let's walk a grid pattern." Olivia gestured in an east-west direction to parallel the direction of the road. Then she began walking, slowly, eyes on the ground. "Watch where you step. If Zoe tossed her phone out the Jeep window, it would be close to the road. If it's deep in the woods, buried under dead leaves, we'll never find it."

Nicki followed. Their footsteps crunched in dry foliage.

After thirty minutes of searching, Olivia stopped. "We don't know if the phone is here, so this feels pointless, like searching a haystack we're not sure contains a needle. We might have to come back with a metal detector. Or the police can search the area with a K-9." Though Olivia wasn't looking forward to an awkward conversation about why she was conducting her own investigation. Also, she wasn't sure they would bother to search for Zoe's phone. They weren't convinced anything bad had happened to her.

But as Nicki would say, *Whatever*. Olivia wasn't giving up. From her true crime research, she knew the police were limited in what they could do to track a missing adult with no evidence that a crime had been committed. Their resources were finite, and an adult was free to leave their spouse if they chose. The police couldn't proceed on their personal knowledge of the missing person, but Olivia could. She would keep looking for Zoe the same way Lincoln hadn't given up on her. Olivia's stomach clenched and her lungs tightened at the thought of Zoe being held captive. Was she cold? Thirsty? What horrible things could already have been done to her?

Stop! You don't know that she was taken.

Olivia led the way back to the car. "Why would Zoe come out here?" She opened her own GPS app and began scanning the area on the map. She zoomed in on the closest dot. "There's a building right over there, just around the corner past the bend in the road. It's only about two hundred yards from us." She looked up at the thick forest that lined the road on both sides. In mid-September, the leaves had begun to turn, but the foliage was still dense enough to block the view. "I don't see any other buildings on the map within a half mile of here." She expanded the lone dot again. The back of her neck tingled as she read the description. "It's a self-storage facility."

Nicki said, "If Zoe needed to store something, why would she drive all the way out here? It's not exactly convenient. Why not rent a unit closer to home?"

"She could have rented it before she moved to Scarlet Falls, or maybe she didn't want it to be convenient." *Maybe she didn't want anyone to know.* Olivia put the car in gear and pulled onto the road. She steered around the bend, and the self-storage sign came into view. The facility was old, run-down, and desolate-looking. She drove into the entrance and parked in front of the office.

Nicki reached for the door handle. "Do we have a plan?"

"We're going to tell the truth. We're looking for our friend, who is missing, and she has a unit here."

"And you think that'll work?"

"You never know what will work. We can only try."

The office was cold and smelled musty. A young man in his early twenties perched on a stool behind the counter, reading what appeared to be a textbook. His gaze passed right over Olivia as if she were invisible and focused on Nicki. "Can I help you?"

Nicki picked up on his interest and stepped up to the counter, cocked a hip, and twirled one of the many locks of hair that had escaped her messy bun. "We're looking for my aunt."

Aunt?

"She's missing, and we think she rented a storage unit here. We're really worried." She turned impressively sad eyes on him. "We think she was here the other day. We're trying to retrace her steps, ya know. Would you look at a picture of her and tell us if you've seen her?"

Olivia was impressed with Nicki's improvisation. She hadn't known her niece could act so fluidly—and lie so easily.

The young man swallowed. "Uh. Sure."

Nicki nudged Olivia with an elbow. "Show him a picture of your sister."

"My sister, right." Olivia fished out her phone from her pocket and pulled up a photo of Zoe. She turned the cell so he could see the screen.

He glanced at it for two seconds at the most. "Yeah, I've seen her here."

"Recently?" Nicki sounded hopeful.

"A few weeks ago?" He didn't sound sure. "I don't remember which day, but within the last month for sure. I remember her because she came in and paid for the whole year in cash. Not many people do that. Most people use a credit card and have their account set to auto pay every month, occasionally I get a check, but this was my first all-cash payment."

Olivia glanced through the window. The office sat in front of the property. Vehicles had to pass through a gate with a keypad and an arm barrier to access the actual units. The fence didn't look hard to climb. There was no razor wire coiled at the top. No notice that the fence was electrified. But you couldn't drive a vehicle to your unit without passing through the gate. "Is there any way to check? Do renters need to punch in a unique code?"

"No." He ripped his gaze from Nicki and followed Olivia's line of sight. "There's only one code for the gate. Everybody uses it. It's our zip code."

Doesn't seem very secure. But then, nothing about the facility appeared to be modern or up to date. A sign on the wall posted very low unit rental rates. *You get what you pay for.*

"Do you know which unit is hers?" Nicki asked.

He shook his head. "It won't matter. The units are locked."

Nicki held up her own keys. "I have her key."

Liar liar.

He looked doubtful. "I don't know if I'm allowed to give out that kind of information."

"We're not asking for her personal information," Olivia said. "We just want to see if the key fits."

"Please." Nicki dropped her chin, her lips quivered, and she contorted her face into a ridiculously sad expression. *Is that a tear?* Her eyes suddenly opened wide. "I wonder if she could have accidentally locked herself inside her unit or had a medical emergency while she was inside. She could be in there right now." She stopped just short of suggesting her "aunt" could have died and was now decomposing in her storage unit. "How many days has she been missing?" She began to count on her fingers. "It's been kind of warm . . ."

The young man caught the implication. His eyes bugged. "Shit." He turned to a computer so old the plastic had yellowed. He typed. "Her name?"

"Zoe March," Olivia said.

"That's her," the young man said.

Bingo.

"Thank you!" Nicki rewarded him with a few bats of her eyes. "You have a really good memory."

"It's unit 160," he said, all concerns of client privacy seemingly banished by Nicki's praise and the thought that a corpse could be decomposing in the facility.

Nicki touched his forearm. "Thank you so much. You might have saved her life."

He blushed. "You'll let me know, right? I mean, if she's . . ." His gaze slid to the window.

"Of course. Thanks again." Nicki led the way out of the office. Olivia hurried after her, and they slid into the Prius.

Olivia fastened her seat belt. "I'm not sure whether to be impressed or concerned at your ability to lie on the spot."

"You can be both," Nicki said.

Olivia drove to the gate and entered the zip code on the keypad. She spotted a security camera high on the side of the building. She assumed it was supposed to be aimed at the gate, but it dangled crookedly from its mount. If it worked, it was taking a video of the ground. When the barrier arm rose, she went through. Unit 160 was a corner space on the first level at the back of the facility. The doors were rolling-overhead-garage types. Zoe's unit was one of the largest. Olivia parked on the side of the building. "We don't have Zoe's key, though."

But Olivia wanted into that unit. She didn't want to wait. Zoe could be a captive at that very moment. Every second that ticked by could be her last. Sweat gathered between Olivia's shoulder blades. She knew exactly how a worst-case scenario could play out. How every second of captivity could feel like an eternity. What it meant to wonder if each breath was your last. She had to find Zoe before it was too late.

Nicki turned in her seat to view the back of Olivia's vehicle. "Don't you keep a tool kit back there?"

"Yes."

They exchanged a look. Nicki raised a brow.

Olivia stepped out of the vehicle, went to the rear, and opened the hatch.

Nicki joined her. Olivia checked her phone again. Still nothing from Officer Billings. Why hadn't he called her back? Wasn't he concerned about Zoe? Frustration bubbled in Olivia's throat.

Olivia glanced at the padlock securing Zoe's unit. Then she fished a bolt cutter from the tool bag. "Check for cameras." It was best not to have illegal activity recorded on video.

Nicki's head swiveled as she scanned their surroundings, her gaze lingering on the exterior of the building. "There's no one around, and I only see one security camera back here."

Olivia unzipped the tool kit. She followed Nicki's gaze. The camera was mounted on the next building and pointed to capture the entire row of units.

"The way it's pointed, it won't see us until we go around the corner," Nicki said.

"One camera is still too many."

Nicki moved to stand under it. She looked up. "I've got this." She tested the downspout, then wrapped her hands around it and climbed up the building.

"You've been climbing?" Olivia watched her niece mimic Spider-Man.

"Only inside. Dad made me promise not to climb without him. But I've been keeping up with my strength training too." Her slim build was deceptively strong. She shimmied to the camera, redirected its lens upward, then slid down like a fireman on a pole. Landing lightly, she said, "We're clear."

"Makes you wonder if Zoe's low-tech, out-of-the-way choice was intentional, doesn't it?"

"It does," Nicki agreed. "But what would Zoe have that she wanted to hide? She seems so . . . normal."

"Let's find out." Olivia clipped off the padlock without any hesitation, like ripping a Band-Aid off a wound. She returned the bolt cutters to the car and pocketed the padlock. There was no point in advertising their break-in.

Nicki leaned over, grabbed the handle, and lifted the door. It creaked and moaned as it rolled overhead, revealing an old black Jeep. The rest of the space was empty. "That's her Jeep, right?"

Olivia stared at a row of rubber duckies lined up along the dashboard. "I don't know her license plate, but I bought her that duck in the Hawaiian shirt when she and Dylan went to Maui for their honeymoon." Olivia circled the vehicle, peering through the windows. "According to Wendy, Zoe was driving her Jeep when she left the studio at midnight."

"So, she was here after that—this morning," Nicki said.

Olivia stopped at the driver's door and opened it. The console was empty. She leaned inside and swept a hand under the seat. Her fingers found something metal and round. Zoe's vehicle key, which was old enough to be an actual physical key that had to be inserted and turned to start the engine.

"This thing is a relic." On the other side of the Jeep, Nicki opened the passenger door and stuck her head inside. "Is that an actual key?"

"Yes. Check under the passenger seat."

Nicki pulled out two items: a phone and a separate battery. "She left these behind." She handed them across the console.

Olivia pulled her torso out of the vehicle. She stood up and inserted the battery into the phone. "I hope the battery has a charge."

Nicki withdrew from the passenger side and crawled into the back seat. "I don't see anything but trash back here."

"Look for receipts or anything else that might help us retrace Zoe's recent activity."

"OK."

Mentally crossing her fingers, Olivia turned the phone on. The screen blinked, then came to life, the battery showing a 53 percent charge.

"Do you know her passcode?" Nicki asked.

"Yes." Olivia hummed the tune as she entered the numbers, eight-six-seven-five-three-zero. She mentally filled in the unnecessary *nine*, then opened Zoe's email and scrolled. Emails appeared to be mostly related to the podcast or spam. "I wonder if her disappearance could be related to a case she's researching."

"Will Wendy know?" Nicki emerged from the back seat with a small stack of receipts in her hand.

"I'm not sure how much Zoe shares with her." Olivia closed the email app. She could dig into Zoe's podcast research later. She moved on to Zoe's texts, tapping on the last message, which she'd received at 12:07 that morning from an unknown sender. Olivia froze and her body went cold as she read the text.

"You're pale." Nicki rounded the vehicle to stand in front of Olivia. "What does it say?"

Olivia read the single word. "'Run.'"

Chapter Eight

During the years Zoe had planned her escape scenario, she'd never actually thought she'd need to implement it. Even though the necessity had always lurked in the background, given what she did. Her life did revolve around murder. But she'd compartmentalized. She'd made plans and then put them out of her mind.

Until last night.

Run.

Fresh panic rose in her throat, hot, caustic, and tasting of copper, like a penny—or blood.

Stop.

She tried a few yoga breaths, like Olivia said had helped her when she'd been abducted. But Zoe didn't have the same level of self-control as her friend. Olivia's trauma was fresh. Her body had decades to understand how it felt to be untraumatized. She had her experience with normal to draw on. Zoe didn't. Her trauma ran too deep. Her heart continued to race, and her lungs refused to loosen. A small, tinny sound echoed in her ears, building and building, threatening to completely block her hearing.

You're safe.

For now.

No one knew where she was going.

She wished she could have told Olivia, wished she had her steady, methodical presence to calm her. But she hadn't dared. Olivia would insist on knowing everything, and she'd have Zoe's back no matter what, which was the very reason Zoe couldn't tell her. Anyone who knew too much would be in danger.

She kept her speed exactly at the limit. She couldn't afford to be pulled over. The van was small and white with no windows in the cargo area. It was the generic kind of vehicle used by contractors of all kinds. She had several different magnetic signs she could switch out, along with an extra set of license plates. Currently, the van sported an A-OK Plumbing logo. It blended, but the vehicle was also registered to a dead person, so it would not hold up to the scrutiny of law enforcement.

She'd been listening to her police scanner app. So far, there had been no response to the BOLO alert the Scarlet Falls PD had issued on her. She touched her auburn wig for reassurance. Chin length, with a straight row of bangs, it drastically altered her appearance. Her real hair was longer, wavy, and blond. She'd disguised her athletic shape with an oversize flannel shirt and baggy jeans. Lug-soled work boots gave her an extra inch or two of height and supported the plumber persona. When she'd stopped to gas up the van, she'd worn a baseball cap to shadow her face and inserted gauze into her cheek pockets to change the shape of her face. Normally, she didn't even go to the mailbox without applying a full face of makeup. Today, she wore none. She barely recognized herself.

The van was the most nondescript, boring vehicle in the world. Plus, if her hideout had been compromised, the van was large enough to sleep in. But for now, she could still hope her plans had held.

She pressed the brake pedal, bringing the van to a halt at a stop sign, then turned right. Another mile down the road, she cruised through a bend and slowed as she approached the turnoff. She'd already driven by twice. Both times, other vehicles had been in sight, and she'd elected to keep going. She didn't want anyone to see her entering the community.

This neighborhood consisted largely of vacation homes. People skied in the winter and hiked, swam, and boated in the summer. There were local caves to tour and a small ski resort that offered zip-lining in the warmer months.

Thick woods flanked both sides of the road. On one side, the ground sloped upward in a steep grade. On the other, the ground fell away into a gorge.

At a sign for Hidden Cavern, a subterranean tourist attraction, she slowed.

There.

The entrance to Hidden Mountain Estates was barely visible. She turned left to get off the paved road. Pine boughs brushed the sides of the van as she eased through the turn. Gravel crunched under the tires as the van roller-coastered over deep ruts. Zoe drove slowly. She could fix a flat tire, but a broken axle would ground her.

Not wanting to tackle the rough road in the dark last night, she'd taken a roundabout route, traveling a hundred and fifty miles in the wrong direction, then refilling her gas tank. Her disguise should hold up, but if she was recognized, it would appear as if she were headed south, not west. Then she'd meandered her way into the mountains, avoiding toll roads. At first light, she'd driven around the area to get her bearings. She hadn't been here in a long time. The van climbed the gravel road like the famous little engine, branches scraping at the roof and sides. Her Jeep would have been safer, but she couldn't risk anyone spotting it. Just like when she'd been a teen, wild blackberry thickets edged the road. If she stopped and picked a few, would their sweet juiciness bring back memories?

At a fork in the road, she bore right and continued to bump up the incline. If the weather turned, she was in trouble. Mud, ice, or snow would make the road impassable to any vehicle without four-wheel drive. She checked the map app on her phone, then navigated the two intersecting loops that composed the neighborhood. Cruising slowly, she scanned each property. No visible vehicles. No movements in windows. No puffs of smoke from chimneys.

No signs of habitation.

Perfect.

She steered the van into a long, steep driveway. The house stared down at her. The cedar structure had been built into the mountain. You could enter on the first-floor garage on the left and exit from the third-level bedroom on the right. On the second floor, a deck jutted out over the valley.

Zoe chugged slowly up the incline. At the top, she stopped the van in front of the garage. She got out and pivoted in a complete circle, then stood still and listened. She saw no one and heard nothing. Holding her breath, she separated the key from her others. It slid into the lock but refused to turn. With a hitch in her pulse, Zoe jiggled it. Would her key work? Had the house been sold?

She returned to her van and opened the rear cargo door. In one of her toolboxes, she selected a can of WD-40 from her supplies. She also grabbed a flashlight before closing the hatch. Inserting the skinny straw into the oil can's nozzle, she sprayed the inside of the lock and tried the key again. It turned easily.

With a relieved breath, she opened the door and called out, "Hello?" When no one answered, she stepped inside. Her boots scraped on the rough concrete. The interior was dark and smelled musty. She pocketed the lubricant and shone her flashlight around the space. The first bay was empty. A small lawn mower, a Weedwacker, and a snowblower occupied the second. A workbench and rolling tool cabinet stood against the bare cinder block wall. Random junk filled the dark corners. On the right side, an interior door led into the mudroom.

Something rustled in dead leaves behind a shelving unit. Zoe startled. With one hand splayed over the center of her chest, she froze. Even with the flashlight, she couldn't see into all the nooks and crannies, not without getting close, and there was enough space in the dark corner for a man to hide. Vacant homes could be targeted by squatters.

Or someone had guessed where she'd gone.

Sweat gathered under Zoe's arms. She waited. Heavy breathing emanated from the darkness. Someone was waiting, hiding, ready to ambush her.

Her pulse pounded in her temples, its echo thrumming at the base of her throat. Outside, the last remnants of daylight faded.

She contemplated moving closer, but her feet refused to do so. She had no choice but to risk turning on a light. She reached for one of two strings dangling from ceiling-mounted light bulbs. What was the chance the bulb still worked? To her surprise, the light turned on, flooding the space, leaving Zoe and a black bear to stare at each other. Three hundred pounds of teeth and claws and raw strength met her gaze, and where was her bear spray? Safely in her backpack in the van.

That bear could rip her to pieces and eat her for lunch. Yet, for a split second, she was relieved it wasn't a human. At least a bear would only kill her. A man could do much worse. She knew this for a fact. She'd seen—experienced—what they could do, and lived through what one particular man had tried to do.

Reality sent a shiver of primitive fear through her bones. The bear stood on its back legs and sniffed the air. But it did not rush her. Zoe wanted to bolt but held her ground. She'd grown up camping. She'd been taught how to handle a bear encounter. Running would trigger the bear's prey instinct. Black bears were not usually aggressive unless they felt threatened, but she was between the animal and the open garage door. If the bear felt trapped, it might attack.

This was not the first time in her life she'd encountered a black bear. They were common enough in the mountains of upstate New York. Normally, on an open trail, she'd stand tall and raise her arms to appear bigger. Bears respected size and would usually go the other way. But in close quarters, she didn't want to trigger a defensive charge.

Mutual respect would be a better option in her current situation. Still standing, the bear was roughly the same height as Zoe.

Don't antagonize it, but also don't act like prey. Be chill.

Her heart continued to pound against the inside of her breastbone. It took all of her self-control to move slowly and with careful deliberation. Any sudden move—even tripping—might trigger aggression. She slid one foot backward on the dirty concrete, shifting her weight slowly, steadily, easing back. Her gaze remained on the bear. She could not bring herself to look away for even an instant to check her progress or to make sure the path behind her was clear. She took another easy step back, putting more distance between her and the animal.

The bear's head nodded as it gave the air another sniff, then it turned and disappeared through the door to the mudroom, leaving the wooden door swinging on its hinges.

Zoe didn't move. Indecision rooted her in place. Did the bear go upstairs into the house? Had it broken through a window or the glass door on the main level? Had it been living in the house? When she'd considered squatters, a bear was not what she'd had in mind.

Fuck.

She had two choices: See where the bear went or find somewhere else to hide. But where? She had nowhere else to go, and she was exhausted.

Make noise!

Her legs shook as she moved forward. "Hey, bear. I'm coming in." She grabbed a rake and slammed the metal teeth into the cinder block wall. No huffing. No grunting. Nothing crashed.

Ten feet of space seemed like forever. Zoe used the rake handle to push the mudroom door open. Nothing happened. A foul stench wafted out. She shuffled forward. "Hello? Mr. Bear?"

She peered through the opening. The mudroom had been trashed. Her gaze immediately locked on the back door and small broken window next to it. The opening didn't look big enough for Mr. Bear's getting-ready-for-hibernation butt, but it had clearly used that exit. Must have been a tight squeeze. She moved closer and spotted the bear running up the back slope and disappearing into the woods. Three smaller shapes the size of dogs followed in its wake. Her knees buckled, and she leaned on the wall for a full minute, catching her breath and willing her heart to stop its mad rush through her chest.

Not *Mr.* Bear. A mama bear. Thankfully, it hadn't brought the cubs into the house. Zoe didn't want to think about how the animal would have reacted if she'd accidentally cornered one of its babies.

When her legs steadied, she pushed off the wall and scanned the room. The washer and dryer sported a few dents, and the laundry sink was askew. The source of the odor, a huge pile of bear scat, sat on the tile. The hooks, bench, and cubbies that once held skis and fishing gear had been pulled from the walls. A small container was on its side, some grainy substance spilling out. The lid had been flung across the room. Zoe shone her flashlight on the floor. Birdseed. The bear had broken into the house for birdseed. In September, it would be foraging almost nonstop to put on as much fat as possible in preparation for hibernation.

She returned to the garage for a shovel and removed the bear scat, carrying it up the backyard slope to the tree line and dumping it in the underbrush. She also emptied the container of birdseed in the woods so Ms. Bear would not be tempted again. Zoe left the back door open to air out the space. She doubted the bear would be back—at least not yet.

She needed to get the van out of sight. She'd wanted to be inside, with the house locked up tight, before full dark. The bear encounter had messed up her timeline.

She climbed the steps to the main level, one large room containing a living space and kitchen. It didn't appear as if the bear had found its way upstairs. Nothing was torn apart.

Unlike other homes in the area, this one had never been renovated. The windows were small, and there was only one set of glass doors leading onto the deck. The dim space looked almost cramped compared to modern standards, but Zoe was grateful for the dark, closed-in space. Fewer windows meant fewer opportunities for anyone to see her, not that she would risk using the lights or fireplace.

The glass doors that overlooked the valley were grimy, but the view was still lovely. The wraparound deck spanned three sides of the house and overlooked the valley below. The wood railing peeled and flaked. Cracks split the deck planks. The house had always been rustic, with its rough-hewn wood walls and wide-planked floors. But when she'd come here, it had been maintained. How long had it been since anyone had visited the mountain house?

She tried a light switch and was almost surprised when the overhead light turned on. She quickly turned it off. On the odd chance that a neighbor had come to the mountain for a leaf-peeping getaway, she would keep a low profile. No one could know she was here. Electricity meant more than lights, though. A well supplied the house with water, and power meant that the pump might work. She lifted the lever. Pipes squeaked and protested, but water sputtered, then rushed from the faucet. The mineral smell of well water filled her nose. The initial stream was tinted brown. Rust or mud? Didn't matter, the water quickly ran clear.

Relief surged through her. She'd brought some food and water, but having a source of water simplified meeting her basic survival needs. The electric stove also worked. Hot food would be a bonus. She let the faucet run while she checked the rest of the house. Three small bedrooms and a single bath on the third level. All empty except for dust, cobwebs, and scatterings of dead flies on the windowsills. Satisfied that the house was empty—and therefore safe—she returned to her van and pulled it into the garage. She used a fallen branch to brush away the faint imprint of her tires in the dry earth of the driveway. The garage was windowless. No one would see her van. From the outside, the house still looked vacant, and she would keep it that way.

Then she went back into the garage, closing and locking the door from the inside. Back in the mudroom, the smell of bear poop clung to the air. Zoe opened the cupboard where cleaning supplies had been kept. She stared at a large bottle of Pine-Sol, memories stirring, eyes moistening. She brushed at her eyes.

No time for remembrances and sadness. Not yet.

She grabbed a small bucket and some rags and cleaned the floor. She was no clean freak, but even she had limits, and bear shit crossed them.

Then she found a square of old warped plywood and nailed it over the broken window. She tested the back door. It seemed strong enough, but the bear could likely break right through if it really wanted to get inside.

She retrieved a box of pantry staples, her backpack, and her sleeping bag from the van and carried them up to the main floor. She had no idea how long she'd have to stay. She'd been ready to run, but she hadn't planned too far ahead. Despite all her preparations, she'd never really believed this day would come.

You'll be safe.

That promise hadn't aged well.

Lying piece of shit.

Unzipping the pack, she fished out a protein bar. There was food in the box, but she was too tired to prepare a meal. She'd been awake and on the move for somewhere around thirty-six hours. All she wanted to do was crawl into her sleeping bag and pass out until morning. Safely inside the house, she removed her wig and freed her hair from the tight cap. She massaged her scalp and ran her hands through her long locks.

She washed a glass and filled it with water, holding it up in the beam of her flashlight. Looked clear. She drank, tentatively at first, then with enthusiasm. Mountain water was cold with a clean, fresh taste that took her back in time.

Some people reveled in their memories. People with good ones, anyway. But Zoe didn't often allow herself to look back. Her past was mired in grief, pain, and fear. She'd barely escaped.

Her phone vibrated in her pocket. Zoe froze. Only one person knew the number of her burner phone, but he knew not to use it. She pulled it out and stared at the screen. A simple text should not generate a ball of dread in her belly. It wasn't a smartphone and she hadn't stored any numbers in it. Every call would be labeled as *unknown*.

But this wasn't spam. She recognized the digits.

Why would he text her? She breathed, then tapped the message to open it. The words tightened her lungs and choked off her next breath.

Need to see you.

Chapter Nine

Anxiety rolled through Olivia like a bowling ball. Zoe was in trouble. Olivia called Officer Billings again. When he didn't answer, she left another—more urgent—message, saying she had important information about Zoe's disappearance. Then she started for her Prius. She needed help. If the police weren't going to assist, then Lincoln would.

Nicki rolled down the overhead door. "Are we going to leave this unlocked?"

"No." Olivia retrieved her lock from her gym bag and used it to secure the door. The smaller padlock looked flimsy, but it was all she had on hand.

"Let's go." She stowed Zoe's phone and receipts in her purse. They got into the car and drove out the gate, noting the arm opened with a motion sensor, with no need to enter the code on the way out. She parked in front of the office, and they went inside once again.

The clerk gave Nicki a questioning glance.

Nicki shook her head. "She wasn't in there."

The poor guy visibly deflated with relief.

"Are there surveillance cameras anywhere around the facility?" Olivia asked, as if she didn't know.

"A couple. The coverage isn't good, though," he admitted.

"How about the one on the gate?"

"Let me see." He returned to the computer. "Huh. I know that camera was working last week because someone hit the gate and I needed to send the footage to the insurance company. But it looks like it went down. I don't see a recording of you going through just now."

Nicki leaned on the counter. "What's the last time it recorded an entry?"

"One forty-five this morning," he said.

If Zoe had left Scarlet Falls when she'd received the *Run* message, then she would have reached Kellsville at just about that time.

He turned the computer so they could see the screen. They watched a video of Zoe's Jeep going through the gate. The time stamp read 1:45 a.m. Zoe's profile was visible, and the passenger seat appeared to be empty. The footage was too dark to see farther into the Jeep. "There's no video after that, but the electronic exit gate recorded opening at 1:58 a.m. The camera should have captured the vehicle leaving."

Did Zoe have a vehicle stashed in the unit? It seemed unlikely that she'd left on foot. There was nowhere to walk to. Unless someone picked her up . . .

"Could you give us a copy of that video?" Nicki asked.

But not even her charms could entice him. "Not without checking with my boss, no."

"I understand." Olivia didn't blame him at all. They weren't law enforcement, and they'd provided no evidence of their story. "But if I were you, I'd make sure it doesn't get deleted in case the police need it."

He nodded. "I'll make a copy."

"Do you know how long ago she rented the unit?" Olivia asked.

He tapped on the computer. "The current owners changed the system when they bought this place eight years ago."

Olivia couldn't have heard him correctly. "Did you say *eight* years?"

He nodded. "Actually, her record is older than that, but I don't have an actual date. Not sure if it's possible to find it either."

Olivia was too shocked to respond. Eight years—or more—was a long time to keep a secret this big. What was Zoe afraid of? It had to be a major threat to go to these lengths to be ready to run *and* to conceal those plans.

"Thanks anyway. You were really helpful," Nicki added.

"I hope you find her," he said.

Back in the Prius, Nicki asked in a worried tone, "What happened to Zoe?"

"I don't know."

"Why would someone tell her to run?"

"I don't know that either." But Olivia was going to find out.

They drove back to Nicki's apartment with much less conversation, as if Nicki was also processing the events of the day and what they could mean for Zoe. Lincoln texted to let Olivia know he'd be home soon.

Olivia pulled to the curb in front of Nicki's apartment.

In the passenger seat, Nicki showed no signs of wanting to get out of the car. "What now?"

"I don't know." Helplessness swirled in Olivia's gut. All of her instincts were screaming that Zoe was in deep trouble. But neither the police nor Zoe's producer had returned her calls. "I need to regroup and talk to Lincoln when he gets home."

"That's it?" Nicki's voice rose with urgency. "*Wait for Sharp* is your plan?" Everyone called him Sharp except Olivia. She refused to call the man she was in a relationship with by his last name. And she'd known from the very first time they'd met that he'd had that potential. Chemistry didn't lie.

"He's very good at what he does," Olivia said. "He found me."

"Yes." Nicki reached over and squeezed her hand.

Olivia squeezed back. "Try not to worry too much. We know Zoe was alive and well very early this morning."

"Not exactly," Nicki said. "We know she drove her Jeep into the storage facility. The gate recorded a vehicle leaving, but we didn't *see* Zoe. We're assuming it was her."

"That's a good point." Olivia was worried.

"What if someone was waiting inside her Jeep for her at the office and made her drive to the storage unit?"

"That's a lot of conjecture," Olivia warned. "We can only go by the facts. But you're right. We didn't see *her* at the unit. We only saw her Jeep. But I still need some time to review and process everything."

"I could cancel my plans for tonight and help. You have Zoe's phone, and the number that texted her to run."

"And researching those things will take time. Lincoln will help, and I have other people I can reach out to." Olivia had established connections over her long career.

"OK." But Nicki sounded disappointed.

"You have a date tonight and work tomorrow?"

Nicki shook her head. "For the tenth time, it's not a date. It's coffee."

"How many *coffees* progress to *dates*?"

"Not very many," Nicki admitted. "I haven't had any luck since *Trevor*." She said the name like it was *dog poo*.

"Trevor was a jerk."

"Can't argue with that."

"You'll meet someone."

"I'm not in a rush," Nicki said. "I'm happy by myself."

"That's good." But Olivia thought she must be lonely. Nicki had ended her relationship with Trevor because he'd cheated with her best friend. She'd lost her boyfriend and her bestie in one day. She and Olivia had always been close. But since the breakup, they'd spent even more time together. Not that Olivia was complaining. She enjoyed her niece.

Nicki continued. "I'm open to a relationship with a man who adds value to my life, but I don't need one just for the sake of having one. Aren't you the one who always told me I should be content with myself first? That I should *choose* to be with someone because I like being with them? I should never hook up just because I don't want to be alone."

Olivia laughed. "Yes. I'm glad you've been paying attention. You shouldn't settle for less than you deserve. Enjoy your evening. Maybe this young man will be worthy. You never know."

Nicki reached for the door handle. "OK, then. I'll call you tomorrow?"

"OK."

"And you'll let me know if you discover anything really important?"

"Sure." *Maybe.* "You're going to change your clothes and comb your hair before you go out tonight, right?" As soon as the questions left her lips, Olivia regretted them. Why was she so superficial?

"Probably." Nicki tilted her head. "But shouldn't a man like me for my intellect and personality rather than for my looks?"

"Yes," Olivia admitted.

"Not everyone needs to look perfect like you all the time," Nicki said.

"I do not look perfect."

"Oh, please." Nicki pointed to Olivia's hand on the steering wheel. "I bet the polish on your toenails matches that gorgeous bronze on your fingertips right now."

Guilty. The heat that flushed Olivia's cheeks was her answer.

"You know how absurd that is, right? You're wearing boots." Nicki pointed to them.

"Point taken. You're right. I'm too concerned with appearances. Does it make a difference that I do it for me and not anyone else?"

"Yeah. It does." Nicki grinned. "And you do always look fabulous. Love you. I'll call you tomorrow." She leaned over and gave Olivia a quick peck on the cheek.

"Love you too." Olivia watched until Nicki was safely inside her building. Then she checked her rearview mirror. She'd seen no sign of anyone following them, but she was not going to relax her vigilance.

She texted Lincoln to let him know she was on her way. He replied with a smiley face, which made her snort. He didn't seem like the sort of man who would use silly emojis, and she loved that he did. She sped up, anxious to talk to him. They'd only been dating for a little over three years, but their connection felt like it had spanned decades. He'd become her anchor. They'd met on one of his investigations. He hadn't wanted her help, and he'd resisted the pull between them just as hard, but he hadn't been able to deny the attraction either.

She drove home without incident. The kitchen smelled like tomato sauce. Lincoln stood at the island grating a block of Parmesan cheese. Water boiled on the stove, and red liquid simmered in a saucepan. A pot of tea steeped on the counter. He looked up as she shed her jacket, boots, and purse.

"Have you been here long?" She kissed him lightly, then rested her head on his chest. He'd recently showered. She breathed in the comforting scent of his citrus body wash.

"About a half hour." He dropped the cheese and grater, wrapped both arms around her, and kissed the top of her head. "Rough day?"

"Yes." Peace washed through her. She leaned back, taking in the weariness on his face. "I should ask the same of you. Your eyes look tired."

"I spent the day lying on a roof squinting into a pair of binoculars. And because absolutely nothing happened, I get to do it again tomorrow. You?"

Stepping out of his embrace, she poured a small amount of tea into a mug to inspect the color. Finding it perfect, she poured them each a cup. Perching on a stool, both hands curled around the mug, she watched him cook and told him everything. When she reached the attempted mugging point in her story, he stiffened but said nothing. "I have Zoe's phone and a small stack of receipts. Thankfully, Zoe is the type of person who crumples and tosses trash into the back of her vehicle."

Without a word, he turned to her and hugged her again, this time with a stronger measure of urgency. Then he released her and tossed a handful of dried spaghetti into the boiling water. "The fact that you were followed concerns me as much as the text message Zoe received."

"Nicki and I handled it."

"It still worries me, though I wish I'd been there to see it." The corner of his mouth quirked. "Have you touched base with Dylan since you found Zoe's Jeep?"

"No."

"Why not?" His voice held no criticism, only curiosity.

"We both know that the significant other is always a suspect."

"But you know Dylan."

"I'm trying to be objective. I've never met Dylan's extended family. I think today was the first time I've been with him without Zoe. I don't feel as if I know him well enough to risk Zoe's life on being able to trust him—at least not yet. Do you approve of that decision?"

"Very much." Lincoln took two shallow bowls from the cabinet and set a colander in the sink. "It can be hard to put emotions aside when you have a relationship with the people in your investigation. Being objective can mean the difference between success and failure."

"Failure means not finding Zoe, so that's not an option."

"But he's going to expect you to call him."

"I know, but I don't know how much to tell him."

"Be vague?" Lincoln suggested.

Olivia pulled out her phone and called Dylan. He answered on the first ring. "Did you find her?"

"No, but I'm still trying." The best way to avoid answering questions was to be the one asking them. "Did you discover anything?"

"No." Dylan's voice slurred. Had he been drinking? "I searched the entire apartment, and I made two hundred flyers. I put them on every windshield in the complex parking lot. Then I drove to her office to do the same, but there were only a couple of cars in that lot."

"That was good thinking," Olivia said. "Maybe someone saw something."

"What are you doing now?" he asked. The sound of ice hitting a glass came over the connection. Had he progressed to hard liquor instead of wine?

"I'm going to regroup," Olivia said. "I left a message for Wendy in case Zoe's research is involved."

"OK. I don't know what to do." His words trembled. "I'm so worried."

"Have the police called you?" she asked.

"No," he snapped. "It didn't sound like they're going to do anything."

"They have to get warrants before they can really dig into her life," Olivia said. She didn't want Dylan to be hostile or oppositional with Billings. That never helped. "I'll call you tomorrow." She didn't tell him not to worry.

"Please, Olivia. You're the only one other than me who seems to care."

"Hang tight, Dylan." She ended the call and turned to Lincoln. "I hope the police don't return tonight to ask him more questions. He's been drinking."

"You said it looked like he'd been drinking last night too. Has Zoe ever mentioned Dylan having a problem with alcohol?" Lincoln strained the pasta.

"No."

"Is that the kind of thing she'd share with you?"

"I'm not sure. I don't share everything about my private life with her."

He watched her through a cloud of billowing steam. "What if Zoe doesn't want to be found?"

Olivia considered never knowing what happened to her friend. "Then she'll have to tell me that herself. I can't be objective about that. Especially not after seeing the text she got after midnight. Someone told her to run. From what or whom? She could be . . ." A flashback rolled through her with the power of a wicked August thunderstorm. The cold, the damp, the dark. The shortness of breath.

The terror.

She shuddered, focused on steady breaths, and closed her eyes to concentrate. When she opened them, Lincoln was watching her. "You OK?"

"Yes. I know what it's like to be kidnapped. I can't take the chance that Zoe is being pursued or held captive somewhere with no one looking for her. If it hadn't been for you . . ." Her lungs quaked again. "I can't let it go."

Before she could recover, he was in front of her, his arms around her, his steadiness seeping into her body, talking into her hair. "Even if you didn't have your own experience driving you, I wouldn't expect you to just accept Zoe's disappearance. If it were one of my friends, I wouldn't give up either."

"The police don't seem that interested."

"The vast majority of people who are reported missing show up in a day or so, and you said he was a patrol officer. He'd be off duty now. He'll probably call you back in the morning. What's his name?" Lincoln had worked for the Scarlet Falls PD before he retired.

"Billings."

"I don't know him." Lincoln turned back to his meal prep, filling bowls with pasta, topping them with sauce and grated cheese. "Jenny Kruger can trace the number that sent the text." Lance's mother was a computer programmer, professor, and general whiz with all things digital. She handled most of the PI firm's technical online legwork.

"Thank you." She slipped off her stool and retrieved her purse, pulling out Zoe's phone and receipts. She returned to the island. Lincoln sat next to her. They sorted Zoe's receipts while they ate.

Lincoln set aside his pile. "The most recent of these is a Starbucks receipt from last week. None of the others seem important. Normal day-to-day stuff. The police will want them, though."

"Yes, but I'll make copies before I turn them over, just in case one of them becomes relevant." Olivia gathered them and put them into an envelope. "I have greater hopes for the phone."

They spent the rest of the evening reading through Zoe's emails and apps. She kept detailed notes about her research on her phone, using a voice recorder and an application specifically for note-taking.

Olivia said, "Usually she digs into a number of cases for the podcast, then narrows down the selections to the one that's the most interesting or intriguing. For Zoe, that's an unsolved case with at least one strong suspect the police were unable to prove was guilty. She has dozens of files in her research folder."

"When you start researching new books, do you end up doing more research on the most promising cases?"

"Yes, and the ones that are less interesting naturally fall off my radar."

"Then try sorting by computer file size."

"Good idea." Olivia re-sorted the file list. "The largest files are titled REYES, MARTIN, GRADY, PATEL, and HAMILTON." She retrieved a notebook from her drawer and began copying notes from Zoe's phone. "I'll ask Wendy if Zoe made a decision about next season's case yet."

"Now let's talk about the storage unit," Lincoln said. "She paid cash to avoid an obvious digital trail, and the only thing inside her unit was her Jeep?"

"Yes."

Lincoln gathered their dishes and transferred them to the sink. He began rinsing dishes and loading them into the dishwasher. "If she left her vehicle there, it seems reasonable to assume she traded it for a vehicle that was already in the unit."

"That seems the most likely conclusion," Olivia said. "What was Zoe into that would require her to have an exit plan?"

"Do you know when she first rented the storage unit?"

"More than eight years ago. The company's records don't extend back further than that."

"So it's possible that she had that unit—or a different one—even longer?"

"Yes." Olivia's phone buzzed. She answered the call.

"It's Wendy Simon, returning your call. Have you found Zoe?"

"No," Olivia said.

"Damn. I really thought she'd turn up by now. Even I'm starting to worry."

"I'd like to see Zoe's office. Can you let me in?"

"Yeah. I guess it would be OK." Wendy yawned. "I can meet you there tomorrow morning. A cop wants to see her office and talk to me too."

Olivia stiffened. "Do you have the officer's name?"

"Yeah. I wrote it down. Hold on." Wendy paused for a second, then said, "Billings."

"When did you speak to him?"

"About an hour ago."

Olivia bristled. Billings was working late, but he hadn't returned her call.

"He's meeting me at eight," Wendy said.

"Can you meet me at seven?" Olivia wanted access to Zoe's office before the police.

"Why?" Wendy sounded suspicious.

"I don't want to get in his way," Olivia said vaguely, though it would be more accurate to say she didn't want *him* to get in *her* way.

"I doubt the police would appreciate me giving you first access," Wendy said in a cool voice. "If you want to see Zoe's office, you can come at the same time or later. I'll be in my office until noon."

The connection went dead. Olivia frowned at her phone. Wendy had seen through her sad lie. "I'm out of practice. I used to be able to talk my way into just about any place."

"Don't be too hard on yourself," Lincoln said. "Wendy works true crime cases with Zoe. She knows a little about law and procedure."

"If she and Zoe regularly need access to information, she might not want to irritate the local PD either," Olivia added.

"What do you know about Zoe's past?"

"She grew up in Brick, New York, which is a few hours west of here. She has no siblings. Her parents died in a car accident when she was sixteen. She spent a couple years in foster care, got a scholarship and a degree in journalism from Syracuse. We met about fifteen years ago, when we worked for the same newspaper." Olivia tried to remember more but failed. "She doesn't like to talk about her past."

"Does she ever talk about trauma or abuse in the foster system?"

"No. In fact, she said she got lucky. The people she lived with were teachers. She credits them with helping her get her scholarship and fresh start."

Lincoln looked skeptical. "You don't know their names, do you?"

Olivia searched her brain. "The woman's name was Clarice. Either Zoe never told me her last name, or I forgot."

"You don't forget much, so I suspect she never told you." He closed the dishwasher door and paused. "Zoe was obviously mixed up in something bad. I can clear my calendar for tomorrow. I might be able to help. I speak fluent cop."

"I appreciate the offer, but don't you have another day of staring into a pair of binoculars?"

"Don't remind me." Lincoln grimaced. "I can work something out."

"No. You do your job, and I'll do mine."

He gave her a reluctant nod. "I will be available if you need me."

"Wendy said Billings will be there. I should be safe enough in police company."

"The keyword in that sentence is *should*." Lincoln gave her a look. "Are you going to give him the phone along with the receipts?"

"Do I have a choice?"

Lincoln stared at the ceiling, clearly thinking it over. "Legally? I don't know. It feels murky. Technically, no crime has been committed."

"Technically, I broke into Zoe's storage unit to get it," Olivia pointed out.

"Did you damage any of the facility's property?"

"No."

"Is Zoe going to file a complaint?" Lincoln asked.

"No, but it still feels wrong to keep it. How can I push for Billings to do a full investigation if I hold back key evidence?"

"What are you going to do?"

Olivia touched the phone. "I'm going to copy the data and *then* hand it over."

"Win-win," Lincoln said.

"But now that I think about it, I don't like that Billings will have first crack at Zoe's office. What if he takes evidence and then doesn't pursue the leads? I'll never know."

"Do you want to see her office first?"

"Like now?"

"Yep."

"I don't have a key."

He scoffed. "Not a problem."

Billings hasn't even called me back. I told him I had important information. Is he interested in finding Zoe or actively looking for reasons not to look?

She stood. "Let's do it."

Chapter Ten

Olivia silenced her phone as Lincoln pulled to the curb of the street that ran behind Zoe's office. Darkness fell over the vehicle as it slid into the shadow of a mature oak. They faced the rear of the complex. The buildings were one story tall, with four offices in each strip. A dumpster sat next to each rear door. The middle units faced a parking lot to the east. The offices on either end pointed north and south. Zoe rented the southern unit.

Lincoln studied the buildings through a pair of binoculars. "There's a single camera in the parking lot and one over the front door." He lowered the binoculars. "Is there a security system?"

"There's a panel in the hallway. I've been in Zoe's studio dozens of times, and I've never seen her use it." Olivia scanned the southern parking lot and spotted the camera mounted on a streetlamp above a small solar-power panel. "It doesn't seem as if the parking lot camera will capture us if we stick close to the wall."

"No." Lincoln turned off the interior vehicle light, opened his door, and stepped out. Olivia followed, taking care to close her door softly rather than slam it. They crossed three yards of grass and paused. A narrow expanse of asphalt—wide enough for a delivery or waste management vehicle—extended between them and the office complex.

As they approached the edge of the tree's shadow, he held up a hand and stopped. Lifting the binoculars, he scanned the dumpster and recycling bins lined up along the back of the building. "Looks clear."

Lincoln wore sneakers, jeans, and a zip-up sweat jacket. He lifted the hood over his head, shadowing his face. Olivia wore black yoga pants and a matching slim jacket, also with a hood, which she also drew over her head. She'd added block-heeled boots because she liked them, and why not match?

They jogged across the pavement and onto the concrete walkway that ran around the perimeter of the building. Sticking close to the brick exterior, they approached the rear door. "I don't see a camera back here. Not a very secure building."

"She chose it because the rent is cheap."

"You get what you pay for." Lincoln jogged to the rear door. He pulled a slim leather case from his pocket, removed two slim tools, and crouched. He closed his eyes and twisted and finessed the tools for a few seconds until the door clicked. "Got it."

"That was fast."

"Not much of a lock." He opened the door. The back entrance led into a narrow hallway. Olivia closed the door behind them. She held her breath, waiting for a beep that would indicate the office had a security system. But the office remained quiet except for the hum of the water-cooler. She exhaled and squinted into the darkness. The air smelled of dust and burned coffee.

Lincoln used a small flashlight to examine the edges of the door. He shone his light on a small magnet in a plastic mount on the doorframe. His light traced the wire from the contact to the corner of the molding, where it dangled, the end cut and frayed. Whatever security system used to be in place was no longer functioning.

Olivia nodded. Even though the office was empty, she inexplicably wanted to stay quiet. Apparently, so did Lincoln. He waved her forward. As they crept down the hallway, Olivia fished her own penlight from a jacket pocket. She didn't want to turn on the overhead lights and potentially draw attention from a passing police patrol vehicle.

Four doors opened off the main hallway. The two offices were on the right, the studio and kitchenette on the left.

Lincoln leaned close and spoke softly in her ear. "Which door is Zoe's office?"

Olivia gestured to the door to their right. Lincoln stepped over the threshold. Something rustled. Olivia froze. In front of her, Lincoln's body tensed. Before either of them could react, a dark shape hurtled toward them. Olivia jumped backward on reflex. Lincoln did the same but had less room to maneuver in the doorway.

The shape seemed male—and also familiar—for the split-second glance Olivia managed before the man ducked and drilled a shoulder into Lincoln's midsection. Lincoln twisted as his assailant made contact, minimizing the impact. His flashlight went flying, landing on the linoleum floor and rolling under the desk.

The assailant wrapped his arms around Lincoln's torso. Lincoln hammered both fists into the back of the man's shoulders. Momentum carried the men into the hallway. They crashed into the opposite wall. Lincoln took the brunt of the impact, his body deflating with a hard exhalation.

Frantic, Olivia searched the office for a potential weapon. There must be something here she could use. Her penlight glimmered on an acrylic podcast award on the corner of Zoe's desk. Dropping the light, she snatched up the award. It was shaped like an obelisk. About the size of a bowling pin, it had enough heft to do the job.

Spinning on one heel, she lunged into the hallway. The men were still locked in a fighting embrace like boxers, with Lincoln's back pressed into the wall. Lincoln had recovered his wind. His attacker bent low into a tackle position and jammed his left shoulder into Lincoln's rib cage. His right fist drew back, prepared to deliver an uppercut to Lincoln's kidney. Lincoln hammered the back of his opponent's neck, forcing him downward a few inches. Then he wrapped one arm around the back of his neck, sliding his hand and forearm across the man's windpipe and trapping him in a headlock. He jerked upright, knocking the attacker off kilter and taking the force out of his kidney punch. But having his back to the wall limited Lincoln's mobility and his ability to shift backward and use additional leverage to increase the pressure of his forearm into his assailant's throat.

Lincoln took a small step sideways and turned. Freeing up a small amount of space between his body and his attacker's, he drove a knee into the man's belly. The man continued to pound Lincoln's flank with short punches. A few years before, Lincoln had been stabbed in the abdomen, and as much as he pretended to be 100 percent recovered, Olivia knew the area around the scar would always be his Achilles' heel.

Momentum—and fury—propelled her into the hallway. Using both hands, she lifted the acrylic obelisk and brought it down on the only target available to her: the middle of the man's back, right between his shoulder blades. He sagged. She lifted the award high and hit him again. Grunting, he released Lincoln.

His body jerked backward. He twisted and sent an elbow over his shoulder at Olivia's face. She turned her face away just in time, the blow glancing off her cheek with a sharp burst of pain. Lights flashed in her vision like a kaleidoscope. The impact drove her sideways. She stumbled and dropped the award, then flung out her free hand to catch her balance on the wall. The obelisk miraculously missed her toe and bounced into the baseboard. Her palm landed on the cool wallboard with a thud. She gave her head a shake to clear it. Adrenaline quickly numbed her face.

Thank goodness she'd turned away. A direct blow could have knocked her out.

"Keep your hands off her!" Recovering, Lincoln staggered forward.

The man turned back to Lincoln to reengage, and Olivia got her first glimpse of the intruder's face in the red glow of the exit sign. The bandanna across his nose and mouth chilled her blood. Even in the dim light, she recognized the eyes of the man who'd accosted her that afternoon.

"You!" she gasped.

He glared back at her and growled, "Bitch."

Olivia lifted a knee and drove the block heel of her boot into the side of the man's knee, using the same move as Nicki had earlier that day. His leg buckled. He dropped to one knee. Olivia lunged for the only weapon at hand, the award at the base of the wall. Pushing off the floor with a gloved hand, the intruder ran, limping, for the rear door.

Panting, Lincoln started in pursuit. "Who's the bitch now?"

The man shoved through the door with Lincoln at his heels. Olivia ran after them. She burst outside onto the concrete. She squinted into the darkness. An engine sounded. Where was Lincoln? A vehicle drove away.

"Lincoln?" she whispered, fear crawling through her belly.

Had the man had an accomplice? Had Lincoln been hurt? Or worse?

A shape emerged from the shadows. "Here."

The breath left Olivia in a rush, leaving her dizzy for a few seconds. She inhaled a lungful of night air. Oxygen flooded her. Her head stilled. He walked toward her gingerly. One hand rubbed his side.

"Are you all right?" She stepped backward into the darkness of the building hallway.

Lincoln followed and closed the door. "I'm fine."

"Do you think he's coming back?" she asked.

"No, but I didn't expect him to be here, so who knows? You OK?"

"Yes."

Lincoln snorted. "No doubt we'll both have some interesting bruises tomorrow. But it could have been worse. Did you recognize him?"

"Yes. His face was covered—again—so I can't be completely certain, but I think that's the same man who tried to steal my purse."

"So, it definitely wasn't a random mugging attempt. He is either following you—though I didn't spot a tail—or he's looking for Zoe, same as us. Could it be Zoe's husband?"

"No. The eyes are wrong," Olivia said. "Do we call the police?"

"Not unless you're prepared to explain how we discovered the break-in while we were breaking in."

"No. I suppose not. Then what do we do?"

Lincoln turned back toward Zoe's office. "What we came to do."

"Right. I'll take her office." She headed down the hall.

"Wait."

Olivia turned back.

Lincoln handed her a pair of blue nitrile gloves. "Try to leave things where you find them."

Olivia glanced around. Other than the award on the floor, the hallway showed no sign of their altercation. Lincoln walked into Zoe's studio while Olivia tugged on the gloves. She picked up the award from the hallway and returned it to Zoe's desk, giving its surface a wipe with the hem of her jacket. Then she started searching. She couldn't tell if the desk's contents had been rifled through because Zoe was no tidier with her professional space than she was with her personal one. Files, books, and sticky notes littered the blotter. One drawer hung open. Zoe used a laptop computer and took it home with her each night, so there was no desktop to hack into. Had the intruder taken anything? Or had he just arrived when they'd interrupted him?

Olivia worked her way through Zoe's desk drawers. She moved a tangle of charging cords and a box of pens to reveal an envelope of receipts labeled EXPENSES. She thumbed through them. None were recent. She tucked the envelope back into place and turned to the files and notes strewn across the desk's surface. In the pencil drawer she rummaged through an assortment of highlighters, index cards, pens, and binder clips to a small notepad. The top sheet was blank. Olivia thumbed through the rest of the pages. In the center, she found a list of seemingly random words, numbers, and symbols. Passwords? She took a photo of the page with her phone and moved on to the next drawer.

Her gaze fell on a file labeled JENNIFER HAMILTON. Opening the file, she found handwritten notes and computer printouts of articles. She pulled out her phone and photographed each page. Then she closed the file. The rest of the materials and notes related to her own case. She took a quick look through them but found nothing new. She checked the trash can under the desk but saw only dirty napkins, empty sugar packets, and used wooden coffee stirrers.

Something red caught her attention. She spotted a red rectangle the size of a quarter under the desk. She picked it up. A flash drive. Had the intruder dropped it when they interrupted him? Or did Zoe knock it off her chaotic desk or toss it toward the trash can and miss? Olivia slipped it into her pocket.

A final scan of the desk yielded nothing else. There were no personal effects. Not a single framed photo. Zoe spent most of her time in this space, and yet it reflected nothing about her. But was the absence of personality a clue?

Lincoln appeared in the doorway. "Find anything?"

"Maybe some passwords. I took a picture." She lifted her phone. "I also took pictures of her notes on one of the cases she was researching for her podcast, the death of Jennifer Hamilton. And I found this." She held up the flash drive. "Just this." She shoved it back into her pocket. "Other than those two things, no. You?"

"Not really. Her studio is small and contains mostly recording equipment. Where does she edit her podcast?"

"Zoe and Wendy use laptops for everything. I'm meeting with Wendy in the morning. I'll double-check." She gestured around her. "Notice anything weird about this office?"

Lincoln's gaze swept the space, corner to corner, missing nothing. "It's impersonal. How long has she been renting this place?"

"Four years?" Olivia guessed.

"You'd think she'd have a funny mug or a wedding photo."

"Maybe she wants to keep the space professional. She does interview people here."

Lincoln raised his brows. "Does she clean up first?"

Olivia shook her head. "She's always been messy. I don't know how she stands it."

"You and Zoe are polar opposites in that regard." Lincoln gestured to the office next door. "Let's check Wendy's office."

Olivia followed him with a vague sense of discomfort. Wendy's office was stark. One cheap plastic chair faced a desk. A printer and copy machine occupied a stand in the corner. A box of computer paper sat on the floor next to it. She approached Wendy's desk with her hands in her pockets. "It feels wrong to be in here."

"Why?" In Wendy's chair, Lincoln paused in searching the drawers.

"Zoe is my friend. I know she'll understand my intrusion. She'll know I'm doing this because I care about her and am worried. But I don't know Wendy."

"Zoe owns the business and pays the rent, right?"

"Yes." But discomfort still gathered in Olivia's gut.

"How long has she worked for Zoe?"

"Not long. Maybe a few months."

Lincoln opened another drawer. "All the more reason to search her office."

"Wendy didn't attack me—or us."

"Which doesn't mean she isn't involved. Criminals can be hired. Or there could be more than one moving part to this situation," Lincoln said. He opened and closed more drawers. "Blah. There's barely anything here."

"She probably keeps everything important on her computer."

Lincoln paused and shot her a thoughtful look. "Do they back up the business files to a business cloud account?"

"I don't know. That's another question for Wendy."

Lincoln stood. "I guess that's it then."

They left the studio through the back door. It locked automatically behind them. Then they went back to her house. Olivia poured them each a small glass of red wine while Lincoln inserted the flash drive into the USB port of his laptop.

He sighed. "The files are password protected. Digital hacking isn't my best skill set."

"Same. I can break into my parents' computer when they accidentally change the passwords and lock themselves out, but that's the extent of my hacking experience."

"Lance's mom can have a crack at it when she traces the number that texted Zoe."

"I have no other options, so thank you."

"What's your plan for tomorrow?" he asked.

"Speak with Wendy. Talk to Dylan. Research Zoe's past."

Who was the man trying to find Zoe? And why?

Chapter Eleven

Olivia parked in front of Zoe's studio at seven forty-five the next morning. Wendy's vehicle and an SFPD patrol vehicle sat side by side in the lot. *Damn.*

She got out of her car. She'd wanted to arrive first to see if Wendy had noticed the previous night's break-in and to observe her initial interaction with the police. The upside to Zoe's disorganized and messy office was that who would be able to tell? Her office and house both looked like they'd been ransacked most of the time.

Her eyes felt gritty from lack of sleep, and the makeup she'd applied to conceal her insomnia wasn't helping with the sticky feeling. She pushed through the glass door. A buzzer sounded to announce her arrival. The front entrance of the office was more guest friendly than the rear. The outer office was still bare bones, though, with a coatrack, three cheap chairs, and a fake ficus tree.

Voices emanated from Wendy's office. Hasty appeared in the doorway. Her scowl said she wasn't happy to see Olivia, but she wasn't surprised either. She held up a hand, stopping Olivia. "Why are you here?"

"I came to talk to Wendy."

"Well, you'll have to wait outside until we're finished."

Olivia went back onto the sidewalk and paced the concrete. Despite the morning chill, she didn't return to her vehicle. She couldn't just *sit.* The window blinds of the office were lowered, so she couldn't see inside.

Were the cops searching Zoe's office? Olivia hoped they were. At least that would signal they were conducting a detailed investigation.

Nearly an hour later, Billings opened the door and gestured for Olivia to come in. Wendy's door was closed, and Olivia could hear Hasty's voice behind it, but she couldn't make out the words. Billings led her into the kitchenette and waved Olivia toward a chair. She sat, and he leaned back against the counter, crossed his arms, and glared down at her. It took effort not to roll her eyes at his obvious attempt to establish dominance. Unimpressed, she folded her hands in her lap, stared back, and waited patiently for him to get over himself.

After a few seconds of clearly not establishing dominance, his weight shifted with discomfort. "Why are you here?"

"I came to talk to Wendy," she repeated.

"She doesn't know where Zoe is, but she isn't as worried about her as you are."

"She doesn't know Zoe as well as I do," Olivia said. "Why didn't you return my call last night?"

"I didn't get the message until this morning."

Bullshit. He was on his phone with Wendy last night, which meant he most likely saw Olivia's message and ignored it.

Olivia said nothing. She let the silence stretch on for a solid minute. If he was waiting for her to blink first, he was wasting his time.

"What is the important information you uncovered?" His tone doubted its importance.

"Zoe has a storage unit." Olivia described the attempted purse snatching, tracking the storage unit through the last known location of Zoe's cell, and finding the Jeep and cell phone inside. She omitted the parts about lying to the clerk and cutting the lock. "The gate to the storage complex opened a few minutes later, so I assume she left in a vehicle. She could have walked out without triggering the gate."

Billings agreed with a nod. "She swapped her Jeep for another vehicle. If she paid cash for the unit, then that implies she didn't want her husband to know about the unit or the spare vehicle."

Olivia didn't disagree. She opened her purse and pulled out two clear plastic bags. "Here's the phone and receipts from Zoe's Jeep." She had scanned the receipts and downloaded the contents of the phone to her laptop the previous evening.

Billings's face flushed like a wicked sunburn. "You took evidence?"

"Evidence of what?" Olivia shot back in a calm but firm tone. "You keep telling me there's no proof of a crime."

Unbelievably, his color deepened to impending stroke. He muttered something that sounded like *fuck* under his breath.

Olivia ignored his anger. She wouldn't be bullied, and he couldn't have it both ways. Either Billings was going to admit something sketchy had happened with Zoe and launch a full-out investigation into her disappearance, or he'd have to deal with Olivia looking for her friend. "Anyway, you're going to want to trace the text Zoe received."

Billings pulled gloves from his pocket and tugged them on before accepting the bag. "What's the passcode for the phone?"

Olivia recited it.

Billings typed with his thumbs. "We requested Zoe's phone records. We would have had this information later today."

"I'm sure."

He read the text, and his mouth went flat. "Wait here." He took the phone into the hallway, closing the kitchen door behind him. A few minutes later, he returned. "The number is linked to a burner phone. We're working on tracing the point of purchase."

Olivia assumed Lance's mother could trace the burner phone faster since she didn't have to adhere to police procedure. Hackers didn't need warrants. "Does Zoe have any additional vehicles registered to her?"

"No," Billings said. "And we put out a BOLO. No one's seen her." *BOLO* stood for *Be on the Lookout.* "But without a description of the vehicle she's in . . ." He shrugged.

Was the vehicle Zoe had driven away from her storage unit registered to someone else? Or was it illegal?

"Is there anything else you need to tell me?" he asked, his eyes unreadable. Did he know she'd broken into Zoe's office last night? She certainly wasn't going to volunteer that bit of information.

"No. What are you going to do besides trace the text?"

"Ma'am," Billings said, his tone making *ma'am* sound distasteful. "I don't necessarily like this situation any more than you, but as you pointed out earlier, we've uncovered no indication of foul play. A woman is allowed to leave her husband. Maybe she had good reasons that she didn't share with you. There seems to be a lot that she didn't tell you. I'll follow up on the text and look into the storage unit. But even this text"—he held up the phone—"isn't proof a crime occurred. The attempted mugging could have been exactly that. The text is weird. I'll give you that. But here are the facts: Zoe kept a storage unit for over eight years, likely with a vehicle inside. She *planned* for her departure. She paid cash for the unit, thereby deliberately keeping its existence a secret from her husband—and you. She was seen at that unit very early Sunday morning, possibly exchanging her Jeep for a different vehicle. These facts—and everything else we've found—support her leaving on her own."

"Why would she do all that?"

"Maybe she'd just had it with her husband. They'd had an argument earlier. The fight was loud enough that the neighbor heard it through the wall. He admitted that the argument was a recurring marital issue. Maybe Zoe didn't like her life. Maybe she wanted to start over. I don't know, but it doesn't matter. She can leave for any reason she likes."

"Have you obtained the surveillance footage from this office complex?" Olivia asked.

"Yes. The footage confirms the time of her arrival and departure. Zoe drove away first. Ms. Simon left a couple of minutes later. No one followed either of them."

"And Zoe must have driven directly to the storage facility," Olivia said.

"With no evidence that she was forced or coerced to do so," Billings added.

"What about her credit cards and bank accounts? Has there been any activity?"

"I can't share any specific financial information with you, but I will say that none of her accounts have seen any activity since Saturday. Wherever she is, she's probably paying cash to cover her needs—just like she did with the storage unit." His next breath whistled out. "Look, if she wanted her husband—or you—to know where she was going, she would have told you both."

This point stung. "But why? Why would she run away? Her podcast was taking off. She'd built a life here. It doesn't make sense."

"I don't have to make sense of it. People are weird. They do inexplicable things all the time. If you uncover proof of foul play, call me and I'll be happy to dig deeper. Otherwise, if these last few leads don't pan out into something illegal, I'll be at the end of the line."

"She's still missing," Olivia said.

"She left," Billings corrected. His eyes softened. "I really wish I could do more, but I have to follow the law. You know my hands are tied."

"I do," Olivia admitted. Lincoln had said the same. "I'm just frustrated and worried about my friend."

"I understand," Billings said. "And for what it's worth, I'm sorry I can't help."

When he and Hasty left ten minutes later, Wendy did not emerge from her office.

Olivia knocked on the door. "Wendy?"

"You can come in."

Olivia entered the room.

Wendy sat behind her desk, chewing on a thumbnail. Anxiety gathered in her eyes as she looked up. "I really thought she'd turn up by now."

"Me too." Olivia walked in and perched on the edge of the desk.

Wendy's phone made a chirping sound. The screen showed a message. Olivia read it upside down. 4 pm today. Wendy caught Olivia watching and quickly turned over the device.

Why didn't she want me to see that?

"Can I help you?" Wendy asked.

"Has Zoe been acting differently lately? Did she seem upset?"

"No." But as she answered, Wendy's gaze drifted away. Was she hiding something? "We worked really hard preparing for your interview. She wanted it to be perfect, more in-depth and serious than the show had been in the past, almost like a documentary. I warned her that style wasn't her brand. True crime is always a little sensationalized. If it stuck a hundred percent to the facts, it would be dull, right? Sometimes you have to feed the drama to get subscribers. Clicks are money. That's the nature of the genre."

Olivia wanted to disagree. With her books, she aimed for truth. But did she speculate just a little to keep the pages turning? With a small internal cringe, she thought, *Maybe*.

Wendy continued. "Zoe wanted to get it right. I can't accept that she would put that many hours into a project if she was planning to cut and run."

"I agree," Olivia said. "Is there anything you can tell me? Anything at all about her movements or phone calls over the past few days?"

"No." But again, Wendy wouldn't meet Olivia's gaze.

"How was the show doing? Was the show making money?"

"She didn't share specifics, but things seemed to be going really well."

"But you don't know the numbers?"

"No." Wendy grimaced.

Olivia caught her eye.

Wendy frowned. "Frankly, that annoys me. I mean, she hired me to improve the show. I've clearly been successful, because our subscriber base increased and we got two new sponsors over the last couple of months."

Or was Nicki's social media plan responsible for the show's increased success?

"How am I supposed to gauge my efforts if she won't share the spreadsheets?" Wendy tapped a frustrated foot under the desk. "I have revenue benchmarks to hit for my bonus."

"Are you worried?"

Wendy shook her head. "I'm sure it'll be fine. Zoe did say the third quarter was looking like her best yet."

"Zoe didn't mention any upcoming debt payments or bills she couldn't pay?"

"No." Wendy ripped off a chunk of thumbnail. When she finally made eye contact, there was something in her eyes that didn't mesh with total innocence.

Olivia pressed. "You didn't disagree about anything?"

Wendy blinked away. "Not really."

Bingo. The vague negative felt like an admission.

Olivia waited. In an interview, silence created tension. Eventually, the subject almost always filled the void to relieve it.

But Wendy didn't bite.

Rather than put her on the defensive, which could make her shut down, Olivia moved on to her next question. "Had Zoe picked a case for next season of the show?"

"Yes. She'd decided to pursue the Jennifer Hamilton murder."

"Do you know the details on that case?"

"Yes. I have my own notes." Wendy opened her laptop and typed. "Twenty years ago, Jennifer's body was found in the woods behind a truck stop just outside of Scranton, Pennsylvania. The police determined she was killed elsewhere and her remains dumped at the rest stop. She lived just a few miles away from the dump site. According to the ME, she'd been dead about a week. Cause of death was strangulation. Though she'd been missing for two weeks, no one filed a report. Her father, Conway, was a drug dealer. Her mother was an addict. Neither parent seemed very concerned. During the initial investigation, the police assumed the father did it because of his record and overall nastiness. But they couldn't prove anything. Two years later, the father went to prison on unrelated manslaughter and drug charges. By that time, the investigation had long gone cold. But Zoe wasn't convinced that Conway was guilty. She'd found two other similar cases in which remains were dumped at rest stops, and she wanted to pursue a potential serial killer angle, looking for someone who had a job that required him to travel the interstates frequently. Jennifer's mother overdosed ten years ago, but Zoe tried to contact Conway multiple times for a possible interview."

"Did he respond?"

"Not that she told me. She was planning to drive to Scranton and knock on his door, which seemed like a very bad idea to me."

"But totally what Zoe would do," Olivia said. She would do the same. "Scranton is only a few hours away by car."

"Since Conway was recently released from prison, Zoe assumed he wouldn't want to go back and would want to talk to her to prove his innocence."

Unless he isn't innocent.

What if Conway Hamilton killed his daughter and didn't want to go back to prison? Would he threaten Zoe to keep her from resurrecting Jennifer's murder investigation? He might want to steal any evidence Zoe had collected. Maybe he knew Olivia had been to Zoe's apartment. She hadn't noticed anyone following her, but she wasn't a PI or a cop.

The most logical reason the man had tried to steal Olivia's purse and break into Zoe's office was that he wanted something Zoe had in her possession. Maybe something he assumed had been in Zoe's apartment and that Olivia had taken.

Like Zoe's cell phone.

Chapter Twelve

Olivia knocked on Zoe and Dylan's apartment door. Footsteps approached inside, and she could feel someone staring at her through the peephole. A few seconds later, the door opened.

Dylan stuck out his head and looked both ways. Then he gestured for Olivia to enter. "Come in quickly."

"Is something wrong?"

"A reporter was here earlier. He tried to push his way inside."

"I'm sorry." She walked in. The odor of rotten food hit her nose.

Dylan closed the door and leaned on it. He was wearing the same clothes as the day before, including the shirt with the wine stain. She suspected he hadn't even combed his hair, and he hadn't showered. He smelled like whiskey and stale sweat. His bloodshot eyes attested to more booze than sleep.

She went to the kitchen. The source of the odor was easy to spot: a garbage can so overfilled the lid was propped open by an empty whiskey bottle. Olivia grabbed the bottle, rinsed it, and put it in the recycling bin. "Have the police called today?"

"Yes. They aren't doing anything. In their opinion, she left me, and that's that." Dylan followed her but stood in the doorway and made no effort to help. Was he afraid of taking out the trash for fear the reporter was watching?

Olivia lifted the garage bag and tied it closed. She brushed past him and carried the bag outside, setting it on the concrete next to the door. Returning to the kitchen, she found a new bag under the sink and put it in the can.

Dylan swayed slightly on his feet. Was he drunk again this morning or still drunk from last night? Both, she decided, with a twinge of irritation. *Give him some slack.* He was no doubt depressed and anxious over Zoe's disappearance. Sure, Lincoln hadn't given up on finding Olivia when she'd gone missing, but everyone was different.

She washed her hands and looked for a paper towel or dishcloth to dry them. With none in sight, she wiped her palms on her thighs. "It's not uncommon for the family of a missing adult to need to hire a private investigator to look for their loved one."

"That's not right. I pay taxes. I deserve their help." His eyes narrowed to mean slits. "They owe me."

"I know that you're upset, and I also would like the police to do more," Olivia said. "But if I put my emotions aside, I know it's not their lack of interest that's holding them back. Privacy laws limit how deeply they can delve into someone's personal accounts without permission. And if it seems the person left of their own free will, they can't legally pursue them."

Do I tell him about the storage unit or not? What would Zoe want me to do?

If Zoe had asked Olivia to keep a secret, she would have never divulged any information. But that hadn't happened, and Olivia couldn't put aside her belief that something truly terrible had happened to Zoe. Something awful enough that she'd felt running away was her only option. If Dylan knew anything that might help find Zoe, Olivia had to try. After a deep breath, she told him about the storage unit and the text message on Zoe's phone.

He listened with stunned attention. "She's had a vehicle stashed in a secret storage unit?"

"Yes."

"You didn't know?" he asked, his voice suspicious.

"I didn't."

"Why would she keep secrets from me?" Dylan sounded hurt. "Why would she need to rent a storage unit? What would she need to hide from me?"

"We don't know why she rented the unit. We don't know the exact date she rented it. It could have been before she met you." After all, if Zoe had rented the unit and stashed a car while she was married to Dylan, that brought up a whole other realm of possibilities, ones that suggested she'd felt the need to hide her escape plans from her husband. Maybe he was the reason. Was Dylan the person she was running from?

"But she still didn't tell me." His words slurred, but he understood what Zoe had done. "If it was so important, she should have shared it with me. Husbands and wives are supposed to share everything."

"I've known her fifteen years, and she didn't tell me either."

"You're not her *husband*," Dylan spat. He moved to the table and swiped at the stack of flyers. They scattered, floating to the floor. Dozens of overlapping images of Zoe's face stared up. The photo Dylan had chosen for the flyer was from their honeymoon. Zoe stood on the beach at sunset. The golden light gave her face a youthful glow, but as usual, her smile was crooked, her mouth pursed just a little to one side. Olivia had always seen her friend's sideways grin as a smirk, representative of her smart-alecky sense of humor. But now, Zoe's expression looked almost secretive.

You're imagining things.

Whatever had caused Zoe to rent that unit *had* happened years ago.

How much do I know about Zoe's past? Not much, considering we've been friends for fifteen years.

Olivia had always assumed Zoe's past was painful, and that's why she didn't like to talk about it. After all, she'd been orphaned and spent some time in a foster home. Even if her foster parents had been kind, the deaths of one's parents would be traumatic, especially for a teenager. Now, Zoe's refusal to share information about her childhood felt intentional rather than emotional. Then again, nothing created better clarity than hindsight.

Dylan kicked at the flyers. "I don't need these if she left of her own free will. If she wants me to know where she is, she'll call me."

"But why hasn't she?" Olivia argued. "The text message suggests she could be running from something or someone. She could be in danger. Whatever the threat is, it must be serious for her to just drop her entire life."

"She should have told me!" Dylan insisted. Was the alcohol making him belligerent? Or was this the real Dylan, minus a public facade—was this the man Zoe lived with?

Olivia wondered how long he'd been drinking this heavily and if he and Zoe had fought about that too. "I know Zoe, and I have to believe she had to have a very good reason to disappear like this."

"She left me!" Dylan shouted. "In the middle of the night, without any explanation. She had a secret escape plan in place. She didn't even leave me a note saying, 'Sorry. Don't worry. I'm alive.'" He threw his hands into the air. "I don't think the *why* matters very much." He crossed to the couch, picked up a glass of amber liquid on ice, and drank deeply. He seemed to have forgotten Olivia was there.

Well, he isn't very useful anyway.

"Fuck!" Dylan yelled, then threw his whiskey glass across the room. It hit the metal coffee table and shattered, whiskey, ice, and glass shards skittering across the table and onto the carpet.

With his sudden burst of violence, Olivia was done with him. She headed for the door, walking around the mess.

"Women. All they do is leave when a man needs them!" Instead of cleaning up the broken bits of glass, Dylan headed to the kitchen, opened a cabinet, and took down a fresh glass.

Olivia didn't grace his nasty comment with an answer. If he wanted to drink himself unconscious, he had the freedom to do so, but damned if she'd endure his behavior. Nor would she feel any further responsibility to keep him updated.

She closed the door behind her, grateful Lincoln had worried more about her than himself. He'd refused to believe she would just disappear. He'd searched 24/7 until he'd found her. There'd been no wallowing in self-pity. Instead, he'd used all his energy to find her. Every comment out of Dylan's mouth had been based on *I* or *me*. He didn't seem worried about Zoe at all.

She left Dylan to pickle himself in self-pity and whiskey while she continued her investigation. On the way to her car, she dropped the garbage bag in the dumpster, which felt like taking out the trash in more ways than the obvious one.

She started for home. She'd dig into Zoe's past, research the Jennifer Hamilton case, and see where that led. As she drove out of the lot, her phone played Taylor Swift's "Shake It Off," the ringer assigned to Nicki. Olivia answered the call on speaker.

Nicki's shout filled the car. "I found something!"

Confused, Olivia turned down the volume. "Something?"

"About Zoe. I'm at your house." Why did conversations with Nicki always seem to start in the middle?

"It's still morning. Why are you up and out?"

"I had a meeting." Nicki's eye roll came through in her voice. Over the connection, kitchen cabinets opened and closed. "You don't have any food." Nicki had her own key to Olivia's house.

"There are overnight oats with strawberries in the fridge."

"Do you really eat that on purpose?"

"Yes. I like it," Olivia said. "Did you really find some real information about Zoe, or do you just want free breakfast?"

"It's real, but I wouldn't object to food."

"I'll make a stop." Olivia ended the call, then detoured to a café in Scarlet Falls. She grabbed a syrupy drink masquerading as coffee for Nicki, a green tea for herself, and two breakfast options. She parked in her garage, plugged the charger into her car, and carried the food into the kitchen.

Nicki attacked the bag as if she hadn't eaten in a week. She set Olivia's parchment-wrapped selection in front of her. "Is that a croissant?"

"Yes. Chocolate."

Nicki unwrapped her bagel, egg, and cheese sandwich. "You always get the healthy egg white and vegetable things."

Olivia sniffed the croissant. It smelled like butter and chocolate and reminded her of Paris. "It's been a day."

"It's only eleven a.m., though it is a Monday."

"Exactly." Olivia sipped her tea and dug into the pastry, giving Nicki a quick synopsis of her morning between bites. "He was seriously drunk when I left."

"Do you think he's an alcoholic?"

"It occurred to me," Olivia admitted.

"Maybe Zoe *did* want to leave him."

"It is possible that their marriage was rocky, but she wouldn't need to vanish to leave Dylan. Zoe kept her own bank accounts and credit cards. She could have knocked on my door at any hour, day or night, if she needed a place to stay. For that matter, the apartment is in her name. His credit was too shaky to add to the lease. She could have kicked him out."

"Unless she was afraid of him."

"That doesn't feel like Zoe, but I guess you never know. I wouldn't have expected Dylan to react to his wife disappearing by drowning himself in whiskey and throwing a glass tumbler either. I expected him to refuse to rest until she was found."

"Like Sharp did when you were kidnapped."

"Exactly."

"You two aren't married, and you hadn't even been together that long when it happened."

All reasons Dylan's reaction was even more disappointing.

Olivia finished her croissant and wiped her fingers on a napkin. "Now what did you find?"

Nicki took a long pull from her straw. "I couldn't sleep last night, so I signed onto Zoe's socials and spent some time looking for stalker-type followers or anyone who set off my creeper alert. The more success her podcast achieves, the more known she becomes, and the more people follow her. Let's face it: People can be weird." She paused to take an enormous bite of her sandwich. Cheese oozed out, and she licked it off her fingertips.

Impatient, Olivia prompted, "Did you find any?"

Nicki unlocked her phone. "Yeah. I mean, it's a podcast about murder. The content can be morbid. There's always a few delulu commenters." She scrolled. "But there was this dude who sent her a direct message two weeks ago. She blocked him, but he re-sent it the following week under a slightly different name, but not different enough that she wouldn't know it was him."

"What was the message?"

"'Remember me? I know what you did. Payback is coming,'" Nicki read from her screen. "The first message came from an account with the name CRYUNCLE25. The next one—which was identical—came from the handle SPARROW25. I doubted the repetition of the number or the exact duplication of phrasing was a coincidence, so I did a little recon. It's definitely the same sender."

"Did the messages go to the podcast page or Zoe's personal one?"

"The podcast. She doesn't post on her personal account at all. It's set to private," Nicki said. "I don't think Zoe even saw the second message. Since she handed over the social media postings for the podcast to me, she doesn't bother checking her accounts very often. She limits her involvement to skimming through the comments now and then, mostly when I ask her to engage. Sometimes I can handle responding, but it's important that exchanges with followers be authentic."

"She doesn't like social media. She once told me that if it weren't for the podcast, she wouldn't even have any accounts," Olivia said. "Can you get any more information about either of the accounts that messaged her?"

"Both CRYUNCLE25 and SPARROW25 are private profiles. You can only see the general information on their account: name, number of followers, number of accounts they follow, and number of posts. The account pictures are so dark, you can't see facial features, just a silhouette of his profile." Nicki reached for her laptop and opened it. "Look here."

Olivia moved her chair next to her niece and squinted at the thumbnail-size photo of CRYUNCLE25. She tapped the tiny image. "That looks like a beard, so let's assume CRYUNCLE25 is a man for now. Could that be the man who tried to steal my purse? He had some facial hair."

Nicki gave the screen a lopsided frown. "I can't tell. Beards are pretty common." She switched to SPARROW25's profile.

"The pages look exactly the same, except for the username."

Nicki continued. "Both of the accounts are new, created shortly before the messages were sent. Neither of them follow any accounts or have any followers."

"Does that mean they're bots?"

"Not necessarily, but they're accounts that aren't used. Bots are computer generated and typically follow a handful of other bots to lend an appearance of legitimacy. I suspect these profiles were created by a real person just to message Zoe."

Olivia read the messages again. "It sounds like the sender knows her—or knew her in the past."

"Yes."

"Would the police be able to get any personal details on the profile creator?"

"I doubt it. The police might be able to get a warrant for the social media company, but the information they get will probably be either entirely fake or what they call an impostor or sock-puppet account, which is one created with some poor rando's data without their knowledge or consent."

"Like social media identify theft."

"Kinda," Nicki said.

"Zoe rented her storage facility over eight years ago. Now this person referenced knowing that she did something bad."

"We need to dig into her past," Nicki said.

"We? Don't you have to work?"

Nicki waved away Olivia's concern. "I can take a few days. I just finished a big campaign."

"I don't like you getting involved." It was the opposite of what Olivia's brother had asked of her. "I already dragged you into an attempted mugging."

"And I'm not about to just accept some dude coming after me and me doing nothing about it."

Olivia shook her head. "It's not a good idea."

Nicki sat back and crossed her arms. "I'm going to help find Zoe with or without you."

Her face was locked in a stubborn expression Olivia suspected matched her own—far too well. The best Olivia could do was set parameters. "You have to do what I say."

Nicki's chin jutted. "Not if you give me some bullshit order."

Olivia gritted her teeth. "Fine. Just be careful, OK? Try to be reasonable."

"I will if you will," Nicki said.

Olivia rubbed her forehead, where a headache threatened. "Let's move on."

Nicki finished her drink with a gurgling-straw noise. "Let's."

"You worked with Zoe and Wendy. What can you tell me about their relationship?"

Nicki pushed her cup away. "It felt like they were still feeling each other out. Zoe was clearly in charge. Sometimes it seemed like Wendy was resentful that Zoe wanted to review all of her work."

"They argued?"

Nicki made a face. "Yes, but the conflicts were minor. For example, the three of us were working on sound bites to use on social media. Wendy had written a few that she thought would generate interest and expand our follower base on the various platforms. Do you know about keywords that prompt some social media platforms to censor a post?"

Olivia nodded. "Like saying *kill* or *murder* isn't allowed."

"Correct," Nicki continued. "The way to get around these filters is to use different or made-up words or even emojis as an unofficial code. Like saying *unalive* instead of *murder* or using the eggplant emoji instead of *sex*. Everyone knows about the censorship and understands the code. Anyway, Wendy wrote copy to use in a trailer for the episodes devoted to your interview. Zoe didn't like her promo text suggestions."

"That seems like a minor disagreement." And yet it didn't in a way that Olivia couldn't pinpoint.

"It's minor in the grand scheme of things, but Wendy wasn't happy. Their disagreement was about the basic trajectory of the podcast. Zoe wanted to stick to the facts and take the show in a more serious direction. Wendy wanted to hype the posts like a reality TV show. She'd added words and phrases that suggested there was a sexual element to your abduction. Zoe said absolutely not. She refused to mislead her listeners. Wendy said sex sells."

"That's . . . I don't have a word for it." Olivia felt a little sick.

"*Sensationalistic* was the word Zoe used," Nicki supplied. "She said she wouldn't reduce her show to the podcast equivalent of a tabloid and that she refused to feed into anyone's sick fantasies. If they were coming to her podcast for that, they'd be sorely disappointed."

Olivia nodded. "Zoe promised me the interview would be authentic."

"What happened to you was horrific. You almost died. There was no need to add extra horror."

Olivia took a sip of her tea to settle her stomach. Zoe's professionalism was the reason she'd agreed to the interview. Wendy's attitude was the reason she'd been hesitant.

Nicki added, "I don't have the text anymore because Zoe deleted it all—which pissed off Wendy even more. But the gist of it is, an argument over some sound bites and trailers should have been minor, but it seemed as if Zoe and Wendy were disagreeing on the very foundation of the show. Would it be hard-hitting journalism, or would the stories be heavily edited to create more marketable drama?"

"At the end of the day, it's Zoe's show."

Nicki nodded. "And she had no problem being in charge. But Wendy wasn't happy. I don't know the details of her contract, but she hinted that she couldn't make her subscriber and sponsorship goals if Zoe wouldn't let her market the show the way she wanted to."

"She told me that Zoe wouldn't let her see the financials, which implies a lack of trust on Zoe's part," Olivia said. "Of course, Zoe kept a lot of secrets, so she wasn't willing to trust anyone completely—including her husband and friends."

She told Nicki about the text message Wendy had received while Olivia was in her office. "I'm going to find out where she's going today at four o'clock," Olivia said. "Whoever she's meeting, she didn't want me to know about it."

"So we *need* to know," Nicki finished.

Olivia's phone played a rumba, the ringtone assigned to her mother. She answered the call. "Hola, Mami."

"Olivia, I'm sorry. I need your help again."

"What is it?"

"I have a doctor's appointment tomorrow. It's on my phone. I'm supposed to check in for it, but I don't know how."

"You have a virtual appointment tomorrow?" Olivia clarified.

"Yes. I was trying to save you a trip, but the office texted me and I can't follow their instructions. Also, your father did something to the computer."

Olivia knew from experience that there was no way to talk her mother through the online check-in process over the phone. She looked at her watch. "I'll be there in an hour."

"I'm sorry you have to drive down here. Is Sharp there? Can he come with you?"

Olivia closed her eyes for just a few seconds, remembering her mother was the one who'd declared her missing when Olivia didn't show up to take her to a doctor's appointment. Was she trying to do virtual appointments because she was afraid to have Olivia drive alone?

She opened her mouth to say she'd be fine driving by herself but changed her mind. "Nicki's here. She'll come with me."

"Oh, good." Her mother sounded relieved.

"It's no problem, Mami. See you soon." Olivia ended the call.

Nicki tapped her phone and read the screen. "We'd better hurry if we're going to get back in time to follow Wendy."

Olivia collected her things. "Let's go."

In the car, Nicki said, "I'll bet you ten bucks Abuelo changed the password on the Wi-Fi again."

Olivia laughed. "No one would take that bet. He does that every week." Her parents tried to keep up, but technology moved too fast for them.

"I'll have it fixed in a minute," Nicki said. "I made myself an administrator on their account."

"I'm glad they call you for all things digital."

"And I'm glad you handle all their doctors' appointments." Nicki laughed.

Olivia could make the drive to Albany in her sleep. She was at her parents' house at least once or twice a week. They lived in a senior community of nearly identical single-story homes. She parked at the curb.

As they walked up the driveway, Nicki said, "I'll take Abuelo. I handle yelling better than tears."

"Works for me." Olivia's mother was easier to help. She didn't love technology—except for the ability to have hundreds of photos of her grandchildren at her fingertips—and was content to hand over her phone to be fixed. Her father still insisted on doing everything himself, and his frustration sometimes took the form of yelling at no one in particular.

They went inside the small house. Her father was in the living room, playing dominoes with Olivia's youngest nephew, six-year-old Brian. Olivia kissed her father on the cheek. "Why aren't you in school, Bri?"

Focused on the game, Brian barely looked at her. "I dunno. School's closed."

"Teacher in-service day," Olivia's father said. "I need to talk to Nicki about my computer. Maybe you can play with your aunt Olivia?"

"No way." Brian shook his head. "She wins all the time."

Nicki laughed. "You think she's good at dominoes. Wait until you're old enough to play Scrabble with her. Aunt Liv is the Scrabble Queen."

Olivia had a firm policy of never letting her nieces and nephews win. Everyone needed to learn to lose gracefully. "Maybe another time. I have to help Mami." She went to find her mother.

As she left the room, she heard her father say, "Nicki, my computer isn't working. I don't know what happened to it."

"I got you, Abuelo," Nicki said with more patience than she ever had for Olivia.

As usual, her mother was in the kitchen. She stood at the sink, scrubbing a pot. She was a petite woman with a head of forever-brown curls.

"Hola, Mami." Olivia kissed her on the cheek.

Her mother gestured toward the phone on the counter and waved her hands over it as if she were very done with the device. "Are you hungry?"

"No, Nicki and I just ate." Olivia picked up the phone and entered her mother's passcode. She scrolled through her apps. "Where is the app the doctor uses?"

"I don't know. It was there yesterday. Today, it's gone."

How did she delete the entire app?

Olivia knew better than to ask her mother. She simply downloaded the app again, signed her mother into her account, and checked her in for her morning appointment. "You're all set. Just leave the app open tonight but don't do anything with it until your appointment time tomorrow, OK?"

"OK," her mother agreed. "Just put it on the charger."

Olivia crossed her fingers. Nicki walked into the kitchen and greeted her grandmother with a kiss.

"Are you hungry?" her mother asked.

"No, we have to go anyway. Sorry, Abuela," Nicki said.

Olivia's mother looked disappointed. "It's OK. I appreciate you coming to help." She turned to the refrigerator. "I made *pastelitos* today. You take them home for Sharp."

She set a container in Olivia's hands. It felt heavy.

"How many are in here?" Olivia asked.

"Not that many." Her mother shrugged. That meant at least a half dozen of the *pastelitos de guayaba*, or guava and cream cheese pastries, that Lincoln loved.

"Yum!" Nicki said.

"They're for Sharp," her abuela admonished.

"Sharp didn't help you with your computer today," Nicki protested.

"Don't be fresh," Olivia's mother corrected with a laugh. "Sharp has done enough for this family." Olivia's mother would do anything for the man who had found and saved her daughter.

Her whole family had been affected by her abduction. Would they ever feel secure again? For now, Olivia could only hope her mother never learned of Zoe's disappearance.

And that they found Zoe alive.

Chapter Thirteen

By three o'clock, Olivia pulled into the parking lot two offices away from Zoe's studio complex. She parked her Prius partially behind a pickup truck. Wendy's SUV was about two hundred feet away and barely visible.

She gestured to her niece. "Could you get the binoculars out of the glove box?"

In the passenger seat, Nicki opened the compartment and removed them. Instead of handing them over, she raised them to her eyes. "Nothing is happening."

Olivia reclined her seat a few inches. "Keep watching. We'll take turns. Watch the door, not her vehicle, in case someone picks her up."

"Gotcha. I don't really need these."

"You will if we need to get a license plate or something like that."

"Good point."

Olivia closed her eyes. She'd barely slept the night before, but despite being exhausted, her mind whirled.

Ten minutes later, Nicki lowered the binoculars. "Stakeouts are boring."

"I bought you coffee, or whatever that is." Olivia gestured toward the tall, milkshake-like drink in the cupholder.

"It's a Frappuccino." Nicki picked it up and sucked on the straw.

"It's a liquid candy bar."

"It's delicious." Nicki slurped harder.

Olivia took a small sip of her tea, rationing her liquid consumption. She didn't want to need a restroom if it wasn't convenient. Her much younger niece had an iron bladder and had to have a giant container of water or other liquid in hand at every moment.

"I'll take a turn." Olivia held out a hand. "If Wendy is meeting someone at four o'clock, then we don't have long to wait."

Nicki sighed and placed the binoculars into Olivia's palm. "Have at it." She opened her phone and scrolled, then set it on her thigh. "Why were you doing the interview with Zoe? Did she pressure you into it?"

"No. It was my idea."

"Why?"

"I was hoping it would help me put the incident behind me."

"How is making your trauma public going to do that?" Nicki asked, but her voice held no criticism, only genuine concern.

"I'm not sure." Olivia kept her eyes on the studio door. "It just feels right, like maybe I'll be purging my shame."

"Shame? Why would you have shame? You didn't do anything wrong."

"I know that in my head, but my heart doesn't believe it."

"You were the *victim*."

"I know it's backward." But shame was exactly what Olivia felt. "My therapist said it's not unusual. Many crime victims have internalized guilt. They question what they might have done differently to prevent the crime from happening."

"I've heard other people victim blame, but I've never heard a victim blame themselves."

"The way people respond to trauma doesn't always make sense," Olivia said. "But if I go public with the details, there's no room for speculation." She'd hoped that the chatter would die down three years after her kidnapping, but the media continued to rehash the story. Olivia didn't want her next book project to be overshadowed by her own past.

Of course, first she had to *have* a next book project. She hadn't even begun to research possible cases.

"So by doing the interview, you hope to take back control of the narrative."

"Yes. I think that's exactly what I'm doing."

"Cool." Nicki took the lid off her cup and chugged the last of the whipped cream. Then she slid the cup into the console holder. "I was worried she was using you."

"Zoe wouldn't—" Olivia cut herself off. "I was going to say Zoe would never, but I guess I don't know her as well as I thought I did."

"Wendy's leaving." Nicki pointed across the parking lots, where Wendy was getting into her SUV.

Olivia set down the binoculars. She waited until Wendy began driving out of the lot before following her. Wendy headed into the business district. Nervous that she'd recognize the Prius, Olivia kept plenty of distance—and at least three vehicles—between them. Maintaining distance and visibility was easy on the highway, but as they approached the main drag of Scarlet Falls, she had to drop back.

Wendy turned down a side street. Olivia switched on her blinker, but didn't make the turn until she saw Wendy's SUV disappear into a small parking lot that ran behind a strip center. Then Olivia made the turn and cruised past the lot's entrance. "Can you see her?"

"Yep," Nicki said. "She's getting out of her SUV."

Fifty feet down the street, Olivia slid into an empty space at the curb.

Nicki's head swiveled. "She's headed for the patio at Petie's."

Petie's Bistro was a sandwich shop with a small dining room that spilled onto an expansive back patio. With the aid of awnings and portable heaters, Petie's made outdoor dining popular even in winter. Olivia put the car in park and turned to look through the rear window. "I can't see her."

"She went behind that hedge."

"We need to get closer." Bringing her tea to look casual, Olivia stepped into the street and joined Nicki on the sidewalk.

The strip center held a used bookstore, a vintage clothing boutique, a Scoops homemade ice cream shop, and Petie's. Of course, Nicki made a beeline for the ice cream shop. Scoops had a take-out window that always had a line. Today, a dozen people waited.

"You can't be hungry," Olivia said.

"You don't have to be hungry to eat ice cream." Nicki got into the queue. "Besides, the line is good cover. I mean, even if she sees us, we're here for ice cream. Just a coincidence that she's here too."

Olivia had to admit she was right. From the line, they had a clear view of Petie's patio. Wendy sat alone at a table, drinking from a mug, her eyes scanning the parking lot. She was clearly waiting for someone.

The line shuffled forward. The staff at Scoops were pros, and Olivia and Nicki faced the clerk over the counter in less than five minutes. Nicki ordered three scoops of chocolate ice cream with multiple toppings. Olivia passed. They stood partially behind a shrub. Nicki ate her ice cream. Olivia sipped her tea as they watched Wendy's table.

Wendy stood as a blond woman approached her. They shook hands and sat down. The blond woman set a tote bag on the patio next to her chair. The waitress approached and took her order.

After the waitress left, Wendy slid a folder from her own crossbody bag and handed it to the blonde. She opened it and flipped through the pages briefly. Looking up, she nodded, then slipped the folder into her tote bag.

"Do you know who that is?" Olivia whispered in Nicki's ear.

"Nope."

Facing away from Wendy, Olivia lifted her phone, angled it, and smiled, pretending to take a selfie of her and Nicki while actually snapping pics of Wendy and her tablemate over her shoulder. "We're going to find out." The waitress brought the blond woman an iced beverage and a sandwich. A few minutes later, Wendy drained her cup, rose, and left the table. The blonde seemed content to finish her lunch alone.

"I'd like to know what Wendy gave her," Nicki said.

"Me too." Olivia held her cup out to Nicki. "Hold my tea."

"What are you doing?" Nicki took the cup.

"Just wait here." Olivia didn't recognize the second woman. So the woman likely wouldn't know her either. She circled the area and walked to Petie's patio, past the PLEASE SEAT YOURSELF sign, and chose the seat behind the blonde. Putting her back to her, she set her own bag at her feet, close to the blonde's. When the waitress came, she ordered a black coffee and said she was waiting for someone.

A phone rang behind her. The blonde answered the call. Olivia lifted her own phone in front of her and checked out the blonde in the screen's reflection. The blonde was focused on her call. Lunchtime had passed, and the patio had mostly emptied out. The waitress wasn't looking. Olivia reached down, slid her hand into the blonde's tote, and transferred the folder to her messenger bag. Then she pretended to get a call, snatched up her phone, tossed a ten-dollar bill onto the table, and hurried away with her phone pressed to her ear.

She kept her back to the blonde as she walked away. Circling around the patio, she texted Nicki. MEET ME AT THE CAR.

With a confident and brisk stride, she left Petie's and made her way to the Prius. Nicki was already waiting, Olivia's tea in her hand. They slid into the car.

Nicki fastened her seat belt. "The way you stole that was pretty slick."

Olivia tossed her bag into Nicki's lap. "I'm not proud. I'm desperate."

While Olivia drove away from the curb, Nicki opened the folder. "This is weird. It's about a murder."

"A murder?"

"Yes. The murder of Evan Brown." Nicki flipped pages. "He disappeared thirty years ago from Summerton, New York. His remains were found last year when his car was pulled from a lake. The case is unsolved." She lowered the folder. "Maybe this is another case Zoe was researching."

"Could be. Dylan said she was there in May for a few days." Olivia checked her rearview mirror, but no one was behind them. She exhaled and headed for home. "But why would Wendy be giving her case file to that blond woman?"

Nicki set the folder on her lap and pulled out her phone. "Let's see if we can find out who she is."

"Reverse image search?" Olivia asked.

"Yep." Nicki scrolled, tapped, shook her head, and scrolled some more. "Aha! Found her!"

"Who is she?" Olivia glanced at Nicki.

"Well, this is super sus." Nicki stabbed at her screen with a forefinger. "The bitch's name is Melissa MacGuiness."

"Who?"

"You've never heard of her?"

"No. Is she famous?" Olivia accelerated as they left town.

"She's the host of *In Our Backyard*. It's a true crime podcast."

"Is she one of Zoe's competitors?"

"You bet your ass she is." Nicki gestured with both hands so dramatically, Olivia worried she'd toss her phone into the back seat. "Locally, she's Zoe's main competitor. She disses Zoe's podcast on her own all the time." Nicki stopped Kermit-flailing to stare at her phone. "I didn't recognize her without all the makeup and tarantula-leg eyelashes." She wriggled her fingertips in front of her eye for effect. "She must use mega filters on every picture she posts."

Olivia stopped at a red light. "Let me see."

Nicki tilted her phone so Olivia could view the screen. The blond woman in the photo barely resembled the one who had just met with Wendy. "Wow. I want her makeup artist."

"Right?" Nicki shook the phone. "Those cheekbones are an optical illusion."

The light turned green, and Olivia continued forward. "Why would Wendy be handing over a file about the Evan Brown murder?"

"Maybe that's the next one Zoe planned to use for her podcast. Maybe Melissa wants to steal Zoe's content."

"I thought the Jennifer Hamilton case was Zoe's next subject," Olivia said.

"Who told you that?"

Olivia sighed. "Wendy."

Nicki snorted. "The last time I talked to Zoe, she hadn't made a decision yet."

"So Wendy could have lied to throw me off."

"Yep." Nicki tapped an absent finger on her leg. "Maybe Melissa paid her to steal Zoe's research."

"When I talked to her, she seemed worried that she wouldn't make the target revenue goals required for her bonus. Maybe she decided to diversify her income."

Nicki added, "Or she was thinking about going to work for Melissa and taking Zoe's ideas with her."

"I'll have to talk to Wendy again." Olivia's phone buzzed. Her car announced the call was from Lincoln. She answered. "Hi. You're on speakerphone. Nicki's in the car."

"Hey, Sharp," Nicki said, reminding Olivia once again that she was the only person to call him by his first name.

"Hey, Nicki," Lincoln replied. "Liv, I'm on my way to your place. Can I pick up dinner?"

Nicki replied before Olivia had a chance. "Where are you stopping?"

"What do you want?" Lincoln asked.

"Pizza?" Nicki asked in a hopeful tone.

"Liv," Lincoln asked, "is pizza OK with you?"

"Sure," she said. "Do you need our orders?"

Lincoln laughed. "I know what you both want. Meet you at home." He ended the call.

"I like that he remembers my order," Nicki said. "He's a keeper."

"He is."

"When are you guys going to move in together?"

"I don't know."

Officially, Lincoln still lived in the apartment over the offices of Sharp Investigations, but it gave her a warm and squishy feeling in the center of her chest when he called her house *home*. Maybe she'd be ready to take the next step in their relationship soon.

"Don't you two spend most nights together anyway?" Nicki asked.

"We do." Olivia didn't want to admit she feared she would become dependent on him. It felt . . . silly? So she kept her response light. "Give us time. We're old and set in our ways."

"You're not *that* old."

"Gee, thanks." Olivia turned in to her driveway ten minutes later. She parked in the garage and plugged in her car. Nicki bounded into the house ahead of her. By the time Olivia joined her, Nicki had helped herself to a lime-flavored sparkling water.

Olivia set her purse on the counter and washed her hands. "I'll get some lettuce for a salad." She went out back into her vegetable garden. They hadn't yet had a hard frost. In addition to some straggly greens, one of her tomato plants was hanging on. She collected two tomatoes, small but ripe, and clipped a basketful of arugula and fresh basil. She brought the veggies inside and washed them while Nicki took plates from the cabinet.

The front door opened, and Lincoln came in, carrying two pizza boxes with a paper take-out bag balanced on top. He walked into the kitchen, set down the food, and kissed Olivia.

Nicki pounced on the food. She transferred two slices of sausage-and-mushroom pie to her plate and inhaled dramatically. "You're the best, Sharp."

"Hello to you too." Lincoln laughed. He handed her the bag. "The fries are for you."

"Salad?" Olivia asked Nicki.

Nicki made a face. "No, thanks."

She never accepted, but Olivia would keep trying. Nicki loved food but still had the palate of a teenager. Olivia set two salad bowls on the island. Lincoln slid slices of the veggie lovers special, light on the cheese, onto their plates. Sitting at the island, he reached into his pocket and set the flash drive from Zoe's office on the countertop. "Jenny Kruger bypassed the password."

Olivia took a bite of salad. "Did she say what was on the drive?"

"It sounded like more research on true crime cases," Lincoln said.

Disappointment filled Olivia. "I was hoping for a clear lead."

"I know. I'm sorry. Go through the files. I might be wrong," Lincoln said, but he rarely was.

"Thank you, anyway." Olivia got up and fetched her laptop. Setting it next to her plate, she inserted the flash drive.

"You're welcome." Lincoln finished his salad and moved on to his pizza.

Nicki returned to the box for two more slices.

"Are you staying over?" Lincoln asked Nicki.

"No." She sat back down. "I have to go after dinner. I have a date tonight."

"A date?" Olivia ripped her attention away from her computer, which was chugging away trying to load the contents of the flash drive. "Is this the same individual from your *coffee*?"

"No." She didn't elaborate, but the word sounded very final.

"Someone new, then?" Olivia asked.

Nicki flushed, which never happened. "I met this guy on an app."

Olivia nodded but didn't respond. She knew most singles used apps to connect, but she never had. It didn't feel organic to her.

"I know you never liked app dating," Nicki said. "But I'm not a club person, so . . ."

Lincoln finished his pizza. "Let me know if you want me to run a background check on him." His tone was light, but Olivia knew he wasn't kidding.

Nicki rolled her eyes. "Not necessary." She scarfed down the rest of her pizza in a few more minutes, then stood, snatching her phone off the island, where she'd placed it face down during the meal. "I should call an Uber."

Lincoln pushed back his plate. "I'll give you a ride home."

He wasn't a fan of rideshares either.

"That'd be great. Thanks." Nicki gathered her things and shoved them into her backpack.

"I'll be right back." Lincoln kissed Olivia on the cheek.

"Thank you." She turned back to her computer. As they walked out of the house, the spinning beach ball disappeared, and the contents of the drive appeared. She scanned the list, then opened the first file. A death certificate popped onto the screen. Goose bumps rippled up her arms as she read the name.

Evan Brown.

The same case file that Wendy had tried to give to Melissa MacGuiness.

Chapter Fourteen

Nicki arrived at five minutes before eight. For first dates, particularly ones arranged via apps, she always made her own way and never gave out her address or actual phone number. She'd broken one of her rules, though. She'd wanted to meet for coffee, but he'd said he worked too late and would be hungry. She'd compromised and agreed to drinks and appetizers. First meets should be short. If it went well, she could always suggest an additional activity, but she didn't want to be trapped for an entire meal with someone she didn't like.

He'd suggested the bar in the Tuscan Grill, which meant he might be a local, and she'd agreed. The restaurant was a ten-minute walk from her apartment. Nicki despised the noise, crush, and chaos of clubs. The restaurant had a nice bar area, but it was generally a quiet crowd. The floors weren't sticky, and you could hear your date talk, rare elements in a town dominated by the college scene. If she didn't like her date, she could make a rapid exit. She didn't even need to wait for an Uber.

For a Monday evening, the dining room was bustling. She crossed the lobby and went to the bar. Every stool was occupied. A grid of tables filled the remaining space. Tall plants, mostly ferns, separated the tables, providing a small amount of privacy and creating an intimate atmosphere. A male voice caught her attention. It sounded familiar. She scanned the long bar and spotted him. If she'd been a cartoon, her eyes would have bugged out of her head.

Was that . . . *Dylan*?

He stood at the bar, a tumbler of amber liquid in one hand, the other propped on the back of a stool occupied by a woman twenty years younger than him. She wore a red minidress that looked prone to wardrobe malfunctions. One less-than-careful recrossing of her legs, and no one would be able to question her biological sex. Nicki had to admit, the dress made her boobs look amazing. The woman squeezed her biceps to her rib cage, highlighting her assets. She was one deep breath away from a nip slip. She lifted a glass of beer, took a sip, then licked the foam from her lips with a slow deliberation that made Nicki do a mental eye roll. Dylan, however, leaned closer. He was practically drooling. He tried an awkward thigh grab, but the woman evaded with an *ah-ah* smile. Nicki wasn't sure who was playing who, but the game was entertaining to watch.

She shook her head and refocused on Dylan. He wasn't looking his best. His eyes were puffy and bloodshot. But he still oozed some kind of stupid charm, no doubt the same quality that had lured Zoe into marrying him—that and his 4 percent body fat and carefully sculpted physique. Though Nicki wasn't into the super-lean look. Sure, she liked a guy to be generally fit, but she didn't want to hook up with anyone who spent *that* much time in the gym—or was *that* into himself. Despite Dylan's obvious intoxication, he looked like he'd preened. The tousled, textured look of his hair required multiple products to achieve, and his three-day scruff had perfectly clean edges. Yeah, he spent a lot of time trying to appear carelessly disheveled.

She contemplated confronting him. She really wanted to let him have it. After Trevor's betrayal, she had some rage to channel. But taking her frustration out on him would do nothing to help find Zoe. Sure, it would probably feel amazing, but it wouldn't accomplish anything. She would watch and see what he did. If Dylan was responsible for his wife's disappearance, then his behavior might be important.

There were only two empty tables. Luckily, a handy fern stood between the table and Dylan. If she peered between the fronds, she could see him, but he wasn't likely to spot her. She watched him continue to drink and drool over the woman's perfect cleavage. What was his deal? Was he mad at Zoe? Aunt Liv had said he was convinced his wife had left him. In that case, he'd already decided to move on, with no confirmation and without putting much effort into finding Zoe. In what? A day and a half? Didn't seem like enough time to recover from being left by one's spouse. His behavior also said a lot about the state of their marriage and his opinion of Zoe. Maybe he wasn't that sad she was gone. Maybe her disappearance wasn't a surprise.

Maybe this wasn't the first time he'd hit up a younger woman in a bar.

Had he cheated on Zoe in the past? She put in a lot of hours with the podcast, and he had tons of free time.

A chill raced up Nicki's backbone. She wasn't enamored with Dylan, but she didn't dislike him either. Her opinion was more neutral. He didn't appeal to her physically or intellectually. Dylan wasn't a great conversationalist. At first look, his smile could be charming, but when you looked deeper, that was all there was. Yet both men and woman seemed to find him attractive, so whatevs.

For Nicki, Dylan was way too old to be sexually attractive. Unlike the Woman in Red, Nicki wouldn't pimp herself out for a couple of free drinks. She could buy her own beer, thank you.

The waiter came by and read off the specials. Nicki ordered a Lonely Chicken beer on tap and continued to watch the Dylan Show. Not much was happening, except he ordered fresh drinks for himself and the woman. He kept leaning over and whispering in her ear. Each time, she'd shrink back and smile. His leering and constant touching were gross to watch, especially since Nicki knew his wife.

A few minutes later, she spotted her date standing at the end of the bar. Cody stood about six feet tall, with short blond hair and a nice body. He matched his profile photo and basic description, which was always a good sign. Her last app date had turned out to be at least twenty years older than he'd claimed on his dating profile. No amount of hair dye or bronzer could have disguised those crow's-feet. Being hit on by old dudes always felt weird and a little ick—I mean, this guy was her dad's age. But the lying itself was a red flag the size of a football field.

A man who misrepresented the very basics of his person wasn't interested in a relationship. He just wanted sex. You couldn't lie that blatantly about your age for long, right? She'd lasted five whole minutes before she'd walked out of the bar.

But Cody was age-appropriate and hotter in person than in his pic.

So far, so good.

Mentally crossing her fingers, she waved him over and stood when he approached the table. "Hi, I'm Nicki." She waited for him to confirm that his name was really Cody. She'd been burned more often than not lately. It paid to be cautious.

He nodded. "I'm Cody."

She held out a hand. He smiled as he shook it, then sat. The waiter brought Nicki's beer and set it on the table. As was her habit, she pulled it close, tucking it protectively near her body. Nicki's parents, even her well-traveled dad, were naive and oblivious about the risks of modern dating, probably because they'd been married, as her mom often said, since dinosaurs roamed the earth. But Aunt Liv had hammered dating safety into Nicki's head since before she was old enough to drink. Her golden rules: Keep your friends close and your drinks closer.

Aunt Liv knew all the statistics too, but Nicki usually zoned out while her aunt made her case with hard facts. Nicki didn't need any more convincing. Aunt Liv was the smartest person she knew.

Cody pointed to her beer. "I'll have the same." He leaned forward, his crossed forearms resting on the table. The light was dim, but she could see that his eyes were a nice shade of brown. His fitted black T-shirt hugged muscled biceps and a hard torso. She tore her gaze off his chest and sat back abruptly, her face heating as their eyes met and it was clear he'd seen her staring at his body.

He smirked, and the confident gleam in his eyes was scorching.

Was it hot in here, or what?

She took a healthy swallow of her beer to cool off. The waiter brought Cody's beer, and he took a long drink, his tan throat moving as he swallowed. He set down the tall glass with a satisfied look. He watched her watching him, his gaze skimming her face like a touch. She felt the tiny shiver deep in her belly.

Cody asked, "So, what did you do today?"

She could hardly tell him she'd helped her aunt steal a file from a true crime podcaster they suspected might be double-crossing their missing friend, so she stuck with her actual job. "I had a meeting with a client." She gave a few details but not too many. She didn't want to bore him. A social media marketing campaign wasn't exciting to anyone except the client it had been designed for. Besides, most people like to talk about themselves. "You?"

"The usual. Work, gym, home," he said with an arrogant tilt to his head.

Better than *gym, tan, laundry*, she supposed. They'd messaged within the app, so she already knew he was an associate at an investment bank—and that he was a little cocky, which wasn't a problem. Meek wasn't a quality she was seeking. Plus, she could be brash too. She wanted someone who'd be a good match, not a man who needed to dominate or one who would be a doormat.

She sipped her beer while he went into more detail about his workout, which frankly wasn't any more interesting than her work talk would've been. She resisted glancing at her watch, but barely. Was tonight going to be a dud? Just because a man was good-looking didn't mean there would be chemistry between them. She required intellectual stimulation. Plus she was reminded that some dudes—like

Dylan—were just too into themselves. But after a few minutes, Cody seemed to notice her lack of enthusiasm.

He flushed. "I'm sorry. I'm boring you."

She smiled and admitted, "Maybe a little. I don't spend much time in the gym."

His head cocked. "You're in great shape. You must work out."

She gave him credit both for noticing the need to change the topic of conversation and the subtle compliment. "I like yoga, Pilates, and rock climbing."

"Those are all great for core strength." He nodded.

"Flexibility and balance too." Nicki might not be able to squat heavy weight, but she could do more pull-ups than most men.

Some guys would have disparaged her choices of exercise as good for women. He didn't, so she gave him another point for respect.

He plucked the menu from the napkin holder. "Are you hungry?"

"I could eat." Nicki spun her beer on its coaster. Oddly, she didn't want it anymore. Usually, beer or cider was her go-to. One drink was her first-date limit, and she could nurse a beer for a long time. Mixed drinks tended to go down too easily, especially the fruity ones, and she saved those for girls' nights. But tonight, her stomach felt weird. Indigestion? Maybe she should have stopped at three slices of pizza at dinner. But seriously, she never got sick. Most of her friends couldn't eat gluten or dairy or had food allergies or something. But not Nicki. She could top off jalapeño poppers with chili and a double latte, then go right to bed afterward. She had the digestive system of a goat.

"How about some nachos?" He laid the menu down on the table and turned it so she could read the font.

"Sure." She skimmed the offerings. Maybe she needed some protein. She was getting older. She might need to lay off the carbs. "Chicken fingers for me."

Cody flagged down the waiter and ordered the food and another beer for himself. "You?" He gestured toward Nicki's glass.

"No, I'm good. Thanks." Nicki nursed her own. "I have a full day tomorrow." She'd only drunk a quarter of her beer, and her head was fuzzy already, which was odd. Her stomach was most definitely not empty, considering the volume of her dinner. She was out of practice. When *was* the last time she'd been out for drinks?

Steph's birthday?

Crap. Her friend had turned twenty-six in August. Steph's boyfriend had hosted an '80s night party, complete with disco music and a dance floor. Nicki had rocked skinny jeans and big hair. No, that had been in July! Had it really been two months since she'd gone out?

She really had to leave her apartment more often. She waved for the waiter and asked for a glass of water.

Cody leaned closer. "Are you OK?"

"Yeah." But she felt hot and a little nauseated. The waiter brought the water and their apps. Cody ate his chips, and Nicki nibbled on a chicken finger.

Cody made short work of the nacho order. He gestured to the remaining small pile of chips. "Last chance."

"Sure, thanks." Nicki set down her half-eaten chicken and ate a chip. Her stomach protested with a cramp. She sipped her water and sucked on an ice cube. "Help yourself to some chicken. I can't eat it all."

Cody did. "Thanks."

What the hell? Was she sick? Food poisoning from pizza didn't feel likely. What else had she eaten today? A bagel breakfast sandwich . . . Wait. The client she'd met that morning had mentioned one of her kids had been down with a stomach virus. Had she passed her kid's germs along to Nicki? A tiny shiver of panic fluttered in her belly. She did not want to embarrass herself in front of Cody.

She needed to go home—now—before she lost her beer and chicken all over herself. "I'm really sorry. I think I might be coming down with something." She turned over her phone and slid a credit card from the wallet attached to the back of the case. "Would you mind if we rescheduled? I like you, but I think my client might have infected me with some kiddie cooties."

"Don't worry about it." Cody waved away her card. "I've got this." He pulled his wallet out of his pocket. "Let me see you home safe. I don't want to leave you like this. You look feverish."

"I'll be OK." Nicki didn't know him. Just because she was attracted to him didn't mean she felt comfortable being vulnerable with him. Olivia's lectures were rooted so deep in her mind, they'd been imprinted on her soul. What were her options? Stumble down the street to her apartment alone and hope she made it? Let him walk her home? Call somebody? Her head felt heavy, and her eyelids sagged. Before she decided, her stomach clenched in a way that obliterated the multiple choice. "I'm going to the restroom. Excuse me." She stood and wobbled.

Cody half rose. "Let me help you."

"No." Panic, chicken, and beer rose in Nicki's throat. This gorgeous man could not watch her vomit. What could be worse than puking on your first date?

She stumbled for the restroom at the back of the bar. She sensed that Cody was right behind her. Inside the bathroom, she leaned on the cool tile wall and texted Aunt Liv. COME GET ME. She pressed "Send." How would Aunt Liv find her? She should text her location. The phone screen blurred. Where was she? She couldn't remember the name of the restaurant. She tried to rise, pressing her back to the tiled wall for support. If Aunt Liv didn't come, what was Nicki going to do? She wouldn't make it home like this. She wasn't sure she could walk out of the bathroom, let alone back to her apartment.

She fumbled the phone and shoved it into the pocket of her jacket before she dropped it. Overhead lights swirled like the disco balls at Steph's party. The room spun, and the lights dimmed. She heard the bathroom door squeak as it opened.

"Man coming in," Cody called out. "Nicki? Are you OK?"

She couldn't answer. Her voice wasn't working. The door squeaked again, and his shadow fell over her. His palm cupped her cheek. His hand felt too hot on her face. *No!* Not like this. "Move." She lunged to her feet, but didn't make it a single step before her stomach heaved, and she was helpless to stop it from purging itself.

Without enough warning, Cody didn't react in time, and she vomited all over his very new-looking white Nike sneakers.

He jerked backward, unsuccessfully trying to avoid the sickening splashback. "Fuck."

"Oh, God. Oh, God. I'm s-sorry," she managed to blurt out. Humiliation amplified her sickness. Her eyes filled with hot moisture. Dizzy, nauseated, *and* embarrassed, she couldn't hold back the tears. Cody would never go out with her again. The first guy she'd liked in ages, and she'd ruined it because of some preschooler's germs.

Feeling her stomach gather itself again, she lurched forward and half stumbled, half crawled to the nearest stall, where her body continued emptying itself, seemingly of everything she'd eaten since she was twelve. On her knees, she retched again and again, until her entire abdomen was aching and tears poured down her cheeks. She vaguely heard the faucet turn on behind her.

By the time she rocked back and swiped a hand over her face, Cody was behind her. "I've got you. Let's get you cleaned up."

He hadn't left? If she hadn't been so sick, she would have been astonished. He led her to the sink and wiped her face with a wet paper towel. "You'll be OK."

Her gaze was on the floor. In her feverish haze, she noticed he'd cleaned his sneakers. Wet spots on his jeans showed where he'd wiped his legs too.

"I'm sorry" were the only words her mouth seemed capable of forming. She could do nothing but stand there, head hanging.

"Don't worry about it. I was in a fraternity. This is not the first time I've seen puke. It's fine. I'll take you home. My car is around the corner. I can bring it up front. Where do you live?"

A voice in the back of her mind nagged her. They barely knew each other. She shouldn't go with him. She'd texted Aunt Liv, but she couldn't remember when or if her aunt had replied. Her brain was too muddled to form a protest. Something felt off, wrong down to her bones, but she couldn't make sense of it. Was it her complete humiliation? Or her utter helplessness? The nausea rose, yet again, and tears flowed on reflex at the thought of more vomiting.

He was being so nice, even though she'd puked on him. But her instincts—and Aunt Liv's warnings—replayed in her head.

You don't know him.

But what choice did she have? She was all alone. Her knees buckled and her legs sagged. A strong arm around her waist steadied her. Her vision dimmed as he steered her toward the ladies' room door. Meek as a lamb, barely able to shuffle her feet forward, she allowed him to lead her out.

Helpless. She'd never felt so helpless in her life.

Chapter Fifteen

Olivia stared at her computer screen and rubbed her bleary eyes. "I thought I'd find something interesting on this flash drive, but all I see is research for the Evan Brown case. Why did Zoe back up this case to a flash drive and not the cloud with all her other research?"

"Maybe because she'd picked this one for her show?" Lincoln tapped the file folder in front of them, the same one Olivia had liberated from Melissa MacGuiness's bag. "Wendy *was* stealing content. Maybe Zoe knew. So she backed up the more important notes on a flash drive instead of on the cloud account."

"Zoe told Wendy she was going to use the Hamilton case when she was really interested in the Brown case?"

"But Wendy figured it out anyway," Lincoln said.

"Yes, but I feel like I'm missing something. There are countless unsolved murders. Why was this one so important that Zoe was keeping her files secret?"

"Wendy's spying would also explain why Zoe refused to share the show's financial information with her. She doesn't trust Wendy."

"With good reason."

"What do the notes on the flash drive say about the Brown case?" Lincoln asked.

"Thirty years ago, an unnamed caller implicated Evan Brown and his brother, Tim, in two murders committed during a burglary gone wrong. Tim and Evan both had rap sheets that included sexual assault, plus short jail sentences for a string of burglaries they committed together a few years before. Warrants were issued for Tim and Evan. The cops arrested Tim, but Evan was nowhere to be found. His car and some other personal possessions were also missing."

"He ran and left his brother hanging?"

"That's what the cops assumed at the time. In his statement, Tim claimed they'd only planned to burglarize the house. They thought the house was empty, but the property owner confronted them as they entered through the kitchen window. He was armed and fired at them. The bullet grazed Tim's arm. Tim wrestled the homeowner and made him drop the gun. He said Evan picked up the gun and shot at the homeowner twice. One bullet hit him in the head, killing him. The second went through the interior wall and killed the homeowner's disabled adult son. Since Tim was wounded, his blood—and DNA—was found at the scene—and on the gun."

Lincoln said, "Under the New York felony murder rule, it doesn't matter which of them committed the murder. If the killing occurred during the commission of the burglary, all participants in the felony can be charged."

"Tim was arrested, tried, and convicted of second-degree murder, plus some lesser charges. Due to the severity of the crime and his previous record, his sentence was harsh: twenty-five years to life in prison."

"I hear a *but* in there," Lincoln said.

Olivia nodded. "Turns out Evan's been dead all this time. His car was pulled from a lake last year. His skeletonized remains were inside. Zoe's notes say he'd been underwater for decades."

"We need to get more information on that case."

"Agreed," Olivia said. "Also, we have that list of potential passcodes I found in Zoe's desk."

"We can use them to try and access her financial accounts," Lincoln suggested. "The money always tells a story."

"It does, and I don't know why hacking Zoe's accounts makes me feel as sleazy as searching her apartment and breaking into her office. I'm only trying to help her."

"She doesn't ever have to know."

"Not telling her feels dishonest too." Olivia's phone buzzed with a text. She ripped her eyes off her computer screen to see Nicki's name. She tapped the screen. Her blood went cold as she read the words aloud. "'Come get me.'" She texted back: WHERE ARE YOU?

Nothing. Not even three dots to indicate Nicki was texting back. Olivia pressed the "Call" button. Nicki's phone rang three times, then went to voicemail.

"She's not answering." She looked up at Lincoln. "She's never texted me while she's on a date. Never. She keeps a tight wrap on her dating life."

"Where is she?" Lincoln was already out of his chair and heading toward the door.

"Let me look. I can find her phone." Olivia and Nicki had agreed to share their locations with each other, but Olivia had never tried to find her before. She'd promised to only use the app in an emergency. Nerves gathered in her belly as she waited for it to open. "I don't like this. I have a really bad feeling."

"Let's go. Use the app in the car." Lincoln was at the front door, keys in hand. "We'll head toward her place."

Olivia's Find My app opened as she followed him. She held her breath until Nicki's phone location showed up as a dot on the map. Olivia expanded the map until she could read street names. "Her phone is a half mile from her apartment. I think this is a restaurant."

They jumped into Lincoln's car. Olivia was still fastening her seat belt as he sped away from the curb.

"Do you want to call the police?" he asked.

"And tell them what?" Olivia tried to quell the sick feeling in her stomach. "That my niece texted me for a ride and now won't answer her phone? It hardly sounds like an emergency." Yet Olivia couldn't help but think that's exactly what it was.

"It'll be OK." But Lincoln's voice lacked conviction. "Maybe she's having a terrible date and needs to be extracted from it."

"Nicki can and has handled bad dates herself, and if she really needs an extraction, she'd call." Olivia couldn't imagine Nicki reaching out to her unless something was seriously wrong. Dread rose in her throat, solid enough to restrict her breath. She closed her eyes and breathed.

The car leaned as Lincoln took the next turn at a fast pace. Olivia grabbed the door handle. With his former job as a cop and her career in true crime, they both immediately thought of all the worst-case scenarios. Possibilities reeled in Olivia's mind. *Stop.* Imagining the worst would not help.

Barely ten minutes passed before Lincoln pulled up next to the restaurant. There were no spots at the curb, so he stopped in the middle of the road. "You go in. I'll park."

Olivia was already opening the door. She stepped out, slammed it closed, and jogged to the door of the restaurant. She went inside. From the lobby, she could hear a commotion. Olivia hurried through the restaurant and past a bar area. A small crowd of customers and waitstaff, dressed in black slacks, white polo shirts, and red logo aprons, gathered in front of a narrow hallway with a restroom sign posted above it. She could hear two men arguing. Olivia couldn't see them over the crowd.

"No. I won't let you."

"Get the fuck out of my way," a second man shot back. "She's my girlfriend. I'll take care of her."

"You didn't come together," Man Number One said. "If she's your girlfriend, show me pictures of you two together. You must have a bunch on your phone, right?"

"I don't have to show you shit."

Olivia rose onto her toes and caught a glimpse between the onlookers' bodies. Nicki sat in the hallway, her body propped up against the wall. Her head lolled, and her legs were splayed to the side as if they'd simply folded. A dark-haired man in a blue button-down shirt knelt next to her. Staring at his watch, he held his forefingers on her wrist. Alarm fired in Olivia's chest.

She shoved her way past a woman. The woman pushed back. Olivia wanted to stab her. "Get out of my way." She pushed her aside.

Near Nicki, a blond man looked agitated. "I told you she said she felt sick. She said she had a virus or something. I'll take her home."

"No. She's been drugged, and she's going to the hospital," the dark-haired man said.

"Drugged?" the blond protested. "No way. She seemed fine before she puked."

"Move!" Olivia elbowed her way through the last few people.

Blood trickled from the lip of the dark-haired man kneeling next to Nicki. Cupping her chin, he pulled down one of her eyelids. "Can you hear me? What's your name?"

Nicki didn't respond.

"Her name is Nicki. I'm her aunt. She texted me to come and get her." Olivia dropped to her knees and grabbed Nicki's hand. "Nicki? It's Aunt Liv. I'm here."

Nicki didn't respond. Olivia brushed her hair away from her face. Nicki was as pale as the white wall behind her, and her body was limp. Normally, she practically vibrated with youth. Seeing her unconscious broke Olivia's heart.

The dark-haired man gave Olivia a one-second glance. "I called 911. An ambulance should be here any minute."

"Thank you." Olivia could barely think.

He turned back to Nicki. "Nicki? Can you wake up? I need you to open your eyes."

Nothing.

Olivia focused on the slow but steady rise and fall of Nicki's chest.

She's breathing.

She felt a hand on her shoulder and looked up to see Lincoln at her side.

"What happened?" he asked.

The dark-haired man answered, "I suspect she was drugged."

Her date? The man who'd claimed to be her boyfriend? Olivia looked for him, but he was no longer standing next to Nicki. *Where did he go?*

She looked through the window overlooking the street. Emergency vehicles were double-parked out front. She could see an ambulance, the paramedics, and a police car. The mood in the restaurant shifted. Diners jumped out of their chairs. Two paramedics hustled through, carrying their med kits. Tables were moved to make room for the gurney.

Paramedics evaluated Nicki and started an IV. In minutes, she was scooped onto the gurney, strapped in, and rolled away. Olivia followed them through the restaurant. A staff member opened the door and held it. Fresh air swept inside. A few dead leaves tumbled across the threshold into the lobby, coming to a rest at the base of the hostess's podium.

Outside on the sidewalk, pedestrians paused, staring at the emergency vehicles. Some moved on after a quick glance. Others lingered, their morbid curiosity overruling their manners. Red, white, and blue lights swirled like a patriotic light show.

The cool air jarred Olivia's brain into action. Who would drug Nicki? She scanned the crowd, looking for the blond man. She nudged Lincoln with her elbow. "When I got here, I heard a man claiming to be her boyfriend. I assume that was her date, but I don't know that for sure."

She wanted to go back to the bar and interrogate the staff. A young woman didn't "get" drugged. Someone did it in a very active sense. The restaurant wasn't that big or bustling. Someone had seen something.

"Nicki doesn't have a boyfriend, right?" Lincoln asked.

"Right, at least not one she's mentioned to me." Olivia's gaze skimmed the crowd. "He's gone. Someone in the bar must have seen him." She closed her eyes and pictured the young man she'd seen in that two-second glance. "He's six foot, maybe a little taller, athletic looking, blond, black T-shirt, jeans."

"He'll be on the surveillance tapes." Lincoln's mouth flattened. "Don't worry. I'll find him."

Olivia had no doubt. "I'm riding with her."

"I'll meet you at the hospital," he said. But instead of heading for his car, which she could see parked illegally in a fire lane a hundred feet down the street, Lincoln followed the patrol officer back into the restaurant.

Knowing she could rely on Lincoln to investigate, Olivia turned her attention back to Nicki, who was being loaded into the ambulance. Olivia climbed up and took a seat on the bench next to the paramedic. He was monitoring Nicki's vitals.

Olivia touched her niece's face. Unconscious, with her guard down, Nicki looked ten years younger, like she was still a teenager. Anger stirred in Olivia's chest. Nicki was smart, independent, and careful. But then, Olivia had been all those things, and she'd still been victimized. Whoever did this to Nicki needed to go down.

"How is she?"

He shrugged. "The same."

Olivia hoped that *the same* meant *stable.*

Chapter Sixteen

Sharp stopped in the restaurant lobby and spotted the responding cop talking to a man of about thirty or so. The man had short dark hair and a split lip. A busboy brought him a dish towel, presumedly filled with ice, which he pressed to his mouth.

Sharp knew the cop. Vince Tuckey had been a rookie when Sharp had retired from the Scarlet Falls PD.

The restaurant staff was straightening chairs and getting back to the business of serving food.

Tuckey flipped his notepad closed. Sharp approached. "Hey, Vince."

"Sharp, haven't seen you in a long time. How's the PI business?"

"Good. Fewer rules, and I like being my own boss." Sharp gestured to the bar behind them. "That young lady in the ambulance is my niece." Claiming Nicki as his own family seemed simpler than explaining their actual relationship. She felt like one of his own anyway.

Tuckey's smile evaporated. "Sorry to hear that. I hope she's going to be OK."

"Me too. What can you tell me?"

"Not much yet. According to the manager, she appeared sick and ran for the ladies' room. When she didn't return to the table, her date followed her. Maybe ten minutes or so after that, the date and that guy"—he glanced at his notes, then nodded toward the dark-haired man—"Brandon West, argued in the hallway. The date tried to carry your niece away, but West wouldn't let him. The date punched West, and West hit him back, but harder."

"What happened to the date?" Sharp asked.

"I don't know, but I plan to find out," Tuckey said. "According to multiple witnesses, he claimed to be her boyfriend."

"I don't know of any boyfriend," Sharp said.

Tuckey shrugged. "They don't always tell their family."

"True." Sharp nodded in acknowledgment. Nicki *was* cagey about her dating life with the rest of the family because they could be intrusive, but if she was serious about a guy, she'd tell Olivia. Those two were tight. But he didn't argue. The cops would only work with what he could prove. "What about her food and drink?"

Tuckey frowned. "The waitstaff had already cleared the table when I got here."

"Damn." No chance of testing the contents for drugs.

"I know. I hope whatever she was given, it shows up in her lab work," Tuckey said.

The hospital would run tests for the usual substances, but if it was a designer or atypical drug, it might not show up.

"Can I talk to him?" Sharp nodded toward West.

"Sure. I already got his statement." The cop waved him toward the witness. "I'm going to have a look at the security vids. See me before you leave."

"Will do." Sharp headed toward West, who was pulling a jacket from the back of a barstool. "Hey, can I have a word?"

West turned, shrugging into the jacket, his eyes narrowed in suspicion.

Sharp continued. "The young woman you helped tonight is my niece. I wanted to thank you."

West's mouth flattened as he nodded. "I was just going to head over to the hospital to check on her."

Sharp lifted his brows. "Oh?"

"I'm a doctor. I work in the ER. That's why I didn't let your niece's date leave with her. I strongly suspected she'd been drugged. I've seen it before." Anger darkened his eyes. "The guy claimed to be her boyfriend, but when I asked to see pictures of them together, he got belligerent." He pulled the dish towel away from his face and licked his split lip.

"I appreciate you stopping him. Where did he go?"

"No idea. I was busy."

"You don't know who he is?"

West shook his head. "I've never seen him before."

"Do you come here a lot?" Sharp asked.

"No. I'm new to the neighborhood. Just moved here when I took this job a few months ago. I work long shifts. I don't go out much."

Sharp fished a business card and his phone out of his pocket. He handed West the card. "Would you mind giving me your contact information in case I have any follow-up questions?"

"I already gave my info to the police." West studied the card. "You're a PI?"

Sharp nodded. "I intend to follow up on this."

"Won't the police do that?"

"They'll try, but they have limited resources." *And procedure to follow.* Sharp was in a rule-breaking mood. When he'd been a cop, he'd been constrained by procedure. He'd been a by-the-book detective. That was not the case anymore. He had no tolerance for this bullshit, and whoever had attempted to prey on Nicki was going to find that out.

"Sure. You can call me." West recited a phone number.

Sharp entered it into his phone. "Thanks, and thanks again for looking out for my niece."

"You're welcome on both counts." West headed for the door.

Sharp found Tuckey in the restaurant manager's office. The patrol officer sat at a computer, studying a slightly grainy video. He gestured toward a plastic chair next to the desk. "You're welcome to watch."

Sharp planted his butt in the seat. "Find anything?"

"Yes and no." Tuckey angled the monitor toward Sharp. "Here's the lounge area of the bar." He clicked on the "Play" button. "And your niece walking in."

On the screen, Nicki sat down at a small table. She was focused on something intently for a short time. Then the waiter came to her table and took her order. "As you can see, she appears to be feeling fine at this point." Tuckey fast-forwarded. A blond man approached the table. They shook hands, and he sat opposite her. The waiter brought her a beer, which she sipped while she talked to the date.

"They shook hands, so they're not in a relationship."

"I agree," Tuckey said. "That's not how a boyfriend and girlfriend greet each other."

The waiter returned and set a tall glass of beer in front of the date. Sharp watched Nicki's beer. Olivia had lectured Nicki long and hard about dating safety. Sharp could hear her in his mind.

Even a Coke never leaves your sight. It only takes a few seconds to be roofied. You could blink and miss it. You don't accept drinks from strangers. You don't drink anything out of a punch bowl or anything *mixed in a bathtub. If you go to the ladies' room, you get a freshie, and you don't trust anyone with your beverage that you wouldn't trust with your life. Date-rape substances can be deadly. Women die from this shit. But do these rapist assholes care? No. They do not.*

Clearly, Nicki had listened, because she protected her beer like a lioness with a zebra carcass.

"I'm letting it run, though not much happens for the next fifteen minutes," Tuckey said. "I didn't see him slip anything into her beer on the first watch, but I'm happy to have your second set of eyes."

The waiter brought two appetizers and a second beer for the date. Barely five more minutes passed. Nicki shook herself. Her face changed expression. She placed one hand on her belly. Not long after that, she bolted from the table, her steps unsteady. The date let her go, following her and waiting outside the restroom for a reasonable five minutes.

Sharp made an attempt to view the video objectively, like he'd done hundreds of times when he was on the force, but it wasn't possible. There was no suppressing the raw rage that filled him.

"She's feeling it." Sharp checked the time stamp on the video. "It's a little less than twenty-five minutes from when she got her beer. Right on schedule if she was roofied."

"And she is clearly not drunk," Tuckey said. "She looked stone-cold sober when she walked into the bar and only drank a quarter of her beer."

Sharp leaned back. "He didn't get close to her drink, and no one approached their table."

"So, if she was drugged, it had to have happened before she got her drink."

"Do you know what time he arrived?" Sharp asked.

"About ten minutes after your niece." Tuckey switched windows. "As you can see, the bar camera is focused on the register, and not all of the bar is visible. But this video of the back hallway is more interesting." He clicked "Play." "Obviously, they don't have a camera in the bathroom, but here is the date trying to drag her down the hallway."

Sharp noted the time stamp again. "She must have texted us while she was in the bathroom."

"She puked in there too, which may have kept at least some of the drug out of her system."

The blond man had one of Nicki's arms over his shoulders. He was carrying the bulk of her weight, while her feet stumbled to keep up. Anger and pity twisted in Sharp's gut. Nicki was smart, and also a smart-ass—a younger version of her aunt. She didn't do stupid things, at least not big stupid things. She'd arrived for her date separately. She'd kept her drink covered. She'd done everything right, and she'd still been doped.

The blond man barely dragged Nicki three steps before Brandon West appeared, blocking their path. The video was soundless, but the confrontation was obvious. The date tried to go around him, but West wasn't having any of that. He sidestepped to block their path. The date let Nicki slide to the floor. West turned toward her, and the date sucker punched him in the mouth. It was a shitty, weak-ass punch, and West took the blow with a shake of his head, then pivoted, using his hip turn to add power, and drove an uppercut into the date's gut. The date doubled over, heaving. West gave him a shove and a command, stabbing the air in the direction of the door for emphasis. Then he turned back to Nicki. Then Olivia pushed through the crowd.

Sharp gnashed his teeth and pointed to the screen. "If West hadn't been there, the blond guy might have gotten her out of the bar." Would he have taken her home? Or would he have taken her somewhere else? She would have woken up with no memory of what had happened to her.

"We don't have any proof he drugged her," Tuckey said.

"What about a waiter or the bartender?" Sharp asked.

"So far, I haven't found any evidence of that, but I will check out both of them for sure."

"OK, thanks." Sharp rose. "I have to get to the hospital."

"I'll download the rest of the surveillance videos and interview the rest of the restaurant staff. I'll let you know what I find out."

"Thanks." Sharp didn't promise to do the same. He was more than willing to overstep a few boundaries to find whoever had drugged Nicki. Lying about being Nicki's boyfriend made her date the very strong primary suspect, but Sharp needed to figure out how he'd managed it. In Sharp's experience, rapists were repeat offenders. Whoever did this had likely done it before—and would do it again. Sharp would not let that happen to some other woman, who might not have a badass ER doctor on hand to prevent her from being further victimized.

He found Olivia in the ER waiting room filling out paperwork on a clipboard. "They're assessing her now."

"How was she?" Sharp sat next to Olivia.

"Still out of it." Olivia tucked the pen into the top of the clipboard. Setting it aside, she rested her head on his shoulder.

He kissed her hair and took her hand, his heart melting. "She's tough."

"I know." But her voice was strained and worried.

They sat in silence. The automatic door swished open. Brandon West walked into the ER, swiped a card, and disappeared through the double doors that led into the treatment area. Ten minutes later, he reemerged. He scanned the waiting room and waved to Sharp and Olivia, who hurried across the room.

West lifted a hand. "First of all, she's starting to come around, and I think she's going to be fine."

Olivia exhaled audibly. "Thank you."

West nodded. "Now for the details. She tested positive for gamma hydroxybutyrate. Do you know what that is?"

Sharp nodded. "GHB." The common date-rape drug was clear and odorless. Its slightly salty taste was easily camouflaged by whatever beverage it was mixed into. Symptoms of GHB poisoning included slow breathing, depressed heart rate, low body temperature, nausea, and vomiting. An overdose of GHB could induce coma and death. Sharp was fairly sure Olivia knew all of this, so he kept his mouth shut. She didn't need to be reminded of the danger. Instead, he asked West, "Her vitals are OK?"

"Rapidly improving," West said. "The good news is that GHB has a relatively short half-life. The body clears it quickly, so quickly that sometimes it's hard to test for. Your niece got to the ER promptly. They're hydrating her. As long as her vitals remain stable and she continues to improve, all they'll provide is supportive care. They'll probably keep her for a couple more hours, until she's more lucid and they're sure she's over the worst of it. Someone will come and get you shortly. Then you can stay with her until she's released."

They thanked him again, and he left the hospital. Sharp seethed, mind spinning, until a nurse brought them back to see Nicki. She was pale, but her eyes were open. Her vomit-soiled top had been replaced by a hospital gown. An IV dripped into the back of her hand.

As Olivia and Sharp entered the room, she struggled to sit up. Olivia rushed to her side, perched on the edge of the gurney, and hugged her hard.

Nicki started to cry. "I'm s-sorry."

"There's nothing to be sorry about." Olivia straightened but kept hold of Nicki's hand. "I'm just grateful you texted me."

"I don't even remember doing that. I don't remember much." Nicki dried her eyes with the short sleeve of the oversize gown. "I don't know what happened. Everything is really fuzzy, but you know I'm super careful with my drinks."

Sharp walked closer, feeling a little like he was intruding, but not wanting her to blame herself for anything that had happened that night. Even if she hadn't been as careful, it would not have been her fault. The blame rested completely on the person who'd poisoned her, because that's what GHB was: poison.

He patted her forearm. "I watched the surveillance footage. You did everything right. I can't figure out how it happened either." He gave her arm a gentle squeeze. "But I will."

"I don't think it was Cody." She lay back, pulled her hands free, and played with the edge of the sheet with her fingertips. "He didn't get near my beer."

"I know," Sharp said. Could Cody have put GHB in the food? He'd reached over both plates. Sharp would contact Tuckey the next day and watch the videos again. There could have been some sleight of hand, followed by the date not consuming any more of the food. GHB didn't put itself into Nicki.

Olivia placed a hand over Nicki's, stilling them. "We'll go through all of that tomorrow. Tonight, you just need to recover."

Nicki closed her eyes. "I'm pretty sure I puked all over Cody, my date," she said. "I'm sure I'll never see him again."

Olivia patted her hand. "If he's worth having, he'll know this wasn't your fault."

But Sharp didn't like that the guy had left. Until he got to the bottom of who'd spiked Nicki's drink, he didn't want Cody anywhere near her. And since he had absolutely no control over Nicki, that meant Sharp needed to figure it out fast.

Chapter Seventeen

Zoe waited until darkness fell.

Then she went to him.

She drove to the rural route that wound through foothills at the base of the mountain, where homes stretched out along the country road. She passed a mailbox every half mile or so. No overcrowding out here. Most people would love the open space, but to Zoe, the vastness felt overwhelmingly lonely and isolated.

She thought of her small apartment, with its paper-thin walls and noisy—nosy—neighbors. If she cried out, someone would call 911. Out here in the country, she could scream all night and no one would hear.

His house was just a few miles from the cabin, but the winding mountain switchbacks made for slow progress. Stopping just short of her destination, she pulled over onto the shoulder on the other side of the road, then turned the steering wheel and backed the van deep into the shadow of huge oak trees. She couldn't take the chance of pulling into the driveway. Though she couldn't see anyone nearby, someone could be watching. She lowered the window an inch and listened. An owl hooted. Wind rustled the branches overhead. A small creature moved through the foliage, unleashing a barrage of acorns onto her vehicle's roof.

An engine approached. Her vehicle should be concealed, but Zoe slid down in her seat until her head was below the window opening anyway. She held her breath until the vehicle passed by. After the engine sound faded, she counted to ten, then straightened. The night was once again quiet except for the sounds of nature.

But the passing vehicle had increased her anxiety. No one could see her in the trees, but she'd have to cross an acre of open ground to get to the house.

She waited another half hour, listening for sounds of more traffic. It was nearly midnight when she finally checked her pockets, where she'd stashed a few necessities: lockpick, bear spray, binoculars, flashlight. Then she turned off the interior dome light and slid out of her vehicle, softly closing the door and bumping it with her hip rather than slamming it.

Standing at the edge of the trees, she lifted the binoculars to her eyes and stared across the road. The house was one story and small. A light mounted over the front door cast a dirty yellow pool of light on the cracked concrete stoop. The yard was still and silent.

She wore a black knit hat to cover her blond hair. Her yoga pants and sweatshirt were also black. But her dark clothes were meant to blend into the shadows, and tonight's moon shone like a golden fucking beacon. Where was the storm front the weather app had promised was on the way?

Best to move fast.

She ran in a low crouch to a tall pine tree at the edge of the front yard. She stopped, peering around the trunk, sizing up the situation.

A chain-link fence enclosed a small yard behind the house. All the windows were dark except one at the back of the house, where dim light flickered. Had he fallen asleep with the TV on? Had he been waiting for her? A memory surfaced with the gasp of a struggling swimmer in choppy water. She resisted the pull of the past. She envisioned last night's text: Need to see you.

Why? Why would he want to see her? They'd agreed that being together was too risky. What had changed? He had to have a good reason to put them both in jeopardy. Not a good reason—she had no doubt the reason was terrible.

She hadn't answered his text, hadn't acknowledged his message, hadn't arranged a time or place. On the outside chance that someone was monitoring his phone, she wouldn't give meeting details. She'd just show up randomly.

But it wasn't really random, was it?

He'd expect her to come, as long as she'd received his message. She'd never given him the location of her safe house, though he knew her well enough that he might be able to find her. But he wouldn't try. Because not knowing where she was made her safer, and he worried more about her than he did for himself. He made no effort at all to hide his own location.

This location.

Where anyone could find him.

Where the one person she didn't want to see undoubtedly knew he lived.

Under her sweatshirt, goose bumps rippled up her arms. She should have answered the text. Should have suggested a neutral rendezvous point. It was too late now.

But then, she always thought of the best response when it was too late.

She raised her binoculars and surveyed the house. She didn't see any cameras mounted under the eaves. That didn't mean there weren't any. But unlike her, he had always seemed resigned to their fate should this moment ever come to fruition. He hadn't bothered to take a single precaution.

She stole to the window with the flickering light, but sheer blinds covered the glass. Peering over the sill, she squinted through a half-inch gap at the bottom of the blind. She could see a slice of the room, a dresser with a TV on it, a dark doorway, and a few square feet of blank wall. She headed for the back of the house and tripped over a tree root. An *oomph* escaped her lips as she went down on her knees, pain bursting through her legs.

From behind the house, dog tags jingled. An animal breathed heavily. Zoe scanned the fence line. The shadow of a dog stood at the gate. The animal raised its head and sniffed the air, then burst into a chorus of piercing barks that sounded as loud as a siren. It was a good thing no one was close enough to hear it. She held still for a few minutes. The dog did not settle. It continued to growl and race along the fence.

Would he know that she was here? Or did the dog bark often enough at wind and wildlife that he ignored it?

The grass was a basic square with no flowers, trees, or ornamental bushes. Rust and mold streaked the concrete walkway that led to the front door. She crossed to it on silent sneakers. She could still hear the dog moving behind the fence. Normally, she would have knocked on the back door. But the dog necessitated she use the main entrance. At least there were no neighbors to see her. She hadn't even seen a car pass by after that one vehicle. Moonlight reflected on the glass panes alongside the door. She cupped her hands over her face and tried to look inside, but sheer blinds blocked her view.

Zoe turned the doorknob. It offered no resistance. *Unlocked.* Her heart skipped.

Did people in the country still leave their doors unlocked? Why on earth would he, knowing who was out there? Or had he left it open for her?

Pulse thrumming, she pushed open the door a few inches and poked her head through the gap. The interior of the house was too dark to see anything except the basic shapes of the furniture: a couch, a chair, a few tables. The floorboards squeaked as she walked through the room, then she stood still to get her bearings. She'd never been in this house before.

From the living room, a hallway led toward the back of the house. She could see an eat-in kitchen with glass doors behind a breakfast area. A night-light was plugged into the wall. The dog was at the back door, furiously barking. It stood on its hind legs and dug at the glass door, rattling the slider in its tracks.

Midway down the hall, another corridor led to what she assumed were the bedrooms. Nerves prickled the back of her neck. If he was asleep, surely the barking would have woken him. Unless he was so accustomed to hearing it that he slept right through it.

She ducked into the kitchen—empty—then tiptoed down the corridor toward the bedrooms.

Dread gathered in her belly until her insides cramped. Maybe he wasn't home. The house *felt* empty. That would explain why the dog was locked out. Knowing him, if he were here, it would be curled up in his bed with him. It was a nice night, though. Some dogs liked to be outside.

But where would he be in the middle of the night? He could have a girlfriend. He could have gone out. Plenty of possibilities. Yet she didn't believe any of them. He wouldn't have gone out after asking to see her. Maybe he worked the graveyard shift . . .

Yes, that was plausible. He'd always been a night person.

Yet her pulse accelerated and sweat dampened the waistband of her pants. The house didn't just feel empty. It felt wrong in a way she couldn't articulate. Wrong in a way that made her feet continue down the hallway. Three of the four doors stood open. She peered into the first room: a home office. The second room was empty except for a pile of boxes in the corner. The next room was a bathroom. Empty.

The fourth door loomed at the end of the hall. She didn't need the floor plan to know this would be the primary bedroom. Fear tightened her chest, but she couldn't stop moving forward. Anxiety compelled her to continue. Worry overrode her terror and she opened the door. Sheer blinds covered the windows, dimming the moonlight. She stood in the doorway, eyes adjusting, forms gradually taking shape.

Outside the dog began barking again. But Zoe barely heard it through the rush of blood in her ears. A scream built in a crescendo and burst from her lips as the terror took over.

Chapter Eighteen

The next morning, Olivia woke in the dark. Exhaustion made her head feel like it weighed twenty pounds. She rolled over and checked the time on her phone. Six fifteen. She'd slept a whole fifteen minutes later than usual. She closed her eyes, willing herself to go back to sleep. But her brain rejected sleep. It wanted to see Nicki. Again. To watch the rise and fall of her chest. To hear the breaths roll in and out of her body.

To make sure the worst thing Olivia could imagine hadn't happened.

She rolled again to face the window, where the faintest hint of light signaled the coming of dawn.

Next to her, Lincoln said, "It's pathetic. Even when I want to sleep in, I can't."

"Same." Olivia sat up and perched on the edge of the bed. "I'm going to check on Nicki."

She rose. After she left the warmth of the bed, a chill swept across her bare arms. She reached for a sweatshirt and tugged it over her head.

They hadn't gotten back to the house until nearly four a.m., and Olivia had stayed awake until Nicki had showered, donned a clean pair of pajamas, and crawled into bed. Nicki had been sleepy—normal sleepy, not unconscious sleepy. She'd seemed mostly coherent, although her memory was still hazy. The doctor had said she might or might not remember much from the night before. Olivia knew some women who were drugged sometimes struggled with panic attacks and disjointed flashbacks. But she kept this information to herself. If Nicki had those symptoms, then they'd deal with them. There was no need to create unnecessary anxiety.

Nicki's discharge instructions were to hydrate and sleep. Despite the doctor's assurances that she should be fine, Olivia worried. She'd never had children of her own, but her family was a tight one. She had good relationships with all her nieces and nephews, but she and Nicki had always had a special bond. Their similarities in personality had often exasperated Stephen and his wife. *She's more like you than either of us,* he'd said practically since the day Nicki was born. Where Stephen and his wife were quiet and reserved, Nicki was outgoing, bold, and fearless.

Like herself, Olivia admitted.

She'd asked Nicki to leave the guest room door unlocked. Now she eased it open a few inches and was instantly relieved at the sound of her niece's soft snoring. She exhaled fully for what seemed like the first time since Nicki had texted her the night before. The knot of anxiety behind her sternum loosened, and she quietly closed the door.

When Nicki woke, they'd discuss whether to call her parents. She was an adult. The decision would be up to her. If Stephen asked a specific question, Olivia wouldn't lie, but one of the reasons she was so close to her nieces and nephews was that they knew they could come to her to talk about anything. She would keep their confidence unless it was a drastic matter that involved their safety. The extended family could be gossipy, but Aunt Olivia did not have loose lips. She had their backs.

Lincoln was in the kitchen already, dressed in his running clothes. "I started the kettle for you."

"Thank you." She crossed the room as he straightened and slid her arms around his waist.

He pulled her close and kissed the top of her head. "She's OK?"

"Sleeping hard." Olivia pressed her head to his chest for a few seconds, then released him. Looking up at him, she read the signs of exhaustion in the bags and dark circles beneath his eyes. "You really want to run today?"

"It'll wake me up." Lincoln lived by the *move it or lose it* motto. He exercised as if it were a religion and ate mostly organic foods. She couldn't complain. He was in incredible shape, currently highlighted by his running shorts and snug athletic T-shirt. He ran circles around men half his age. A quick rush of warmth spread through her. She wouldn't do anything about that in her immediate state of exhaustion, but maybe later . . .

Lincoln started for the door. When he opened it, Olivia heard the tweeting of birds.

"Enjoy," she said.

"I highly doubt that I will." He chuckled and closed the door behind him.

A wisp of steam swirled from the kettle. Olivia made a cup of green tea, then changed into yoga pants and took her mat outside into the small backyard.

Sunrise warmed the brick patio. She moved onto a small patch of grass and unrolled her yoga mat. She loosened up with sun salutations, then moved through a flow of stretches, balance poses, and inversions.

The patio door opened and closed. She heard Lincoln lifting the cover of his cold plunge tub. His face contorted for a few seconds, then smoothed into an uncomfortable but resigned expression as his body adjusted to the shocking temperature.

Olivia shuddered and went into the kitchen to restart the kettle. Just watching him made her cold. For a second, she was transported back to the dank cellar where she'd been imprisoned. A dark space, the creeping chill settling into her lungs, the smell of damp and mold. She wheezed, lungs tightening, asthma threatening to flare. The water in the kettle boiled, yanking her out of the flashback and bringing her back to the present. She focused on her next few breaths, inhaling deeply and exhaling slowly, steadily, until the tightness in her chest eased.

Would those flashbacks ever end? Yoga helped, but Olivia would much rather they not happen at all. It was a helpless, out-of-control feeling that she hoped Nicki would not experience.

She brought two cups of tea out onto the patio. Lincoln's timer dinged. Despite his proclamations about how great the ice baths made him feel, he didn't waste any time climbing out of the frigid water. Shivering, he reached for the thick spa robe she'd bought him for his birthday. He'd stripped down to compression shorts before using the tub, and his skin was coated with goose bumps. After wrapping the robe tightly around himself, he accepted the tea.

She could feel the change in season on the morning breeze. A quick check of her weather app confirmed the approaching weather shift. Storms and a thirty-degree drop in temperature were forecasted over the next twelve hours.

She stuffed her phone into the thigh pocket of her yoga pants. "There's a cold front coming in."

Lincoln wrapped an arm around her shoulders and gave her a companionable squeeze. Through the thick robe, his body emanated cold like an ice cube. "Winter is coming."

She chuckled at the *Game of Thrones* reference, but for her, the steady encroachment of winter did feel like an attack. Since her kidnapping, the struggle felt more intense, with the chill and gloom reminding her of the belowground prison she'd been kept in. She closed her eyes and turned her chin to the sun, letting the warmth on her face banish the memories. Then she carried her mug and mat to the glass door, which Lincoln opened for her. "I'm going to check on Nicki again."

"The ER doc said she just needed to sleep it off." Lincoln turned in to the primary bedroom suite.

Olivia continued to the guest room. She didn't relax until she cracked open the door, peered around it, and heard Nicki breathing one more time. Relieved, she went to the bedroom. Lincoln opened a dresser drawer and pulled out a pair of jeans and a T-shirt. "What's your plan for the day?"

She hadn't forgotten about Zoe, but Olivia's priorities had been temporarily reshuffled. Now that Nicki was no longer in danger, Olivia would return to finding her friend.

"I'm not leaving Nicki today, but I have plenty to do: continue reviewing the Evan Brown case, take a second pass at Zoe's iCloud files, and follow up on the Hamilton case. What about you? Do you have work?"

"No. The active part of our investigation is complete, and Lance can handle the reports and paperwork," Lincoln said. "While you get back to finding Zoe, I'd like to dig into Cody's life and background. If necessary, I'll pull in Lance's mom to do a deep dive into Nicki's date. This morning, I plan to check in with Officer Tuckey. I'm going to figure out who poisoned Nicki and how they did it."

"Thank you." Olivia kissed him. Splaying a hand on his chest, she felt him shiver. "You know how important she is to me."

He kissed her back. "I never had any kids of my own, but Lance, his wife, her little girls, Nicki . . . They all feel like they could be mine."

"I know exactly how you feel. There's more than one way to build a family. Love and trust mean more than a family tree, and a blood relationship doesn't guarantee an emotional connection."

"I investigate plenty of people with toxic families," Lincoln agreed.

Thirty minutes later, they returned to the kitchen for breakfast. The rustle of fabric drew her attention to the hallway. Nicki walked toward them. Despite some puffiness and paleness, her eyes were clear.

"Hey," she said.

Olivia felt the smile pull at her cheeks. Relief was a powerful emotion. "Do you want some food?"

Nicki frowned. "Not yet."

"Coffee?" Olivia mentally ran through a list of Nicki's favorite foods. "I could make you a latte and a breakfast sandwich."

Nicki shook her head and placed a hand on her belly. "Sadly, I don't think I can stomach coffee yet. Not sure about food either."

Lincoln set a glass of water in front of her. "You need tea?"

Nicki nodded and slid onto a stool at the island. "Tea sounds good."

Lincoln refilled and started the kettle. "I'll make you toast too. I have some fresh sourdough. You'll need protein, something easily digestible." He bustled around the kitchen and muttered to himself. Deep down, he was equal parts tough guy and mother hen. A few minutes later, he brought Nicki a mug of tea, a slab of toast, and a small pile of fluffy scrambled eggs with fresh dill. He set a small plate with butter and honey at her elbow.

Nicki stared at the loaded plate and grinned. "I didn't think I was hungry . . ." She proceeded to clear her plate, using her fork more like a shovel. Sitting back, she gripped her mug with both hands. Her color had improved, and her eyes were brighter than before her meal. "I feel much better now. Thanks, Sharp."

He beamed. *Total mother hen.*

"You should be back to normal by tomorrow," Olivia said. "Do you feel up to talking about last night?"

Nicki's face scrunched. "Last night is a blur, but sure. I want to know what happened."

Lincoln brought his laptop into the kitchen and settled at the island. "What do you know about your date, Cody?"

Nicki scanned the kitchen. "Aunt Liv, where's my phone?"

Olivia brought it to her.

Nicki opened it. "His name is Cody. The dating app I use doesn't give last names. He gave me some personal information, but I have no way of knowing what's true and what's false." She reviewed her in-app message exchanges with Cody. All were relatively tame, even wary from Nicki's side. She held back her most personal information. She told him she worked in social media marketing but gave no details. She said she lived in Randolph County but didn't specify which town. His messages were equally reserved.

"He said he lives in Randolph County and works as an investment banker," Nicki said. "He mentioned playing lacrosse for the university. I'm assuming he went there."

"You didn't exchange phone numbers?" Lincoln asked.

"No. I don't give out my number until I've met someone in person, verified some of their data, and know that I want to see them again. I've been ghosted, and I've met some real assholes."

Obviously.

"Good policy," he said. "You know how I feel about dating apps."

"I do, but everyone uses them. I love working from home, but it doesn't give me many opportunities to meet people, and I like the efficiency of weeding out people who don't have any interests in common with me. I don't want to waste my time with anyone with a worldview that's drastically different from my own. I have tons of respect for women who want to focus on motherhood and aren't interested in a career. But that's not for me. It's all about free choice. I can't tell you how many times I've been out on a date talking about how much I love my work, and the guy spends the entire date telling me I'm wrong. I shouldn't want that. I should want to focus my life on making biscuits and babies. And the whole 'submit' thing makes me want to bite people." She took a breath. "All I'm saying is that a dude who wants a tradwife should date women who want to be tradwives, not look for a career woman like subduing her is some kind of personal conquest or such bullshit. Apps let me make my interests and goals clear and make appropriate connections."

Lincoln shook his head. "I can appreciate your frustration. But it's still too easy to make a fake account on most apps. It's too easy to lie. Too easy to con someone. The whole setup is as sketchy as social media." He held up a hand. "I know these things are here to stay, and I'm well aware of my dinosaur status."

"Won't the police try to find Cody?" Olivia asked.

"Tuckey will probably make a preliminary effort to find him and question him, but the police need a warrant to pursue Cody's private information. They can't get that without probable cause. The surveillance tape clearly shows Cody *not* slipping anything into Nicki's beer."

"No probable cause," Olivia concluded.

"Right," Lincoln said. "Thankfully, I have more freedom. Technically, PIs have to adhere to the law, but there's plenty of gray area." And if the stakes were high enough, Lincoln would take that gray to charcoal. "I'm also not a hundred percent sure it was Cody who drugged Nicki. Assumptions can wreck an investigation. I have to follow the evidence, not lead it."

As a writer, Olivia tended to work on evidence *and* theories. "He was the one who has motive, though. Why would a random stranger slip GHB into Nicki's beer or food?"

"I've no idea," Sharp said. "Can we see his profile?"

Nicki nodded and pulled it up on her phone.

"Can you text me his profile pics and basic information?" Sharp asked.

"Sure." Nicki used her thumbs. "His profile says he's a thirty-year-old investment banker."

Sharp's phone dinged. He squinted at the screen. "How long has his profile been active?"

"Ten months," Nicki said.

"Can I borrow your cheaters?" Sharp asked.

Olivia passed her reading glasses to him, and he put them on to scrutinize the data. "I'll verify what I can."

"Thank you." Nicki set down her mug with a loud *thunk*. Tea sloshed over the rim onto the recycled glass countertop. "Oh, my God." Her mouth gaped. She closed it and shut her eyes for a couple of seconds. When she opened them, her gaze was filled with disbelief. She rubbed her temples with both hands. "I can't believe I forgot."

"Forgot what?" Olivia asked.

"I saw Dylan at the bar last night," Nicki said.

"Dylan? Are you sure?" Olivia was stunned, but then again, was it really that shocking considering his behavior?

"I'm sure." Nicki lowered her hands and curled them around her mug. "He was at the bar, and hitting up a woman about my age."

"Did he see you?" Lincoln asked.

"I don't think so." Nicki shook her head. "He was focused on the woman."

"Do you know if he left with her?"

"No idea," Nicki said. "After I spotted him, I kept a big fern between us. After Cody arrived, I stopped watching Dylan."

Olivia's mind whirled. "He was drunk when I saw him yesterday." She recounted her conversation with him from the day before. "I've never seen him behave like that."

"But maybe Zoe had," Nicki said.

"Sounds like there are two Dylans," Lincoln added.

"In his defense, I would be upset if my spouse of nearly ten years kept major secrets from me, and then walked away without a word," Olivia admitted.

"I can understand Dylan being angry and confused, but giving up on her already?" Lincoln shook his head. "And not even trying to find her? The *Run* text message suggests she's fleeing danger. What if she left to protect herself—and not telling him was her way of protecting him? We don't know who she's running from."

Nicki lifted her mug. "I doubt Dylan has the imagination to think of all those possibilities. Plus, his own insecurities are probably influencing his conclusions. When we worked on his fitness videos, he was very self-conscious about his body and face. His crow's-feet really bothered him. He blamed the lack of engagement on his videos on him not looking young enough. He even joked that he should raise his age on his social media account to fifty-five. Then people would be impressed by how he looked."

"So, he'd lie," Olivia said.

"Grifters gonna grift." Nicki shrugged. "People lie on social media all the time. Have you ever seen some woman with no body fat lifting weights, selling her exclusive fine-milled capybara collagen powder, and claiming to be sixty-five when she doesn't look a day older than forty?"

"Yes," Olivia admitted. She wasn't immune to beauty and anti-aging ads. Who didn't want to look younger? "You're saying she probably isn't a day older than forty."

Nicki gave her a *bingo* look. "Also, she's probably using special lighting and filters."

"This is why I don't do social media," Lincoln said. "It's a cesspool of disinformation."

"Do you think Dylan is a social media grifter?" Olivia asked.

"No, but I think he'd like to be," Nicki said.

"That makes sense," Olivia said. "He's frustrated that he isn't making it big and is blaming Zoe for holding him back. But how does this reflect on his relationship with Zoe? Most people see them together and ask why he is with an older woman. Even Billings suggested Dylan could get a much hotter wife."

Lincoln snorted. "Zoe is ten times smarter than him. Financially, I bet he needs her a lot more than she needs him. And he knows it."

Nicki spun her mug. "He once complained that Zoe wouldn't pay for Botox for him, but she'd gotten it for herself."

"Zoe did Botox?" Olivia asked. "I'm not judging. Just surprised."

"That's what he said." Nicki lifted a palm. "He implied she was to blame for his lack of success as an influencer."

Lincoln rolled his eyes. "His career is in the crapper because he has the IQ of a beach ball."

"True," Nicki said. "But how does this help us figure out who drugged me? Cody didn't have the opportunity. Why would anyone else give a strange woman a date-rape drug?"

Lincoln huffed. "Maybe it was an accident. Maybe whoever put the GHB in your beer thought it was meant for someone else. Lonely Chicken is pretty popular with the local set. I'm going to ask Tuckey to let me watch the surveillance tapes again. Sometimes you need to view those multiple times before you see something that's off. Plus, he said he's obtained additional footage. He was going to take a look at the bartender and waiter as well." His phone buzzed and he glanced at it. "Tuckey wants to meet now."

"Is that a good sign or a bad one?"

Lincoln set his glass in the dishwasher. "There's only one way to find out."

Chapter Nineteen

Sharp sat next to Tuckey's desk at the Scarlet Falls Police Station. The SFPD hadn't changed much since Sharp had been on the force. Some of the faces were different, but the beat-up desks and filing cabinets looked exactly the same, because they were exactly the same. The small town didn't have the budget for furniture upgrades.

Tuckey gestured toward his computer screen, where the bar surveillance videos played in multiple windows on the computer. They'd already watched the front entrance feed twice, noting the time Nicki and her date had arrived and left the restaurant. Now the video of the bar area played in the center of the screen.

Tuckey attacked the keyboard. "Give me one second."

While he typed, Sharp casually scanned his messy desk. Tuckey had been writing reports. His personal notepad lay in the center of his blotter. Sharp squinted to read Tuckey's notes upside down.

Cody Vass

1226 State Street, #278

Scarlet Falls

Sharp committed the name and address to memory.

"Here we go." Tuckey tapped the "Enter" key with a dramatic forefinger. "I want to start with the same video we watched last night. I want your eyes on it too, to make sure I didn't miss anything."

They rewatched the camera covering the lounge area, including the table where Nicki and Cody sat. Sharp leaned in to get a closer look. He didn't take his gaze off Cody's hands. He barely blinked.

Tuckey stopped the video when Nicki ran for the bathrooms. "He did not put anything in her beer. Not at the table, anyway."

The cop's comment piqued Sharp's interest. "Did he have another opportunity?"

"Maybe," Tuckey said. "I watched the feed from earlier in the evening to make sure that Nicki's date didn't lie, that he hadn't been in the bar before their date to scope out the place."

"Was he?" Sharp asked.

"Again, maybe if we're splitting hairs." Tuckey opened another window to play the video covering the bar cash register. He dragged his mouse backward. "We'll start at seven o'clock." He played the video in quadruple time.

The camera didn't cover the entire room. About 20 percent of the bar area wasn't visible, but no one could approach the bartender or front-facing portion of the bar without passing through the camera's view. At seven o'clock, there was no sign of Nicki's date, but Dylan Sanders arrived at 7:15. He'd gone directly to the bar, ordered a drink, and scanned the other patrons. He zeroed in on an attractive young woman and worked his way over to her. They flirted. He bought drinks and tried to cozy up. The young woman skillfully avoided his straying hands while accepting the free booze. Dylan's maneuvers looked almost comical on the sped-up video—as did his growing frustration.

"My niece also knows this guy." Sharp pointed to Dylan. "The one hitting up the woman half his age."

"He seems focused on the blonde." Tuckey slowed the video to real time. "I would bet he won't be getting anywhere with her. She just wants free drinks."

Sharp agreed, but he couldn't sympathize. Dylan was too aggressive for anyone's pity. He didn't wait more than five minutes before his hand landed on the woman's thigh and squeezed. She shifted and recrossed her legs, deftly dislodging his kneading fingers with an elbow as she swiveled on her stool. Dylan draped a hand over the back of her seat, his knuckles brushing against the side of her breast. She tossed her hair, putting a few inches of space between his hand and her body. Dylan was not a quitter. He continued to touch her in any way possible, while the young woman exhibited more impressive evasive maneuvers than an NFL running back. They both seemed adept at their roles. Sharp bet this wasn't the first time Dylan had strayed in his marriage. He might be a little awkward, but he didn't appear hesitant.

Tuckey pointed to the monitor. "Keep your attention on this corner of the screen."

Sharp watched the bartender mix two gin and tonics, add slices of lime and cocktail straws, and place the drinks on the bar, just out of the camera's line of sight. He drew a beer and did the same.

Tuckey switched back to the lounge camera. He made a quick pencil sketch on a blank piece of paper. He drew a long *U*, then added a dozen little circles. "Here's the bar and the tables, and here's that spot where the bartender is leaving the drink orders for the waitstaff to pick up."

Sharp pictured the room and tapped on the drawing. "The hallway to the restrooms is right here. Anyone who went to the restroom would have passed right by the drinks sitting there."

"Yep." Tuckey turned back to his computer and opened a third window. "Here's the hallway leading to the restrooms." He advanced the feed to show Cody in the hallway. "Here's your guy entering the bathroom at 8:03 and exiting at 8:07."

Sharp went back to the bar camera. "Can you tell what time the bartender placed Nicki's beer there?"

"About that time. The problem is select beers on tap were on special that night. Lots of people ordered beer."

"Hold on." Sharp switched back and forth between camera feeds, noted the time stamps, then drew out a quick timeline. "So Cody did arrive after Nicki, but he went to the men's room before approaching her. Nicki's beer arrived while he was in the restroom. He *could* have had time to doctor her beer before it went to the table."

"Correct," Tuckey said. "But given the amount of beer sold that night, and the fact that we don't have eyes on the drinks as they go from the bartender to the waitstaff to the tables—there are forty other people in that bar and more in the restaurant who could have spiked your niece's drink. It was a busy night. The drugged beer could have gone to the wrong person. It could have been an accident."

But Sharp didn't believe in coincidences. "Did you interview her date yet?"

"Yes. He used a credit card to pay at the restaurant. I talked to him this morning. He denies everything, and his record is clean."

Using his credit card made Cody either stupid or innocent.

"What about the bartender and waiter?" Sharp asked.

"No footage shows either of them spiking a beer, and neither have a criminal record."

Sharp stood. "Thanks, Tuckey. I appreciate the look at the vids."

"Anytime, Sharp. I wish I could have been more help, but this is why we don't catch many of these guys. They're smart."

Rapists went free more often than not.

On his way out of the police station, Sharp called his partner, Lance Kruger. "You busy?"

"Typing reports. Nothing that can't wait."

"Wanna look threatening while I shake down a couple of assholes?"

"Sure," Lance answered without missing a beat.

Sharp didn't need help interrogating anyone, but they both knew the risks in knocking on the doors of strangers, especially those you suspected of criminal activity. "Neither visit is connected to a paying client."

"No worries." Lance sounded ridiculously chipper these days.

"You at the office?"

"Yep."

"I'm on my way. I'll pick you up in ten."

"Let's take my SUV. It's hard to look intimidating getting out of a Prius."

Even though he was alone, Sharp rolled his eyes. "I don't own a Prius because it looks badass."

"Clearly."

"No minivan today?" Sharp couldn't resist his own good-natured dig. Since Lance had married, he'd become the stepfather to his wife's three little girls. Some days, he drove his wife's minivan, which was filled with crumbs and covered in sticky fingerprints.

"Not today!" Lance replied happily.

Sharp laughed. He knew Lance loved every minute of his new chaotic life. "Would you get quick background basics on Cody Vass and Dylan Sanders?" He spelled their names and provided their addresses.

"I can do that."

Ten minutes later, Sharp parked his car at Sharp Investigations. His partner met him outside. Lance was big and beefy. Dressed in his tactical cargos, a black T-shirt, and well-worn boots, he looked intimidating as hell. They climbed into Lance's new ride.

"May as well enjoy one of the last nice days of the year," Lance said as he opened the sunroof. "Which asshole are we shaking down first?"

Sharp checked the map for proximity. "Cody Vass." He summarized the happenings from the previous night and the surveillance videos he'd watched with Tuckey earlier.

"And you think Cody drugged Nicki?" Lance's blue eyes narrowed.

"Maybe," Sharp admitted. "I'm not sure what happened, but that's why we're talking to him."

Lance emitted a noise that sounded like a growl. "Do we need a lawn-and-leaf bag and a shovel?"

"Not just yet, but I appreciate the sentiment."

The GPS guided them to Cody Vass's apartment in a newish, moderately priced complex.

Lance parked. "Cody has lived here for two years. He works at a bank branch in town. His credit rating is OK but not great. He has a ton of student debt. No criminal record." Lance pointed to an older-model silver Honda Accord. "That's his vehicle."

"So he's probably here." Sharp got out of the SUV.

Lance joined him on the sidewalk.

Cody's apartment was on the second floor. They took the concrete steps to the landing and knocked on his door. Sharp looked back at Lance. Maybe he was too intimidating. "You might want to step to the side." He nodded at the peephole. "Be ready to flex something when I need it."

"Right." Lance shifted out of sight.

Inside the apartment, footsteps approached the door, then stopped. Sharp could feel his attention through the peephole. The door opened a few inches. He recognized Cody from the videos.

Sharp held up a business card. "Cody Vass?"

Cody hesitated, then took the card without answering. He stared at it, then turned a confused and suspicious gaze to Sharp. "What do you want?"

"To ask you a few questions."

Cody moved to close the door. "You're not a cop. I don't have to talk to you."

Sharp stuck his foot in the opening, preventing its closure. "As you said, I'm not a cop."

Lance sidled into view and shoved the door open with one hand. Cody still had his hand on the knob, and the force of the push sent him stumbling backward a few inches. Sharp advanced through the doorway. Normally, when he was working a case, he *mostly* obeyed the law.

But this time, he wasn't on a case. This was personal. This was about finding a rapist.

Who. Drugged. Nicki.

Sharp felt the anger bubbling up in his chest and tamped it firmly back down.

Lance followed him inside, closed the door, and stood in front of it. He knew his role and crossed his arms, biceps bulging. Under his short blond hair, his blue eyes stared coldly.

Cody swallowed. He looked strung out, as if he hadn't slept. Purple circles darkened the hollows under his eyes, and his hair was greasy and disheveled.

"Not working today, Cody?" Sharp scanned the apartment. The front door opened right into the living room and kitchen combo. He assumed the hallway led to the bedroom and bathroom. Cody's keys and wallet sat on the kitchen table. The wood veneer on the corners of the coffee table was peeling, but the place was neat enough. A few dishes sat in the sink. No visible trash or dust.

"I took the day off." Cody inched backward, but the apartment was small. There wasn't anywhere to go. The living room didn't even have a balcony, just double windows that overlooked the parking lot.

"I'm not going to jerk you around." Sharp stepped forward, closing the distance between them. "You know the young woman you went out with last night?"

Cody swallowed and nodded.

"She's my niece."

Cody shoved shaking hands into the front pockets of his jeans. "I already talked to the cops. I didn't do it. I didn't do anything. She—" He stammered. "She ordered her drink before I even got there."

"You're sure about that?" Sharp asked. "Because you went to the bathroom before the table. You passed right by the bar. You could have spiked her beer on the way by."

"I didn't!" Cody's eyes bugged. "How would I even know what she ordered?"

Fair point.

But Sharp was not deterred. "Maybe you asked the waiter or bartender and slipped them some cash." Something they'd be unlikely to admit.

"Why would I do that?"

Sharp gave him a look. "GHB is a date-rape drug. You were Nicki's date." He hesitated, allowing Cody to make the logical leap to *you intended to rape her*. "Why would anyone else have spiked her beer?"

"I don't know!" Sweat beaded on Cody's upper lip. "But it wasn't me. The bar was busy. Anyone could have done it."

"But why? What did anyone else have to gain?" Sharp asked.

Cody threw up his hands. He looked like he might toss up his breakfast. "Nothing."

"You told Nicki you're an investment banker, but that's not exactly true, is it?" When Sharp thought of an investment banker, he pictured someone in a corporate office, not a branch employee.

"I work in a bank," Cody said in a vague tone.

Sharp raised his brows.

"OK." Cody held up his hands in a surrender position. "So I work at the branch in town. I'm not exactly an investment banker. I'm a customer service rep. I open accounts and help people access their safe-deposit boxes, things like that."

"You lied."

Cody rolled his eyes. "Yes. You caught me. I embellished my job a little to impress a girl." He tried to sound flippant but failed.

"A lie's a lie." But Sharp admitted it wasn't even close to the same scale as attempted date rape.

"I would never hurt a woman. Never." Cody licked his lips. "But dating is hard. Girls want successful guys, and with apps, you don't even get a chance to get them to like you. They won't even bother to talk to you. When I was in school, I could meet girls at parties or classes. Personality mattered. Now it's just data and algorithms. For the dating pool of thirty-year-olds, I don't make the computerized first cut."

"That must be frustrating," Sharp said. "Maybe frustrating enough to slip a little something into a date's drink to make sure you got what you wanted from her."

"No!" Cody's face reddened. Anger edged his words. "I might exaggerate on my dating profile a little, but that's just to get a meetup. After that, what happens between us happens." He sighed. "I just needed a leg up to get the first date. All I want is a chance."

The guy was still a liar, but he sounded more pathetic than dangerous. "Why did you leave her at the restaurant?"

"I tried to take her home. That asshole wouldn't let me."

"That asshole is an ER doctor. He called 911 for her. He made sure she was all right. You didn't."

"I didn't think she was that sick." Cody's eyes went white around the edges. "She said something about a virus."

"You could've stayed with her. Waited for the ambulance. Offered to call her family."

Cody's gaze dropped to the floor. He studied his sneakers for a few seconds. "You're right. *I* was the asshole."

Sharp hadn't expected the flash of humility.

Cody continued. "That other guy pissed me off."

"So you just left."

"Yeah." Cody blinked. "I'm not proud of it. I should have made sure she was all right. But I swear, I was just going to take her home. I mean, she puked all over me. That's not exactly a turn-on."

Sharp knew it wouldn't necessarily have stopped an actual rapist. "Instead of taking care of your date, you lost your temper and stormed off."

"Yeah." Cody sounded genuinely regretful. "I did that."

"OK."

"OK? That's it?" Cody glanced between Sharp and Lance. Lance glared unforgivingly.

Sharp said, "For now."

Cody sighed. "For what it's worth, I'm sorry."

"I'm not the one you need to apologize to." Sharp turned toward the door. "But if I find out you're lying to *me*, I'll be back."

Though he didn't think Cody was dumb enough to open the door a second time. They'd have to ambush him at work to get a second interview.

Lance followed Sharp out onto the concrete walkway. They jogged down the stairs and climbed into the SUV. Lance slammed the door hard enough to rattle the windows. "If someone ever drugs one of the girls, I will rip off a head."

"Unless Morgan gets to him first," Sharp pointed out. Lance's wife was more than a star defense attorney. She was a force. "And yeah. That's what I want to do. But I have to find the guilty party first."

Lance grumbled.

"You believe him?" Sharp asked.

Lance considered his question for a minute. "Either he's a good actor or he didn't do it."

"Fuck." Sharp rubbed the top of his head. "Maybe he *is* innocent."

"I wouldn't rule him out completely. He lied to Nicki, and he left the bar not knowing what happened to her. He didn't bother to check on her the next day either. But I'd investigate him a little more and move him down the list unless you get new information."

"Maybe he's just an asshole," Sharp said. "No law against that."

"Unfortunately not."

"That would mean someone else drugged Nicki."

"The GHB could have been intended for someone else," Lance said. "Morgan and I could use a date night. What if we go to the bar and stake out the place?"

"That's not much of a date night."

"She would enjoy it as much as I would. Rapists are repeat offenders. They hardly ever get caught."

"If the risk is low, why not keep doing it?" Sharp felt anger rise hot up the back of his neck. Cody could whine all he wanted about not being able to get dates, but women dealt with the possibility of being poisoned, raped, or even killed. "Would the perp use the same location? After all the attention Nicki's case brought to the restaurant?"

Lance lifted a shoulder. "Who the hell knows? They got away with it. Sometimes, criminals get off on that. They feel emboldened. We've both seen it."

"A smart one would lay low for a bit, then start up again in a fresh location."

"Most of them aren't as smart as they think they are."

But it didn't feel right to Sharp. He was allergic to coincidences, and this case was too full of them.

Chapter Twenty

"Now what?" Nicki propped her chin in both hands, elbows on the table, cheeks smooshed.

"You rest?" Olivia suggested, though she had to admit Nicki looked much better.

"I'm bored."

"Already?"

"Yeah." Nicki nodded. "I feel pretty good after the food. What are we doing today?"

"We?" Olivia asked. "Don't you have work?"

Nicki sighed. "Work is boring. I'd rather help you."

"Don't you need to make money?"

Nicki huffed. "I make enough to pay the bills. What you do is more interesting."

But Olivia did not vocalize her actual plan—watching Nicki all day—because mother-henning from Olivia would annoy her niece. Ironically, Nicki would accept unlimited fussing from Lincoln without bristling. Whether that was due to his personality or Nicki and Olivia's shared history didn't matter. Nicki needed rest. If Olivia had to be sneaky about how she got it, as Nicki would say, *whatever*. They were no closer to finding Zoe, so taking a step back and doing more research was the most logical move anyway. "Reviewing the information we have so far and making a plan to find Zoe."

"Good. I'll help." Nicki brightened. "Where do we start?"

"Our leads so far." Olivia consulted her list. "First up: Dylan."

Nicki wrinkled her nose. "I could see him as the reason she left. After last night, I could believe he cheated."

"His temper seems very short lately."

"Yes," Nicki said. "Could Zoe be teaching him a lesson? Paying him back for an affair?"

"I don't know." Olivia considered it. "Is Zoe that manipulative?"

Nicki frowned. "Did she catch him cheating? Because that might make her angry enough to lash out at him."

"That would sting," Olivia admitted. Was it possible that Dylan only stayed with Zoe because he was financially dependent on her?

"She's self-conscious about their age gap."

"She recently started dyeing her hair, and apparently, she tried Botox too," Olivia said.

"Most women dye their hair, at least for a while."

"But Zoe never wanted to before. If she thought Dylan was losing interest, that might have changed her mind. And if she caught him cheating, especially with someone significantly younger . . ."

"She must've been shook," Nicki said. "Not much we can do if she left to punish him."

"That doesn't explain the text she received telling her to run or the fact that she didn't let *anyone* know that she's OK. I also can't see her abandoning the podcast she's spent years developing even if she's angry."

"No," Nicki agreed. "We can still find her."

Olivia had to know what happened to her friend. "I won't let this go. She must be somewhere."

"Agreed."

"Anyway, Lincoln is following up on Dylan, so that leaves us with the two cases we think Zoe was investigating, plus whatever Wendy was up to." Olivia rubbed her temples.

"Wendy gave Zoe's research on the Evan Brown murder to Zoe's competitor, and Wendy admitted to being unhappy with Zoe as a boss."

"But would she harm her?" Olivia asked.

"Maybe she just wanted to scare her," Nicki suggested. "Wendy strikes me as a manipulative person. She handed Zoe's research to the competition."

"So, Wendy frightened Zoe with a text so she'd leave? What does that do for Wendy?"

"I dunno." Nicki's lips pursed in concentration. "Maybe to get this other job, Wendy needs to do significant damage to Zoe's podcast."

"We only have Wendy's word for what happened at the studio Saturday night." Olivia rubbed her forehead. "Maybe Wendy arranged for that creeper to call in to the show. Maybe she did something else to scare Zoe." *But what?*

"Zoe heavily promoted your upcoming interview on social media. She's using your interview and story as the material for the next three or four weeks of her show. If she doesn't make the episodes or do any shows at all, where does that leave her podcast? She'd have to replay old episodes, a huge disappointment to her fans who've been waiting for the show."

"Losing ratings, losing listeners."

Nicki nodded. "Downgrading Zoe's podcast helps Melissa MacGuiness's show. Aaaand if Melissa picks up the Evan Brown case that Zoe was going to use for next season and Melissa produces a show on that case and airs it ahead of Zoe . . ."

Olivia dropped her hand to the table. "Then Zoe wastes all her work and doesn't have a show for next season. I mean, she couldn't air the same murder case that another podcaster just covered."

"Zoe would have no way of knowing that Melissa was stealing her content. She'd just keep working her case and writing her show copy thinking she had the next season in the bag," Nicki said.

"That would be devious on Wendy's part."

"We already know Wendy is devious. She tried to sabotage Zoe."

"Good thing Melissa didn't actually get that file," Olivia said.

"I wonder what she did when she discovered it was missing," Nicki said. "Will she assume she dropped it? Ask for another copy? That could be awkward."

"That might depend on the actual content and if Melissa thinks the Brown case is worth investigating."

"Zoe did."

Olivia fished the folder she'd stolen from Melissa MacGuinness's bag from a pile of papers and waved it. "Lincoln and I didn't have much chance to dig into it yet."

Nicki gestured toward the computer. "What do we know about this Brown case?"

Olivia opened the computer folder and the physical file. "Evan Brown and his brother, Tim, were burglars." She repeated the case basics. "Tim went to prison. Evan disappeared. At the time, the police assumed he ran and left his brother to deal with the fallout."

"But he was dead the whole time," Nicki finished. "That is an interesting twist to the case."

Olivia said, "Yes. I can understand the appeal to study and/or solve the case for the podcast."

"Do they know if Evan was murdered?"

"There were four possibilities for manner of death: accident, suicide, homicide, or natural. Unfortunately, the medical examiner was unable to determine which one applied because of the condition of the remains."

"Did the ME rule any of them out?" Nicki asked.

Olivia skimmed Zoe's notes. "Natural seems unlikely, unless he had a stroke or heart attack while driving."

Nicki tapped her chin. "Could he have driven off the road by accident? He could have been under the influence of alcohol or drugs. He could have fallen asleep at the wheel."

Olivia shook her head. "I don't know. The lake has a steep bank and is far enough from the road that there isn't a guardrail. There's a photo." She pushed a photograph across the island.

Nicki studied it. "He would have had to drive across all this weedy ground and right into the lake without stopping. It would have been a rough ride. Unless he'd been unconscious, the bumps would have jarred him awake. Maybe he did it intentionally."

"Suicide?" Olivia frowned. "They found a backpack in the trunk. It was full of jewelry. They haven't been able to trace all the pieces, but a few of the items were reported stolen before Evan disappeared. The bag of loot supports the idea that he ran."

"He could have felt guilty," Nicki suggested, then shook her head. "Nah. The kind of person who repeatedly burglarizes homes for a living isn't generally the remorseful type."

"Agreed. It seems Evan and his brother were career criminals."

"Manner of death is different from cause of death, right?" Nicki asked.

"Correct. Again, since the remains were skeletal, the cause of death was also undetermined on autopsy. He had some skull fractures that occurred at or around the time of death. The ME suggests that the head trauma could have resulted from the impact with the lake, but he cannot certify that."

Nicki pulled the photo closer to her face. "It looks as if the drop to the water is only about ten feet. Is that enough impact to break bones?"

Olivia shrugged. "He wasn't wearing a seat belt, and the car didn't have airbags." She paused. "I'd like to get a look at the entire autopsy report." She pointed to the computer. "All that's here are Zoe's notes from phone calls with the detective. Evan's case is officially still open, but it doesn't appear as if anyone is actively trying to solve it. We'll see if the detective in charge is still feeling cooperative, and if he's willing to talk to yet another true crime writer."

Autopsy reports were considered medical records and were not subject to the Freedom of Information Act. Access was usually restricted to next of kin and officers of the court: lawyers, police officers, judges, the DA, et cetera. But Olivia had been able to talk her way into restricted files before. It all depended on the detective. With a case this old, on which there had been no progress, she had a shot.

"The detective currently assigned to the case is Deputy Ted Arnold of the Loon County Sheriff's Department." She shuffled papers. "But the original detective was a Deputy Robert Jones. He probably retired or left the department. I'll call Deputy Arnold and see if he's feeling friendly." Olivia crossed her fingers. In her experience, the detectives who handled a murder case from the beginning tended to have more emotions attached to it. They knew the victims' families and sometimes took a personal interest. When a case changed hands over the years, the emotional attachment naturally ebbed. Sometimes, long-cold cases were handed down multiple times, and the current officer in charge had never cracked the file.

Nicki held a copy of a report in both hands. "I don't see why he'd object. In this case, the victim was a criminal who likely committed second-degree murder. His next of kin was also a criminal. This is not the kind of case I'd expect a cop to be overly attached to."

"You never know. Some officers are by the book." But Olivia hoped Nicki was right. She called the number Zoe had listed for Deputy Arnold and left a message asking him to call her back. If he refused, Olivia would do what she hated doing: She'd ask Lincoln to intervene. As much as she preferred to do her own work, as a former cop, Lincoln would have a much better chance of getting information from Arnold.

Nicki's head cocked. "This is sus."

"What?"

"There's an obituary stuffed in with the Evan Brown reports." Nicki held up the paper. "Clarice Martingale, died in May at the age of seventy-eight."

Olivia froze, her veins suddenly cold. "Did you say her name was Clarice?"

"Yes."

It can't be.

"You know her?" Nicki asked.

Olivia shook her head. "Did you know Zoe was in foster care?"

"No."

"Her parents died when she was a teenager. She spent a couple of years in the system. Her foster mother's name was Clarice. I don't know her last name. But Zoe told me her foster parents were dead. She told me this when we first met fifteen years ago."

"Could be a different person named Clarice," Nicki said. "It's not the most common name, but it's not the most unusual either."

"Where did this Clarice live?" Olivia asked.

Nicki glanced at the paper. "Summerton, New York."

"When did she die?"

"May sixteenth. The funeral was on May twentieth."

The date and location rang several bells in Olivia's memory. "Dylan told the police that Zoe was on a work trip to research a case from May nineteenth to May twenty-second. She stayed at a B and B in Summerton, New York, which can't be a coincidence. Evan Brown disappeared in Summerton. So I assume that's the case."

"Seems logical, but what does it mean?" Nicki's forehead wrinkled. "Is this Clarice related to the Evan Brown case?"

Olivia's mind whirled. "As Lincoln said, there's only one way to find out." Yet she knew in her gut that they'd just uncovered another of Zoe's secrets. Was her friend's entire past a lie? "Does the obituary list any family members?"

Nicki read aloud. "Clarice is survived by her loving husband of fifty-five years, Harold Martingale, age eighty."

"We need to talk to Harold."

"We go to Summerton tomorrow?" Nicki looked excited.

"We?"

"I'm going with you."

"Because you're bored?"

Nicki gave her an emphatic nod. "Yes."

Olivia thought about saying no, but Lincoln hadn't found the person who'd drugged her niece yet. Until the suspect was apprehended, maybe it was better that Nicki stay with her. How much danger could an eighty-year-old widower pose? "I'll appreciate the extra eyes and ears. Plus, you can take notes."

Nicki made a face, then grinned. "Fine. What other leads do we have?" she asked in a TV show detective tone.

"We're not TV detectives," Olivia said dryly.

"Says you," Nicki quipped, but then turned sad eyes on her. "I don't really want to be home alone."

Olivia's heart sank. She understood her niece's sense of vulnerability all too well, and she hated to think that Nicki's experience would make her struggle with independence the same way that Olivia had since her abduction. She'd give her a few days to decompress. If Nicki was still anxious, Olivia would recommend she get a therapist.

"Can I stay with you for a couple of days?" Nicki asked.

"Of course."

"Can we run over to my apartment so I can get some clothes and stuff?"

"Whenever you're ready."

"Cool. Thanks." Nicki relaxed. "I'll hang out with you for a while. I could use a distraction."

"You're always welcome here. I'll keep you busy," Olivia said. "We also have the Jennifer Hamilton murder case to review, which is the one Wendy *said* Zoe had chosen next." She shuffled her notes. "Jennifer's body was dumped behind a truck stop near Scranton." She summed up the case for Nicki. "Jennifer's father, Conway Hamilton, was the prime suspect, but he was never arrested for the murder. He served time for selling drugs instead and was recently released from prison."

"Ooooh, a criminal. That sounds promising."

"According to Wendy, Zoe wanted to interview Conway. She left messages for him."

"She left messages for a drug dealer who just got out of prison, asking about the murder of his daughter, for which he was a suspect?" Nicki asked in a dry voice.

"Yep." Olivia pulled her laptop closer and accessed Zoe's files. "She has a phone number listed for him."

"So you're calling a killer?" Nicki sat back.

"A possible killer," Olivia corrected.

"Cool, I guess?" Sarcasm laced Nicki's voice. "Have you done this before?"

"I have. It's part of the job." Olivia didn't tell Nicki about the more dangerous calls and meetings she'd had with gang members and killers. As a journalist, her job had been to shed light on the truth. As a true crime writer, she did the same. She'd never shied away from risk. Her stubborn determination had almost gotten her and Lincoln killed once. She didn't mention that either. She put a finger to her lips to ask Nicki to be quiet. Then Olivia entered the numbers and pressed the green button.

The call rang three times and bounced to voicemail. Olivia left a vague message that she was following up for Zoe March's podcast.

"What if he doesn't call back?" Nicki asked.

"We'll address that possibility after we've played out the other leads." Olivia almost hoped he didn't, which made her angry. Years ago, she would have jumped at any chance to solve a cold case without hesitation. But now, her friend was missing, and she was worried about herself? Her kidnapping had changed her. She didn't relish the idea of solving a mystery and interviewing a potential murderer.

Chapter Twenty-One

In the passenger seat of Lance's SUV, Sharp moved on to the next item on his agenda. "Dylan Sanders."

Lance plugged the address into the GPS.

Sharp gave a quick synopsis of Zoe's disappearance. "The cops won't investigate because there's no clear sign of foul play. But Olivia isn't buying it."

"That's good enough for me."

"You don't think Liv's personal experience might cloud her judgment?"

Lance glanced sideways at him. "Do you?"

Sharp paused. "I think it might drive her to follow the investigation like a bloodhound, but her judgment is sound. If she says Zoe wouldn't just leave, then I believe her. Also, Dylan has been acting suspicious."

"OK, then." Lance nodded.

Sharp's heart warmed. Loyalty was a thing, wasn't it? Three years ago, Sharp wouldn't have found Olivia without his partner's help. When Lance was a boy, his father had gone missing. Sharp had been the lead detective on the case. When he'd seen Mrs. Kruger's mental illness made her incapable of raising her son, Sharp had stepped in to help. Lance was the closest thing Sharp would ever have to a son. He started to choke up a little but shook off the emotion. Getting old was a bitch. He got more sentimental with every year that passed. He was one step away from crying at Folgers commercials.

"When a woman goes missing, the husband or boyfriend is always a suspect." Sharp added, "Nicki saw Dylan at a bar last night, hitting up a pretty *young* woman."

"Ugh." Lance slowed the SUV and made a left. "Dylan might be a cheating asshole, but his criminal record is clean." He turned in to the parking lot. "He drives a black pickup truck." He drove up and down the rows of cars. No pickup trucks in sight. "Maybe he's not home."

"Let's knock anyway. He might have left his vehicle at the bar."

Lance parked and they made their way to the apartment door. Sharp knocked. No one answered. He knocked again, then put his ear to the door.

"Anything?" Lance asked.

"Crickets." Sharp considered their options. In a low voice he said, "Our first option is the most obvious. We could unlock the door and search the apartment." *Unlock* was code for *break in*.

Lance glanced over his shoulder. "There are people in the parking lot. What are our other options?"

"Do a deeper dive into both Cody and Dylan."

"Research might lead us to other places we can look for Dylan or to other people to question about him. Plus, if we can find some financial data, that might suggest a motive."

"Excellent point. Following the money is always a good idea." As much as Sharp was in action mode, his partner was right. Information was key.

They returned to the SUV, and Lance drove them back to the office. Five minutes later, Sharp printed out the list of potential passwords Olivia had found in Zoe's office. "I'd love basic financials on Dylan and Zoe," Sharp said. Since PIs couldn't get warrants for financial institution records, there was only one way to obtain that info and it was slightly less than legal.

"No problem." Lance pecked away at his keyboard. "My mom is too busy for random hacking today, but I can get us in."

"Without getting caught?"

"Pfft." Lance snorted. "Of course. Easy peasy. My mom and I built this computer with a few enhancements."

"I have a list of potential passwords." Sharp handed over the list. "And Dylan gave Olivia the sign-in for their iCloud accounts."

"That will speed things up."

Sharp made a cup of green tea while Lance worked. Then he returned to the office and paced the space in front of his partner's desk.

"You need to start drinking decaffeinated tea," Lance said without looking up.

"Is this going to take a long time?"

"Not at all." Lance sat back. "I'm not hacking into the bank's server. I'm accessing Dylan's and Zoe's accounts via the customer portal." He shifted back and forth between multiple windows on two monitors. "Thankfully, most people care more about remembering their passwords than security. Zoe picked decent passwords, but she wrote them down. Dylan's were easy to guess from his personal information. Dylan used a combination of their address and his birthday." Lance rolled his eyes.

Sharp leaned closer.

Lance adjusted a monitor to give him a better angle. "Dylan and Zoe have one joint account and they each have a few individual ones. Zoe transfers money into the joint account for rent, insurance, and other household bills, but they don't keep a balance there. Dylan stopped contributing to the household account about ten months ago. Here's his individual account. As you can see, he's broke. He generates decent money from personal training but spends it all—and more—on marketing, clothes, hair and skin products, self-tanning, photo editing software, et cetera."

"He's starting up a fitness influencer business."

Lance continued to scroll through statements. "So far, all he's generating is a loss. He's been solidly in the red for many months."

"It takes time to start up a business. What about Zoe?"

"Her podcast turns a nice profit, and the income has been steadily increasing over the last several years. Recently, she's had a nice uptick, but she hasn't prepared a profit and loss statement for this quarter yet. Unfortunately, Dylan's business has been eating up much of her excess cash. But look at this." Lance pointed to the screen. "Whatever is left over each month, she withdraws in cash at the end of the month. In August, it was roughly fifteen hundred dollars. In July, she took out almost two grand. Yet neither one of them have any real money in savings. Dylan's savings account balance is less than a hundred dollars. Zoe keeps about five hundred in her account. That's it."

"What does she do with the cash?"

Lance typed. "No idea. Unless she has another account somewhere."

"Maybe she doesn't want a clear trail from one account to another." Sharp pointed to Dylan's account. "She might be afraid her husband would spend it if he could find it. Do you see any transactions from Saturday night or Sunday morning?"

"Yes. She withdrew the max from an ATM a little after midnight. Three thousand dollars. She didn't leave much behind, and that's the last time her card was used."

"So she's been socking away cash for how many months?"

"I can only see twelve months of statement history, but she's been doing it the whole time." He scratched on a notepad for a few minutes. "The total for the last year is just over nineteen thousand dollars. Plus, the three thousand ATM withdrawal totals twenty-two thousand dollars."

"She could live off that for a while if she's frugal."

"We don't know where she's keeping the money, how much she started with, or how long she's been stashing it away. She might have considerably more than that," Lance said. "Here's something else that's interesting. Dylan withdrew one thousand dollars from their joint account yesterday. He didn't leave much behind. Looking at their typical monthly activity, their rent will be due in about ten days. If Zoe doesn't come back or transfer some money, he's not going to have that rent money."

"What about credit cards?" Sharp asked.

"Zoe doesn't use hers that much. There's been no activity on her cards since she disappeared. Dylan uses his more, but he has a low credit limit. I don't see anything unusual on either card." Lance shook his head. "No charges from the Tuscan Grill."

"He had cash to spend," Sharp said. "While we're here, can you access Cody Vass's accounts?"

"Let me pull up his personal data and see what I can do." Lance cracked his knuckles and worked his keyboard for about ten minutes. "For a guy who works for a bank, he's very lax with online security. Cody's financials are very boring. Wait. This is interesting. Last month, Cody received a payment from the Mindi Warwick Talent Agency." He opened a new window and googled the name. "They represent models and actors."

"You're kidding?" Sharp couldn't believe it. "Usually, when one of us says 'he's either innocent or a good actor,' we're not serious about the acting bit."

"Let me see if I can find out more."

"Try a reverse image search on Cody's dating profile pics."

"Already doing it." Lance banged away on the keyboard with more enthusiasm. "Ha! Got him." He turned the monitor so Sharp had a better view.

"I'll be damned."

Cody's face stared back at them, with all his even white teeth, chiseled jaw, and perfect tan. He was holding a tube of toothpaste.

Lance changed the image, showing Cody with an equally blond and attractive woman and their Gerber-commercial-clone baby. "Here he is again, selling diapers this time."

"So, he *is* an actor."

Lance leaned closer to the monitor. "His agency bio says actor slash model."

"I guess we move Cody back up the list." Sharp would never have guessed Cody was an actual actor. "This is a first for me."

"Same," Lance agreed. "Professionally, he uses the name Cody Vaughn."

"What if Cody didn't tell Nicki about his acting because he was embarrassed about his lack of success? Or because he's being modest."

"He didn't strike me as the modest type."

"No," Sharp agreed. "We need to talk to him again." He checked the time. "Tomorrow, we can pay him a visit at the bank."

"Sometimes it's helpful to surprise people at their place of work," Lance said. "What do you want to do now?"

"Find Dylan." Sharp drained his tea. "Speaking of surprising people at work, we could look for him at the gym where he does personal training. If he's not around, it might be interesting to see what his coworkers think of him."

Lance checked his notes. "Dylan trains at Titan Fitness."

"Let's roll."

Fifteen minutes later, they stared through the SUV's windshield at the front to Titan Fitness. Plate glass windows across the front of the building created a fishbowl effect. A handful of clients were lifting weights.

Lance said, "I don't see Dylan."

"Me neither. Liv and I have been to dinner with him and Zoe a few times. He'll recognize me." Sharp pulled out his phone and called the gym. He asked for Dylan.

A man answered, "He's not working today. Do you want to leave a message or send him an email?"

"I'll send him an email," Sharp said.

"Send it to Dylan at Titan Fitness NY dot com."

"Thanks." Sharp ended the call. "He's not there." He scanned the gym's interior. The woman at the counter looked like she'd marinated in self-tanner. Her skin was dyed the color of a brown paper bag. "Let's take a dual approach. I'll ask about personal training. I'd really like to get a look at the back rooms in case Dylan has a locker or desk or something." He glanced at Lance. His biceps were the size of baby heads. "No one would believe you'd need a personal trainer since you already look like one. Do you think you can distract the woman at the desk?"

"I can try." Lance underestimated his appeal. He looked like a Hollywood action movie star. You couldn't take him out in public without women—and men—staring at him.

"Flex something."

"Everyone in there is flexing something," Lance said.

"But they don't look like Brad Pitt's better-looking brother." Sharp opened his car door. "Give me five minutes, then come in and work your magic."

He crossed the parking lot and opened the glass door. A chime sounded as he stepped inside.

Titan Fitness was a hardcore bodybuilder gym with a combination of free weights and machines in the main space. In the corner, a heavy bag hung from the ceiling. Racks held medicine balls and kettlebells. A row of cardio machines lined the rear wall, but they didn't look like they got much use. Sharp watched a grunting guy clean press a stack of weights the size of a Volkswagen. The cords of his neck looked like bridge cables. Lance should fit right in.

Sharp approached the desk.

The tanned woman smiled, revealing blindingly white teeth. She was about fifty, with a body that said she trained hard. The name tag pinned over the Titan Fitness logo read HEATHER. "Can I help you?"

"Hi, Heather. I'm interested in personal training. Can you help me?"

Heather nodded enthusiastically. "Absolutely. We have several really good trainers on staff. You'd have to join, though. Training is only available to members."

"Of course," Sharp said.

Heather pulled out a trifold brochure and set it on the counter in front of him. Placing reading glasses on her nose, she picked up a pen and circled some numbers. "Here's our monthly payment plan, but you can get a twenty percent discount if you pay for the whole year up front."

Sharp made a noncommittal noise.

Heather opened the brochure flat. "Here are the gym hours and a list of our trainers. You can go to our website and look up their bios to see what each of them specializes in." She peered at him over the glasses and gave him a once-over. "You don't look like a beginner. Have you worked with weights before?"

"Yes, but I'm old-school." Sharp's workout plan of push-ups, sit-ups, and running hadn't changed much in the last thirty years. He'd added a little yoga since dating Olivia.

"I hear ya," Heather said. "I didn't start lifting until five years ago." She lifted an arm and made a muscle. She might be able to kick his ass.

"Impressive," he said.

"Thanks." She beamed. Closing the brochure, she gestured behind her. "We have a sauna and a tanning bed in the back near the locker rooms."

The chime sounded behind him. Sharp turned to see Lance enter the gym.

Aaaand Heather lost all interest in Sharp. "Excuse me. Why don't you look this over while I help him."

Sharp picked up the brochure. "OK if I take a look around?"

"Sure." Heather didn't even look back as she turned to Lance. "Can I help you?"

Unfolding the brochure and pretending to scan its contents, Sharp drifted away from the counter. He wandered around the main space, checking out the treadmills. He'd thought about joining a gym once, to avoid running in the worst of winter. But impersonating a hamster wasn't his thing. He glanced back. Heather was in Lance's thrall, so Sharp ambled down the corridor that led to the locker rooms. There were a couple of glass-walled offices back there as well, but a short, jacked dude sat in one of them, talking on his phone. So Sharp couldn't have a look-see.

He went into the locker room, brochure in hand. No one was in there, but it smelled like sweat and fungus. He glanced at the showers and the sauna. There wasn't a pair of shower shoes thick enough to get Sharp's bare feet onto that moldy tile. Titan could use a few gallons of bleach. He might disinfect the soles of his sneakers when he got home. He scanned the rows of lockers. Most were empty, with a half dozen bearing locks, likely being used by the people on the floor. The lockers in the last row were labeled with initials. Sharp guessed only the staff could keep their crap in lockers when they weren't on the premises. From the variety of locks that secured them, he assumed it was a bring-your-own situation.

His gaze froze on a label marked DS. Dylan Sanders? Sharp's lockpick was burning a hole in his wallet. He listened. No breathing. No footsteps nearby. He slid his lockpick out of his wallet and went to work. He opened Dylan's locker in twenty seconds. Inside, he found spare clothes and shoes. A cardboard shoebox sat on the skinny top shelf. Sharp photographed it, then pulled it down and lifted the lid. Scraps of silk and cotton? Panties. Women's panties.

For fuck's sake.

Were these Dylan's conquests?

Sharp used his phone to snap a photo of the inside of the box. Then he'd almost closed the lid when he spotted something shiny. A plastic bag peeked out from under the panties. Sharp pulled a nitrile glove from his pocket and put it on. It paid to be prepared. He lifted the baggie clear of the box. It was filled with white powder. Sharp couldn't take the bag. It was evidence. If he took it, then it was compromised. He could make an anonymous call to the SFPD, but what if it was laundry detergent, baking soda, or something equally innocuous? Only one way to find out.

He pulled out a second glove, opened the baggie, and tipped a small amount of the powder into the glove. Then he tied off the wrist opening. If the powder was what he thought it was . . .

He didn't need to cross that bridge just yet.

Footsteps approached in the hall. Sharp returned the baggie to the box, the box to the locker, and secured the lock on the outside. Then he ducked into the bathroom, shoved the purple glove he'd been wearing into his pocket, and washed his hands. The guy who'd been powerlifting walked in and nodded to him.

Sharp nodded back and left the locker room. Heather was giving Lance a personal tour, leading him by the elbow. Was she petting his biceps?

Sharp waved on his way out. "Thanks, Heather. I'll get back to you."

Heather waved back absently. Hanging on Lance's arm, she did not give one fuck if she ever saw Sharp again.

He went outside. He didn't have a key to the SUV, and it wouldn't do to have him and Lance get into the vehicle together. Heather would be watching Lance until he was out of her sight. He walked around the corner and waited. Five minutes later, Lance pulled up, and Sharp stepped into the passenger seat.

"Did you find anything?" Lance asked.

Sharp closed the door and told Lance about the contents of Dylan's locker. "Guess what was inside?"

"I don't know."

Sharp dangled the glove in front of him. "A bag of white powder."

"Bodybuilders take all kinds of protein powders and supplements."

"This is true, but why would he keep protein powder in a baggie inside a box full of panties?"

Lance pulled away from the curb. "That is suspicious."

"We'll send it to the lab for testing."

"We can pick up some drink-testing strips at the drugstore too."

"Good idea," Sharp said.

Lance frowned. "Dylan was hitting up a younger woman at a bar. Maybe he does that regularly. Do you think the panties represent his conquests?"

"At first, that's exactly what I thought. He couldn't keep them at home, obviously. The apartment is small. Zoe might find them." Sharp set the glove of powder in the console. "But then I wondered if the powder is GHB. Bodybuilders take that too. In small amounts, it's supposed to deepen sleep and enhance muscle growth. Unfortunately, the benefits are short-lived."

"So, if he has GHB on hand, he might also give it to the women he 'dates'?" Lance made air quotes with his fingers over the steering wheel.

"It crossed my mind," Sharp agreed.

"If so, is it a coincidence that Dylan was in the same bar as Nicki the night she was drugged?"

Sharp shrugged. "Maybe the GHB was intended for the young woman he was interested in." Mentally, he replayed the bar surveillance video. "She was also drinking beer."

Lance exhaled hard. "Maybe the panties aren't his conquests. Maybe they're his trophies."

Sharp considered the box in Dylan's locker. "There had to be a dozen pairs of underwear in that box."

Could Dylan be a serial rapist?

And did Zoe suspect or even know? If she did, Dylan could be the person she was running from.

"Olivia wants to go to Summerton tomorrow," Sharp said. "She has a lead on Zoe."

"OK. I can keep looking for Dylan, if you want to go with her."

"Thanks." Since her kidnapping, Sharp tried to play it cool, but he obsessed about her safety. He hadn't found love until later in life, and he wouldn't lose her now. "Olivia's smart. She can handle herself."

"But?"

"No buts about that," Sharp said. "It's my concern for her that isn't entirely rational."

"I get that." Lance nodded. "I feel the same way about Morgan. You go with Olivia. Don't worry about Dylan. I'll find that scumbag."

Chapter Twenty-Two

The cold front arrived overnight, frost covered the backyard, and Olivia did her morning yoga inside the next morning. Despite claiming to be fully recovered and bored, Nicki had gone to bed at eight o'clock the previous evening and had slept for—Olivia checked the time on her phone—eleven hours, so far. She wasn't awake yet. When Olivia had passed her door at six o'clock, she'd heard snoring.

She was sipping her morning tea when Lincoln walked into the kitchen holding a small bag bearing the name of the local hardware store. Curious, she lowered her cup.

He set the bag down on the island with a small *thunk*. "I know you're perfectly capable of keeping yourself safe, but I've assembled a few things that you might want to consider carrying."

"My plans involve interviewing an eighty-year-old man, and you're coming with me."

"Plans change, and it's good to be prepared for anything. First of all, I switched vehicles with Lance. So we'll have four-wheel drive for the trip." He cleared his throat, then pulled a multi-tool from the bag. "And I bought you this."

"I already have a well-equipped toolbox in my car."

"This is for your purse or your pocket. Pocket is better."

Olivia picked it up and turned it over. "Bottle opener and corkscrew." She glanced up. "For wine emergencies?"

"You never know," he said. "Keep unfolding."

She continued to reveal the various components: pliers, scissors, both types of screwdrivers, wire cutter, wire stripper, a tiny saw . . . She flipped out a curved blade slightly larger than a crochet hook. "What's this?"

"Rope cutter."

She didn't want to obsess over possible uses for that, but a memory of being bound flashed in her mind. A chill swept through her. She shook it off and unfolded the small knife.

"Technically, it's a tool, but the blade is under four inches in length and totally legal," Lincoln said.

She folded the pieces back into the handle and tucked the tool into its case. "It's very compact. Thank you. This could come in handy." She rose onto her toes to kiss him. "Now, what's going on with the white powder you found in Dylan's locker?"

He kissed her back. "We're waiting for the test results from the lab. I'm hoping to get the results back ASAP. Until then, Lance is looking for Dylan. Keeping an eye on him is important until we know if he is or isn't a serial rapist. If the rapid test is positive, then we also need to find the woman Dylan was talking to at the bar."

"Someone should make sure she's OK," Olivia agreed.

"And see what happened to her the other night. Did she go with Dylan? Did she wake up at home with no memory of the night before? She could have been assaulted and not know it."

"That would be traumatizing." Which reminded Olivia that Nicki bore her own trauma from the other night. "Nicki asked to stay with me for a few days." Olivia almost asked if that was all right with him. He didn't technically live with her. The house was all hers, and he still had his own apartment over his office. Though she couldn't remember the last time he'd slept at his place, and the portion of the closet she'd allotted him looked fuller. The changes felt organic rather than planned, which Olivia liked. They were spending more and more time together because they wanted to, not because they'd made a formal arrangement. "Of course I said yes. She's nervous about being alone."

"Good. I'd rather she stay with us and not go back to her apartment until we determine who spiked her drink."

The doorbell rang, and Lincoln brightened. "That's my online order." He hurried to the front door and retrieved a small package from the doorstep. Back in the kitchen, he opened it and dumped out two small cardboard boxes.

"What are those?"

"Over-the-counter strips to test your drink for common date-rape drugs." Lincoln opened the boxes. "The drugstore was out of stock yesterday. These aren't a hundred percent. Their accuracy can be affected by the drink the drug is mixed into and the concentration of the mixture. Using plain water should negate some of the variability. Also, they only test for specific drugs. I sent most of the powder to the lab, but I held back a small amount. It's in the safe."

Another item that had made its way to her house: a gun safe. Lincoln prioritized safety.

He disappeared down the hallway, returning with a small plastic bag containing about a teaspoon of white powder. He added a few ounces of water to a glass, then tipped some white powder from the tiny clear baggie into it. He stirred it with a spoon, then picked up one of the boxes and read the directions. "This one tests for GHB, ketamine, and Rohypnol. The other covers only GHB and ketamine."

He removed a strip from the first box. Using the spoon, he added a few drops of the mixture to the colored squares. "The box says, 'If it turns orange or gray, do not drink.'" In less than ten seconds, the square turned bright orange. "Positive." He repeated the procedure on the second strip and compared the result to the key on the box. "Also positive." He set down the strip. "Well, the lab can confirm, but both tests lit up fast and bright."

Olivia tilted her head to read the sides of the boxes. "But it could have been either GHB or ketamine, since both of these kits test for those two drugs."

"Yes, I'll need confirmation from the lab before I make a discreet call to the SFPD."

"It's convenient that you used to work there and know so many officers."

"It is." He cleaned up the counter, stowing the test kits in the cabinet with the first aid supplies. He returned the powder to the safe. "In the meantime, Lance will try to get eyes on Dylan."

"Was that the doorbell?" Bleary-eyed, Nicki shuffled into the kitchen wearing flannel pajama bottoms and a hoodie at least two sizes too big. A hardcover book with a blue dragon on the cover was tucked under her arm. They'd made a stop at her apartment the day before, and she'd packed a small bag.

"I have to text Lance with the results of the strip tests. He can start looking for the woman Dylan was hitting up at the bar the other night." Lincoln walked toward the bedroom.

Nicki wandered to the cabinet and selected a demitasse cup. She made herself an espresso in the pod machine Olivia kept for guests, settled at the island, and picked up one of the used test strips. "What are these?"

Olivia explained.

Nicki set down her demitasse cup. "Dylan had GHB?"

"Or ketamine," Olivia said.

Nicki ignored her qualifier. "Do you think *he* drugged me?"

Taking the stool next to her, Olivia shook her head. "We don't know yet. Lance is looking for him today."

"Why would he do that?" Nicki looked stricken. "I *know* him."

But how well?

"We don't know for sure what happened. Lincoln even suggested that he could have spiked your beer by mistake, thinking it was the one intended for the woman he was talking to." Olivia looped an arm around Nicki's shoulders. "But remember that over seventy percent of sexual assaults are perpetrated by people the victim knows. Do not blame yourself."

Nicki downed her espresso like a shot of whiskey. "Fuck that. And fuck him. I'm shocked that he would drug and rape women, but it's no reflection on me."

"That's the spirit."

Nicki's eyes narrowed. "I hope Lance finds him."

Olivia finished her tea. "Until he gets his man, you stay with me."

"Right. We're going to Summerton today to interview Mr. Martingale." Nicki brightened.

"Yes. I was thinking about calling him and making an appointment. The drive is a couple of hours."

Nicki's face scrunched. "I wouldn't. What if he calls the person Zoe is running from? You could be placing her in danger."

"Good point. We'll drive out there and take the risk that he's home. Pack an overnight bag in case we want to stay over."

"OK."

They were both ready in a half hour. Olivia dressed in jeans and a light sweater. She stood in front of her closet, deliberating on footwear when Nicki walked in.

"What are you doing?" Nicki asked. She wore black leggings and a cropped flannel shirt with her giant lug-soled boots. She draped a boxy army-green jacket over one arm.

"Deciding on shoes."

"It's cold, and we're going to the mountains. Those hiking boots are perfect."

Olivia scrunched her nose.

Nicki rolled her eyes. "You're such a clothes snob."

"I'm not." But Olivia totally was. "I was thinking about the black suede ankle boots."

"The ones with the skinny heels?"

"Yes."

Nicki blinked at her. "You're serious?"

Olivia stared back for a few long seconds, but Nicki didn't flinch. "Fine." Olivia grabbed the hiking boots. They were ankle high and not *that* ugly. But she added gold hoop earrings and a silk scarf for a splash of color.

She selected a powder-blue puffy jacket. Since being trapped underground in the cold and damp, Olivia was sensitive to the chill. She added two knit hats, gloves, extra-warm socks, and two waterproof shells to her backpack. The temperature was forecasted to drop even further, rain was moving into the area, and Summerton was in the mountains. The higher elevation would be even colder. She checked her portable power bank to make sure it was fully charged. Her inhaler went into a zippered jacket pocket. She hadn't used it in ages, but she'd never make the mistake of not having one with her again.

"Did you pack snacks?" Nicki asked.

"Snacks?"

"Road trips require snacks. Either we pack them, or we stop for food."

"You just ate."

"I'll need to eat again." Nicki's tone implied just a touch of *duh*.

Olivia waved toward the kitchen. "Pack whatever you want. Grab water."

"I never leave home without it," Nicki called out from the hallway.

Olivia hoisted her backpack over her shoulder and grabbed her purse. She stuffed the multi-tool into the pocket of her jacket and reached for her cell phone. It vibrated in her hand. The incoming phone call was from an unknown number. She pressed "Answer" and put the phone on speaker. "Hello."

"Is this Olivia Cruz?" a man asked in a weak voice.

"Yes." She didn't recognize the voice.

"I'm Conway Hamilton. You called me." The man let loose a wet, raspy cough that sounded painful. He sucked in some air, then audibly swallowed. "Whatcha want?"

"I'm following up for Zoe March," Olivia said vaguely. "Have you received a call from her?"

"Yeah. I did." He cleared his throat. "I'll tell you exactly what I told her when I talked to her a few weeks ago. I won't have this conversation on the phone. You'll have to come here. I talk in person only—and no recording!"

"Did you meet with Ms. March?" Olivia asked.

He ignored her question, giving her an address instead. "Today. Noon." Then the connection went dead. Olivia frowned at her phone for a few seconds.

"Was that Conway Hamilton?" Nicki asked from the doorway.

"Yes."

"Let me look for that call in Zoe's phone records." Nicki disappeared.

Olivia hauled her things into the kitchen. Nicki stood in front of the island working on her laptop. A reusable grocery bag sat next to her. Olivia peeked into the bag. Empty.

"You don't have any snacks," Nicki said. "I found the call in Zoe's phone records. They talked for two minutes four weeks ago. No further contact after that. Maybe she didn't want to have another conversation with Conway Hamilton. She blew him off?"

Olivia opened the pantry and pulled out a box of protein bars. "Zoe doesn't back down on an investigation."

Nicki shot one back. "I would have blown off that guy too. He's an asshole. Maybe she didn't *need* to talk to him again. Also, those aren't snacks."

"Because she'd already decided to use the Brown case?" Olivia packed the bars.

"Yeah." Nicki consulted her phone. "Conway's address is in the same direction as Summerton. It's on the way. We should go there to talk to him, then head to Harold Martingale's house."

A sliver of panic bolted up Olivia's spine. "Hamilton could be dangerous. You don't need to go with me."

"But you shouldn't go alone, right?"

"Some people are more willing to talk if it's just me." Olivia hadn't planned on taking anyone with her. Usually, she conducted interviews alone, even when she was talking to convicted criminals. "I'm careful about making sure people know where I am and who I'm meeting with. I make sure my interview subject is also aware of this."

Olivia had been in some hairy situations in the past. She'd always come through them, though she admitted there were a few times her safety had been in jeopardy. She still hated to think that her kidnapping had made her a coward.

"Sharp will be with us, and we'll give Lance our itinerary," Nicki said. "Besides, Conway sounded old." She tucked her laptop under her arm. "We're stopping for snacks."

And just like that, Olivia was taking her niece to meet a drug dealer and potential murderer.

Chapter Twenty-Three

Olivia stared out the windshield. On both sides, the forest was too thick to see much.

Lincoln slowed to a crawl, the tires grating over rocks and sticks. Following the GPS's instructions, he made a right turn onto a dirt road. The SUV bounced over a pothole the size of a golden retriever.

In the passenger seat, Olivia's teeth rattled. She grabbed the chicken strap. "I'm glad you borrowed Lance's SUV."

He nodded. "It's built to handle the terrain."

"We are in the middle of nowhere," Nicki said from the back seat.

The forest opened up into a sloping meadow on one side. Olivia spotted a lake in the distance. Another slow mile later, and a rusty, numbered mailbox on a bare four-by-four marked the entrance to Conway's property. Lincoln eased the car over a deep rut. In the center of a square patch of mowed grass sat a tiny one-story house. A row of mums brightened the flower bed, and two rocking chairs sat on the front porch. Behind the house, whitecaps topped the lake. A pair of kayaks sat on the back lawn within dragging distance of the water.

"This is more quaint than I expected." Lincoln parked in front of the house.

Nicki said, "It's cute."

Olivia agreed. The encroaching vast wildness juxtaposed with the tidiness of the yard. They got out of the car. An icy blast tore at her hair. She fished a scrunchie out of her pocket and tied it back in a ponytail. There were no road sounds. No voices. Just plenty of absolute silence broken by the occasional rustle of foliage and the tweet of a bird. They'd left civilization behind miles ago. She wondered how long it took for law enforcement to respond way out here. The shiver that traveled up her spine was half cold, half apprehension.

Olivia looked at Nicki. "You could wait in the car with Lincoln." They'd already discussed that he looked too much like a cop to interview Conway.

Nicki's face was completely covered by the hair whipping around her head. "Today, I'm your assistant. I'm here to take notes. Besides, even with Sharp in the car, isn't it safer if you're not alone? Teenage horror movies demonstrate that separating is a bad idea."

Before Olivia could respond, Sharp butted in. "I agree. You two should stay together."

"See?" Nicki started toward the house.

"Fine." Olivia hurried to catch up. They climbed the single step to the porch and knocked on the door. The floorboards looked new, and the trim on the house had been freshly painted.

A woman of about fifty answered the door. "Yes?" She wore jeans, a flannel shirt, and wool slippers. Her face was clear of makeup, and her graying brown hair was coiled into a loose bun. Her gaze held suspicion but no hostility.

"We're here to see Conway Hamilton." Maybe they had the wrong address, Olivia thought.

"You must be Olivia Cruz." The woman nodded. "Could I see some ID, please?"

"Sure." The request caught Olivia off guard. Did she want to give this woman her address? No. She opened her backpack and dug out her business card and an old journalist ID. As she offered them, she gestured to Nicki. "This is my assistant, Natalie."

Nicki raised a brow at the impromptu alias, but she was smart enough to say nothing. She would only have a driver's license, and Olivia didn't want her to reveal her name or address. Conway was a convicted criminal who might have killed his own daughter.

The woman scrutinized it, then handed it back. "I'm sorry. Since Conway was released, he's had nonstop harassment from true crime junkies, bloggers, and reporters. People were standing on our sidewalk chanting 'murderer.' Someone threw a brick through our window. We left our house in town and came up here to get away from them. They haven't found us, but I'm sure it's only a matter of time."

"This isn't your full-time residence?" Olivia asked.

"No." She opened the door wider and gestured for them to enter. "This is our vacation home. We come up here in the summer to get away from the heat. We fish and kayak, et cetera."

"You and Conway?" Olivia stepped across the threshold.

"No. My husband and I." She closed the door after Nicki. "I'm Eleanor, Conway's cousin."

"Nice of you to take him in," Nicki said.

Eleanor lowered her voice. "My husband wasn't happy, given Conway's history, but I'm his only living relative—and it won't be for long."

"He's moving?" Olivia unbuttoned her jacket.

Eleanor shook her head. "He's dying. Lung cancer. He only has a few months to live. Otherwise, my husband would have insisted he go somewhere else." She walked through a living room to a glassed-in back deck with a spectacular view of the lake. Conway sat in a recliner, attached to an oxygen tank on wheels by a tube. Eleanor waved toward a love seat facing him. "I'll give you some privacy." She left the room.

Nicki sat on the love seat and took a small notepad out of her pocket.

Olivia extended a hand toward Conway. "I'm—"

"I know who you are." He waved off her introduction and her offered hand. "Sit."

Since he wasn't hung up on formalities, Olivia didn't bother to introduce Nicki. She perched next to her niece, leaning forward, hands clasped on her knees.

"I don't have a lot of time before I take my next dose of painkillers." He shook his head and wheezed. "It's funny. They sent me to prison for selling drugs. Now *they* give *me* as much as I want."

Olivia spotted hospice papers on the end table. "I'll get right to the point then. I'm following up for Zoe March. She called you."

"Yep," Conway said. "I called her back weeks ago. She was supposed to come here and interview me, but she never did."

"I'm sorry Zoe didn't get back to you. Would you mind answering a few questions for me now?"

Next to Olivia, Nicki clicked her pen and assumed a ready-to-take-notes position.

"This is about Jennifer's murder, right?" Conway didn't sound emotional, not one bit.

"It is," Olivia said. Interviewing victims' families was tricky. Some wanted to talk about their loved one. They could be frustrated by the lack of progress in official cases or angry that law enforcement was unable to obtain justice for their loved one. Others refused. Olivia always tried to feel them out before asking any hard questions. She didn't want to traumatize anyone all over again. They'd suffered enough. On the other hand, Conway was a suspect in his daughter's death. Olivia wanted him to talk, so she erred on the side of compassion. "I know it's been a long time, but I'm sorry for your loss."

"Sure. Right." His voice reflected no grief. Once in a while, a reaction just didn't feel genuine. Not all parents are good ones. "Are you calling because they caught the guy who killed her?"

She froze. Had she heard him correctly? "Excuse me. Did you say they caught the killer?"

"Yeah. The cops were here a couple of days ago. Some truck driver got arrested in Maine for killing a girl. His DNA matched some found on Jennifer's body. Motherfuckers didn't even apologize for accusing me of killing my own kid." He sounded indignant.

"I'm sorry." Olivia didn't know what else to say. "Were you close to Jennifer?"

"Um. Yeah." Again, there was no emotion in his voice. He could have been responding to a question about his favorite sandwich. His eyes weren't the least bit misty.

Olivia wondered how well he had even known his daughter and if he'd shed tears when she died. "Can you tell me a story about Jennifer?"

Conway leaned back and crossed his arms over his chest. His eyes went small, and his posture stiffened in defiance. "I'll tell you the same thing I told your friend. I'd be happy to give you the inside scoop—every dirty detail—for a price."

Speaking of motherfuckers . . .

"You want to sell the story of your daughter's murder?" Olivia wasn't against sharing the proceeds of her work. When she'd written about the Chelsea Clark kidnapping, she'd shared the royalties with the family. They'd needed money for therapy and medical expenses and to move away from the place where the trauma had occurred. Plus, Chelsea had spent dozens of hours answering Olivia's questions and telling her story.

No one had offered to sell the "dirty details."

Olivia had also made sure the book factually represented Chelsea's experience, without embellishment or sensationalism. It encompassed the toll the kidnapping had taken on Chelsea and her entire family. The book had been a solid bestseller. Chelsea and her family were able to get the care they needed. They'd had the money to relocate to be near Chelsea's parents. Also, Chelsea had said that telling her story had helped her recover. She'd gone public with the truth to ward off misinformation and because she'd had nothing to hide, nothing to be ashamed of. Her kidnapping was 100 percent the fault of the man who'd hurt her. Chelsea's truth was part of Olivia's motivation for telling her own story. Put the truth into the world. Own the trauma. Accept it as part of you and understand that it always will be.

There was no way to run from your own memories.

"Me being broke won't do her any good. I got needs. Medicare doesn't cover luxuries, and I'd like a few while I'm dying." Conway shrugged. He just wanted to make a buck, and he didn't care how. "And I ain't got time to wait for you to write your article or whatever neither. I don't have a lot of time left. I got stuff I want to do."

"What was Jennifer's favorite food?" Olivia asked.

"I don't remember," he snapped. "Chicken nuggets, maybe. It's been twenty years. If you want any more answers, you'll have to pay up!"

Olivia would bet a thousand dollars he'd never known what his daughter's favorite food was, but also that he would make up whatever details he thought might pay the best. "If I have any further questions, I know how to reach you. Thank you for your time, Mr. Hamilton."

"Hey, don't you want my story?" he protested, his face reddening.

"No, I was interested in Jennifer's story." Olivia rose.

Nicki shoved her notepad into her pocket and followed Olivia from the room. They passed Eleanor in the living room. "Done already?" she asked.

"Yes," Olivia said. "It seems he doesn't have the information we're looking for. Thank you anyway."

Eleanor walked them to the door. "I'm not surprised. He's usually full of shit and always focused solely on himself."

Nicki snorted. "Thanks for your time."

"You're welcome. I'm sorry he wasn't much of a help. Then again, he's never been anything but a leech his entire life." Eleanor closed the door behind them.

They left the house, walked back to the car, and summed up the interview for Lincoln.

Nicki said, "People suck. He didn't care about his dead daughter at all."

"I suspect he didn't know his daughter that well. Somewhere in the case materials," Olivia recalled, "Zoe noted that Jennifer was mostly raised by her mother."

"So, Conway would just make up stuff to get more money, whether it was true or not." In the back seat, Nicki fastened her seat belt with hostility. "You'd never be able to trust anything he said."

"You're right. That could have been one of the reasons Zoe abandoned the case."

Nicki used both thumbs to work her phone. "Her theory about who killed Jennifer was spot-on, though." She leaned forward and thrust the phone between the seats. "Here's the story in the *Scranton Press*. DNA SOLVES TWENTY-YEAR-OLD MURDER. It says the killer has been linked to more than two dozen cases so far."

"Zoe has a nose for the truth," Olivia said.

"That's why her show is successful." Lincoln turned the SUV around and headed back down the dirt road.

Olivia watched storm clouds gather on the horizon, looming heavy and dark, like harbingers of doom. She hoped the rain held off until they got back to the main road, but luck was not on their side. Drizzle began to dot the windshield.

Nicki withdrew her phone and sat back. "Zoe didn't run because she's afraid of Conway Hamilton. Hopefully, the Brown case will have the answers."

Chapter Twenty-Four

Lightning streaked across the sky. A boom of thunder reverberated in Olivia's bones. The storm picked up intensity with the speed of a moving train. Within minutes, the wipers couldn't arc fast enough to clear the windshield.

Lincoln switched on the headlights and maintained a slow but steady speed.

Water poured from the sky in a solid sheet. Olivia white-knuckled the armrest as the SUV swerved sideways. Mud spewed from the tires. The mud puddles looked deep enough to mire even a four-wheel drive.

Lincoln fought the slippery conditions with a grimace.

When the tires hit the paved main road, Olivia exhaled in relief. Lincoln lifted his hands from the steering wheel one at a time and flexed his fingers.

Nicki, who hadn't spoken since the rain began, exhaled with her. "That was hairy."

"It was." Lightning flashed again, and Olivia started. The clouds turned an ominous shade of greenish gray.

Nicki leaned sideways, looking up at the sky through the sunroof. "Feels like the storm is right on top of us."

"Because it is." Sharp slowed the vehicle and straddled the yellow line in the center of the road. Water gushed from the sky faster than it could run off the road. The SUV hydroplaned. He eased off the gas pedal even more. The sign for the Roadside Diner beckoned. He checked the side mirror. "I can't see. I'm going to stop. We can have lunch while the storm passes."

They lost two hours before the rain let up enough that it was safe to continue driving. Back in the Jeep, they entered the address for Harold Martingale into the GPS. Lincoln took the exit and followed the directions toward the town of Summerton, which was nestled at the base of Devil's Mountain. The tires rumbled as they drove onto a two-lane bridge.

Olivia peered over the guardrail. Water teemed and roiled just a few feet below. "The water seems high."

Lincoln glanced out the driver's-side window. "Too high."

They continued into town. Hours behind schedule, they drove onto a lovely street lined with stately old homes and giant oak trees. Harold Martingale lived at the top of a hill. His expansive two-story home sat behind a sloping green lawn. A small porch held a swing and boasted a spectacular view of the valley. It was so wholesome looking that it screamed picnics, baseball, and apple pie.

Olivia squinted through the window. "Makes me want a glass of lemonade or a mint julep."

"It's charming." Lincoln parked at the curb.

The leaves on the oak tree in the center of the front lawn were turning and sported bright splotches of color in an otherwise gloomy day, like a solitary colorized item in a black-and-white film. The wind gusted. Clusters of gold and red leaves tumbled across the deep-green lawn. Olivia imagined Zoe coming here after the deaths of her parents. She'd been sixteen, lost, and grief-stricken. With no family, she'd been forced to go to strangers. She must have been in shock to have her whole life ripped out from under her. What had the home she'd been raised in been like? Had she been close to her parents?

How could Olivia be friends with Zoe for fifteen years and not know any of these answers? Because her friend had always shut down personal conversations about her childhood.

Lincoln parked on the street where he had a clear view of the house. He squinted through the windshield and stiffened. Olivia followed his gaze. Large gashes marred the wooden front door, as if someone had tried to break in.

"Do you see those?" Lincoln said.

"Yes."

"What?" Nicki asked, peering out the side window. "Oh. The front door! That's not good."

"No." Lincoln checked his weapon.

Olivia glanced over her seat. "You wait here."

"But—"

"No buts." Lincoln opened his door. "Lock up."

Nicki sulked but agreed. "OK." She slid down in the seat and crossed her arms. But Olivia heard the click of the door locks as she walked away from the vehicle.

Olivia followed Lincoln to the front porch. The rain had slowed to a light drizzle. The house had been built on a raised foundation. She'd need a ladder to look in the first-floor windows. Her pulse thrummed in her ears as she pressed the doorbell and waited while chimes echoed inside. Nothing happened.

Lincoln motioned for her to move away from the center of the door. He'd warned her in the past about being in the line of fire if someone inside a house shot through the door. He pulled his weapon from its hip holster.

She pressed the doorbell again. The chime sounded again. No one responded. She pressed the button a third time. The chime repeated, sounding louder. Fabric rustled and something moved at the back of the house.

Olivia banged again, then called out, "Mr. Martingale? Are you all right?"

Shuffling footsteps sounded inside. A shadow appeared at the end of the hallway. It paused, then approached. A shaky voice asked, "Who are you?" He sounded old.

Olivia called, "My name is Olivia Cruz."

"I don't know you," the old man answered. "Go away."

"I really need to speak with you. I'm a friend of Zoe March." She waited, but he didn't respond. "Please, Mr. Martingale. She's missing."

"Be quiet," he admonished. "Stop yelling her name. Someone might hear you!"

"Then talk to me." Something was very wrong here. Zoe was still missing, and Olivia was ready to play hardball.

The dead bolt slid away, and the door cracked. A blue eye and half of a wrinkled face appeared. "She's not here, and I don't know where she is. Now go away before someone sees you."

"If you don't want someone to see us on the porch, let us in," Olivia said. "We're not leaving."

The old man hesitated, then opened the door and stepped back. "Come in quickly." He motioned for them to hurry.

When they were in the foyer, he closed the door and locked it again. He was a tall, lean man in excellent shape for his age. He didn't require a walker or cane. His trim frame was dressed in jeans, a button-up shirt, and loafers with tassels. He looked like a college professor. As her eyes adjusted to the dim, she could see his face more clearly. Wrinkles creased his skin, and his hair had thinned and faded to cotton-ball white. He also had a black eye and a swollen lip. Blood trickled from the corner of his mouth. A red splotch marked an impending bruise darkening his cheek, his shoulders stooped, and he held himself with stiffness that suggested pain.

Lincoln moved past him, scanning the house. "Is anyone else here?"

"No." The old man stared at his gun. "Who are you?"

"I'm going to make sure the house is empty." Lincoln walked down the hallway, clearly intent on confirming they were alone.

"It's OK," Olivia said. "He's a retired police detective. We're not criminals. We're not here to hurt you."

Harold didn't look convinced.

"You're Harold Martingale?" Olivia asked.

"Yes."

"Mr. Martingale—"

"You can call me Harold." Pain scratched in his voice. "And you are?"

Olivia introduced herself again. "Do you remember Zoe March?"

"Of course I do. I remember every one of the kids we helped raise." His words were sharp. "Why are you asking about Zoe?"

"She's my friend, and she's missing." Olivia studied his injuries. "What happened to your face?"

"It's nothing." He touched the scab on his mouth with his fingers.

She tilted her head. "Someone hit you. Obviously more than once."

He lifted a shoulder. "It doesn't matter. I'm fine."

"You don't look fine," Olivia said. "Do you need to see a doctor?" The color of his bruises suggested the beating was fresh.

Harold held up a hand. "I'll be fine."

Lincoln returned, shoving his gun into its holster. "House is clear."

"I already told you it was," Harold snapped.

Lincoln ignored his response and looked him up and down. "Who beat you up?"

Without answering, Harold turned and limped down the hallway. Olivia and Lincoln followed him. They passed a study. Built-in bookcases gleamed on either side of a gas fireplace. Wide-plank wood floors shone. The leather chairs were contemporary but also rustic. The hallway ended in a large kitchen, recently renovated in the modern farmhouse style. The island was as big as Olivia's car. Harold was not a broke senior barely surviving on social security. He lived comfortably.

Lincoln moved from window to window, pushing aside curtains, surveying the surroundings. "I'm going to check outside. I assume whoever attacked you tried to break through the front door?"

"He tried," Harold admitted. "But the joke's on him. That's a custom door, solid poplar. It held."

"Then how did he get in?" Olivia asked.

"He didn't. He hid out back and caught me on my way in from the garage. Then he forced me to use my key in the back door."

The boldness worried Olivia. A home invasion in broad daylight suggested an assailant who wasn't concerned about being caught.

"When did this happen?" she asked.

"This morning," he admitted.

"Did you call the police?" she asked.

"No," Harold said. "He had pictures of my grandchildren. He said he'd kill them if I called anyone."

Lincoln said, "I'll double-check your doors and windows. I'll bring Nicki inside too. I think she'll be safer in the house."

"I doubt that he'll come back." Harold perched on a leather stool. "He searched this house for Zoe and learned that she isn't here."

"Who is he?" Olivia went into the kitchen. Without asking, she opened drawers until she found a dishcloth, then filled it with ice from the freezer. She handed it to Harold.

He frowned but followed instructions. "What do you want?"

"To find Zoe," Olivia said.

"Why?" Harold asked around the ice.

"Because she's missing, and she's my friend," she repeated.

"How do I know she's really your friend?" Harold asked.

Olivia pulled out her phone and opened her photos app. Perching on the stool next to him, she selected several photos of herself with Zoe, then turned the screen to show him. He withdrew reading glasses from his shirt pocket and settled them onto his nose one-handed before examining the images. He leaned forward to study the photos, then sat back and appeared to make a decision. "How do you know Zoe is missing?"

"No one's heard from her in days, not even her husband."

"That's concerning." He lowered the ice and tested his lip with his tongue. "When did you say she was last seen? I listened to the opening of her show Saturday night. That was a live show, so I know she was OK then."

Olivia said, "She left her studio that night and never arrived home. She just disappeared." She didn't mention the storage unit or change of vehicle. Harold didn't need the details. Olivia wasn't sure *she* could trust *him* yet.

Harold shook his head. "That doesn't sound like something Zoe would do."

"No, it doesn't," Olivia agreed. A gust of wind rattled the porch swing outside. "When was the last time you saw her?"

"In May," Harold said without hesitation. "She came to Clarice's funeral." Sorrow clouded his eyes. He closed them for a few seconds to compose himself. He opened them and said, "Clarice and Zoe were close." His eyes went moist. He plucked a white handkerchief from his pocket and mopped his face. "I'm sorry. I just miss her so damned much."

"I'm so sorry for your loss." Olivia felt his grief in her soul. She remembered Zoe's B and B stay. "Why didn't she stay here with you?"

"I have five bedrooms, but they were all taken the week of the funeral. Clarice and I fostered a lot of kids. Some live here in town. I see them regularly. About half our kids moved out of state, but almost everyone came back for her funeral. I even have a couple of honorary grandchildren."

"Those are the ones he threatened?" Olivia asked.

"Yes. Clarice was special. She had this gift for reaching kids in challenging situations. It was her superpower. She never gave up on them, no matter how far gone they seemed. She worked some downright miracles. Over the decades we were foster parents, I can only remember one or two kids who could resist her."

"She sounds very special indeed."

"I was lucky she chose me. I couldn't have kids. I had mumps as a teenager. People nowadays don't realize it can do that." He sighed. "I thought I was destined to be alone. I couldn't believe she still wanted to marry me after I told her, but she didn't particularly want her own kids. She'd been the oldest of thirteen. She said she already raised enough babies. She wanted to help older kids. So that's what we did. Over the years, we took in dozens of them. Some only stayed with us for a few days. Others were with us for years."

"How long did Zoe live with you?"

"Two . . . no, almost three years. Clarice always asked for teenagers because they were hard to place. That woman had the patience of a saint."

"Zoe came to you after her parents died?" Olivia asked.

He gave her a quizzical look. "Her parents didn't die, at least not back then. They passed away years later." He polished his glasses on the hem of his shirt. "I don't know if it's my place to tell you her story." He tilted his head, giving the thought careful consideration. "I suppose since you're a journalist you could find all this information if you looked hard enough. Criminal records are public. Zoe was about sixteen when her parents were arrested for insurance fraud. They stole tens of thousands of dollars from senior citizens. She was miserable. Having incarcerated parents makes one a loner, as if high school in general isn't hard enough."

Olivia's mind whirled. Why was she so surprised? Zoe had lied about other things. But fabricating the deaths of her parents seemed . . . worse, somehow. It felt like a betrayal of their friendship. She said nothing, however. She didn't want to discourage Harold from talking.

"But Clarice worked her magic. Zoe was smart. So smart. She needed some tutoring, but she caught up quickly. I was a mathematics professor and Clarice taught English, so between the two us of, we had the skills."

"Did she have any close friends back then?"

"Only her boyfriend, Jacob. They had a lot in common. His father had also been in jail. They were both ostracized. I wish we'd have had the chance to help Jacob, but he was eighteen when his family crisis happened."

"Crisis?" Olivia asked.

Harold nodded. "His father disappeared, and his uncle went to prison for murder."

A chill passed through Olivia. *Definitely not a coincidence.*

Harold's gaze wandered to the ceiling. "I think his mother had been dead since he was little, but I don't remember the details. My memory isn't what it used to be."

He seemed sharp as a knifepoint to Olivia.

"Anyway," Harold continued. "He was an adult, so he wasn't forced into the foster care system. Though it might have been better if he had been. He lived in the same house, all alone, until he graduated high school. He had a job, but he couldn't pay the bills. The county tried to take the house for back taxes, but it took a while to evict Jacob. Clarice and I helped him fight it." He cleared his throat. "At least long enough for him to find another place to live."

"What happened to him?" Olivia asked.

"Nothing," Harold said. "He got an electrician's license. I believe he still lives in the area, though I haven't seen him in a while. He was a quiet boy. Except for his relationship with Zoe, he kept to himself. I expect he does the same as an adult."

"Did he come to Clarice's funeral?" Olivia asked.

Harold hesitated, just for a split second. "I don't remember seeing him." This answer also felt intentionally vague.

"Do you know where he lives now?"

"Somewhere on the mountain." He gestured to the window, which had a view of it.

Olivia zeroed in on her real question. "Do you know if Zoe saw him while she was here for the funeral?" Had she cheated on Dylan in retaliation for him cheating on her? Or because she needed the connection with a human being she could confide in, someone she'd known and trusted during her most vulnerable years?

He stood and began pacing. "I wouldn't know."

He didn't say *I don't know*, though that would be the more natural response. *I wouldn't know* left technical wiggle room, as if he didn't want to lie, but he also didn't want to tell her. His answer felt like a politician saying *I do not recall* in a congressional hearing.

"Do you remember Jacob's last name?"

Olivia knew the answer before Harold said, "Sure. It's Brown."

"He's related to Evan Brown," Olivia clarified. "The man whose remains were recently pulled out of a lake."

"Yes. Evan was his father." Harold stopped and stood still, seemingly lost though he was in his own home.

"Do you have any idea where Zoe might have gone?" Olivia asked.

Harold shook his head. "I keep in touch, but Clarice was closer to Zoe." He absently rubbed his ribs. How badly had he been beaten? And by whom?

"Who broke in here?" she asked in a quiet voice.

Harold dropped onto the stool again, his mouth set in a stubborn line.

"You said *he* earlier." Olivia had to convince him to talk. "He's after Zoe, right? I want to find her before he does. We can help her."

Harold stared at his shoes.

"Do you think she would go to Jacob?" Olivia asked.

"Maybe." Harold lifted his gaze. "She might be worried about him. Jacob could also be in danger. The man who is looking for her is Jacob's uncle, Tim."

"Evan's brother? I thought he was in prison."

"He was released a few weeks ago." Harold met her gaze. "His sentence was twenty-five to life, so he more than met the minimum. The parole board decided he was no longer a risk to society." Disdain dripped from his voice. He pointed to his face. "Clearly, they were wrong."

"Why does Tim want Zoe?" Olivia asked.

"Because Zoe is the one who put him in prison," Harold said. "He blames her for ruining his life and stealing thirty years out from under him. That's nonsense, of course. He was a criminal who committed a murder. But that's not the way he sees it."

Lincoln stood in the doorway, his expression puzzled, as if unsure that he'd heard Harold correctly. Nicki stood behind him.

Olivia was also confused. She quickly got Lincoln and Nicki caught up on her conversation with Harold, then turned back to him. "Did you say Zoe put Tim Brown in prison? Was she the unnamed caller?"

Harold nodded. "Yes. It was her phone call that tipped off the police that Tim and Evan were the burglars who'd killed the homeowner and his son."

"But Zoe was just a teenager back then," Nicki said.

Harold lifted both palms. "This is all I know. Zoe brought Jacob home one night, distressed, saying that they'd been at Jacob's house and that Tim was going to kill them. The kids were scared and panicking. Neither one of them were making much sense. They refused to give us any more details. But the one thing that was clear was their terror. They'd seen something at Jacob's house, something that implicated Tim in a murder. He's always been a violent, cruel man." He touched the bruise on his face. "It seems prison has only made him worse."

"So they called the police and told them what they knew?" Lincoln asked.

"Yes," Harold said. "They drove to a pay phone and Zoe made the call. The police searched the Browns' house, found evidence Tim and Evan had committed a bunch of burglaries, including one where two people died. The police arrested Tim and issued a warrant for Evan. We know why they never found Evan—he's been dead the whole time."

Olivia said, "The police originally said they thought Evan ran off with the jewelry, leaving Tim to answer for their crimes."

Lincoln added, "But Evan was dead. Maybe Tim killed him. You said he has a temper. Would he kill his own brother?"

Harold nodded. "I believe he would."

"But you don't know what Zoe and Jacob saw that night?"

"No." He shook his head.

"But when Tim came here, he wanted information about Zoe's whereabouts?" Lincoln asked. When Harold nodded, Lincoln continued. "What did you tell him?"

Harold said, "I told him I don't know where she is because it's the truth. I haven't seen Zoe since May." He pursed his lips, then winced. "I'm surprised he didn't kill me. Not that I care all that much. I'm old. I've had a wonderful life, and I'd sacrifice my few remaining years for Zoe. Life isn't the same without Clarice. I'd be OK joining her."

"Do you have any ideas about where Zoe might be?" Olivia asked.

Harold stared at the ceiling. Olivia couldn't decide if the old man was racking his brain for ideas or if he was deciding whether to tell them. Finally, he met her gaze. "Clarice and I have a cabin on the mountain."

"Zoe knows about it?" Lincoln asked.

"Yes. When we had kids in the house, we took them skiing and hiking there. Zoe just liked to sneak out into the woods with a book. It was a great getaway, a place they could go to forget their troubles. Nature is healing. After the kids were all grown, we rented it out, but it needs repairs. I haven't kept up with maintenance for the last few years. But I also couldn't bring myself to sell it."

"So, she could have gone to Jacob or to this cabin?" Olivia asked.

"Yes." Harold gave them the address of the cabin. "Last I heard, Jacob was living on Simmons Road. I don't know the exact address." He lifted the ice to his mouth. "You have to find Zoe before Tim does. He is determined to make her pay."

Chapter Twenty-Five

Sharp's mind whirled with possibilities. He'd been a detective long enough to know people were capable of truly horrible things. "Is it possible Zoe and Jacob saw Tim kill Evan?"

Harold froze. "That never crossed my mind, but it would explain the kids' shock and panic. Tim could have put his brother and his vehicle into the lake."

Sharp's phone buzzed with a weather alert. He read it aloud. "There's a flash flood on Jenkins Road. The bridge is out. Where is that?"

"Other side of the mountain." Cradling his ribs, Harold crossed the room and turned on a TV mounted on the wall. He found a weather report, and they read the breaking news scrolling across the bottom of the screen. "If this rain continues, more bridges are going to be underwater."

"Is this house safe?" Olivia asked.

Harold eased back onto his stool, placing the ice pack on his side. "It's withstood storms for seventy years. We're at the base of the mountain, but on high ground. I have a generator and plenty of supplies." He paused to take a few shallow breaths.

"Are you all right?" Olivia asked. "Could you have broken ribs?"

Harold grimaced. "It's possible, but I'll be fine."

Olivia didn't look convinced. "You didn't go to a doctor?"

"No." He coughed, and his face tightened in pain. "A doctor would ask questions I couldn't answer."

Sharp pulled Olivia aside and whispered, "Between the weather and inherent dangers of chasing Tim Brown, I don't want to take Nicki with us. Also, I think Harold should call the police."

"I agree." Olivia nodded. "She'll be more agreeable if *you* ask her to stay here and take care of Harold. She'll try to butt heads with me."

"OK." Sharp wasn't inclined to take no for an answer, so he didn't ask. "Nicki. Can I talk to you for a second?"

"Sure." She followed him into the hall.

"I'm worried about Harold. I think he's hurt worse than he's saying, but Liv and I need to go find Zoe."

Nicki frowned. "You want me to stay here with the old dude?"

"I would appreciate it," Sharp said.

She nodded. "OK. He seems cool."

They went back into the kitchen. Sharp faced Harold. "Nicki is going to stay here with you. I want you to call the police and tell them what happened. They need to put out a BOLO on Tim."

Harold shook his head hard. "No. He said he'd hurt my grandkids."

"Tell the police that he threatened them." Sharp wasn't taking no for an answer from Harold either. "He needs to be stopped. If he's out on parole, he's already violated his requirements by breaking and entering, assaulting you, and threatening your family. Once they catch him, they'll march him right back to prison. Besides, do you want Tim's presence hanging over you and your family for the rest of your life? The sooner he's back in custody, the sooner you can all relax. If he gets away, you'll have no peace, and your family will be in danger forever."

Harold sighed. "You're right. I'll call them."

Sharp would feel better if Nicki was armed. "Do you have any kind of weapon here?"

"I have a shotgun under my bed," Harold said.

Pleasantly surprised, Sharp asked, "Shells?"

"Plenty of them. For the record, I stored the gun at my gun club when there were kids in the house, but now that I'm alone, I brought it back home."

"I'm glad." Sharp jogged upstairs and found the weapon and ammunition. He brought both down and set them on the kitchen island. "Keep it handy."

Olivia pulled Nicki aside and whispered, "Will you be OK? You feel safe here?"

Nicki waved off her concern. "I've got this. Dude's like, eighty. My biggest concerns are him dying on me or making me reset his Wi-Fi. Keep me in the loop. I want to know where you two are, OK?"

"OK," Olivia agreed.

Sharp brought Nicki's overnight bag inside. Not that he was planning on being gone all night, but with the flooding, he couldn't promise they'd be back by nightfall either.

"Make sure he calls the police," Sharp said to Nicki.

"Will do," she assured him.

Sharp herded Olivia toward the door. She seemed reluctant to leave Nicki.

Outside, he said, "She'll be safer here than with us." They were looking for a killer.

"I know." Olivia climbed into the SUV.

Behind the wheel, Sharp called Jenny Kruger, who got him Jacob Brown's address in two minutes. He entered the address into the GPS. "Jacob's place is closest. We'll go there first. Harold's cabin is higher up on the mountain."

"If we're lucky, we'll find Zoe with Jacob and we'll be done."

But Sharp wasn't so optimistic. The way he saw it, Tim would have looked for Zoe at Jacob's place too. Jacob was his nephew. He'd know where he lived.

As he shifted into gear, Olivia's phone blared an alarm. She read the screen. "Another flash flood warning."

"Let's not waste any time then."

The rain remained light as they drove, and Sharp crossed his fingers it stayed that way. Puddles accumulated at the edges of the road, forcing him to straddle the yellow line at times. Vehicle headlights approached. He eased back to the right. The tires hit water. The vehicle hydroplaned, and he eased off the gas pedal.

"They need wider roads." Olivia gripped the chicken strap with white knuckles.

"Yes." A truck blew past, hitting a puddle. Water cascaded over the hood.

"Shit." He squinted through the windshield, waiting for the wipers to catch up and clear the glass.

"This is miserable," Olivia said. "Maybe we should just go back to Harold's place."

Sharp glanced at the GPS. "We're almost there." His eyes ached from straining to see the road. "The weather app says it's going to rain for the next few days, so the conditions up here are not going to get any better." He eyed the roadside water. "I'm glad we saw Conway Hamilton when we did. This storm system is huge. If they're getting rain like this, their road will be impassable."

"So will these roads," Olivia said. "We'd better not waste any time."

According to the GPS map, Jacob Brown lived about halfway up the mountain. Thankfully, all the roads they'd driven on so far had been paved. Sharp turned left. The country road narrowed and serpentined. They rounded a bend, and the car announced, "You have reached your destination."

"Where?" Olivia's head swiveled as she looked right and left.

Sharp slowed the car to a crawl. Thick forest covered the area on one side of the road. Open ground sprawled out on the other. There was no shoulder to pull onto, just a ten-foot expanse of weeds and mud before the tree line.

"There!" Olivia pointed to a mailbox.

Sharp turned in to a driveway that bisected a meadow the size of a football field. At the end of it, a small house huddled in the rain. A dim porch light glowed weakly, barely cutting through the gloom. "Do you see any lights on?"

"One around back."

"Somebody's home." He parked the car in front of the front door. He wanted to talk to Jacob, but he also wanted to get off this mountain before the visibility went to zero. "I'd rather not be on this mountain after nightfall."

"Same." Olivia stepped out.

Sharp joined her, hurrying to the covered front stoop. From around back, a dog barked.

"He left his dog out in the rain?" Sharp scowled and banged an angry fist on the door. What kind of man left an animal outside in this weather?

No one answered.

"He's ignoring us." Sharp banged louder. "We know you're in there!"

"He might not be home," Olivia said. "Also, angry knocking and yelling doesn't open doors."

"Right. Sorry." Sharp cracked his neck. "I'm just mad about the dog."

"I understand. They might have a doghouse. It might be a working dog. This is the country. Things are different here."

Sharp didn't look convinced. "It sounds like an ankle biter, not a working dog."

Olivia rapped on the door. "Mr. Brown? My name is Olivia Cruz. I'd really like to talk to you."

Nothing but silence.

Sharp raised a fist and gave the door a few more solid thumps—and it opened a few inches.

Olivia mouthed, "Now what?"

Sharp leaned toward the opening. "Mr. Brown?"

Nothing.

"I don't like this," Olivia said.

"Me either." Sharp used a forefinger to push the door farther open.

"We shouldn't go inside."

"Of course not." But he'd driven halfway up the mountain in a storm. He wasn't leaving without finding out if Zoe was here. He stepped over the threshold. A night-light glowed at the end of the hall. They walked through an empty living room toward it. They entered a kitchen at the back of the house. Their wet boots squeaked on the tile. Through glass patio doors, they saw a small dog on a covered patio, yapping at them.

"At least it's out of the rain," Olivia whispered.

Sharp backtracked to the other hallway, which likely led to the bedrooms. His belly knotted as they crept along. A floorboard creaked under his boot. The first few rooms were empty. The doors stood open. The last door stared at them, firmly shut. The hairs on the back of his neck lifted. His instincts had kept him alive for twenty-five years on the police force. They'd never failed him.

He stepped in front of Olivia. Something was wrong here. He could sense it. He motioned for her to move to the side of the hall. Then he took the opposite side.

She should go. *Run.* Get out of this house.

But he was compelled to keep going, and he knew Olivia wouldn't back down.

His heart thudded. His pulse echoed in his ears. He could still hear the dog, but it seemed far away. Cold, clammy sweat broke out on his palms. He wiped them on his thighs before reaching for the doorknob.

It turned. Not locked. The hinges protested with a squeal as he pushed it open. Coppery and foul odors that he knew all too well hit his nostrils. He automatically covered his nose and mouth with the collar of his jacket.

Olivia gagged.

The room was dark. Sharp pulled out his flashlight and switched it on. He shone the beam across the room and flinched. He'd seen plenty of crime scenes, but he'd never become immune to the shock.

"Oh, my God," Olivia said, her voice flat, as if she couldn't believe what they were seeing.

A man was tied to a chair in the center of the room, ankles secured to the chair legs with zip ties. His arms were bound behind his back. His face had been beaten, but Sharp recognized him from one of the articles from when Evan Brown's vehicle had been pulled from the lake. "Looks like Jacob Brown."

"Is he still alive?" Olivia started forward.

Sharp knew from the smell that he wasn't, but he should make 100 percent sure. He grabbed her elbow. "Wait. We don't want to destroy evidence."

Olivia stopped in her tracks.

He moved the beam of light lower. A vast splotch of dark red encircled the area around the chair. Blood. A lot of blood. Was it his? He'd been beaten, but the damage to his face didn't explain the sheer volume of blood.

Or had Zoe been here? Could the blood be hers?

It felt as if every organ inside Sharp's body curled inward, like a fist clenching ever tighter. He didn't want Zoe to be dead. He also didn't want Olivia to find her friend's corpse. He didn't want that memory for her. He focused the light on the blood. He couldn't step in it. He'd compromise the evidence. Even worse, he'd leave his own boot prints in it. He could become a suspect, which would just make the case even more complicated. He shone his light around the room but didn't see another body.

"Wait here," he said.

"I intend to," Olivia answered.

Sharp stepped closer to the man. He stopped at the very edge of the stain and reached forward. Stretching, he could barely reach him. He pressed two fingers into the side of his neck. The skin was cold and stiff. Clammy. No pulse beat under his fingertips. "He's dead."

"Can you tell when he died?"

Sharp shone his flashlight on the corpse, giving it a once-over. "Looks like he's been dead a day or two."

He stepped back, careful with his footsteps, light shining on the floor. He examined the dried blood puddle, moving his light in a grid pattern. "Oh, no."

"What?" Olivia asked.

He stared down at the spotlight. Stuck in the crusty, dried edge was a long blond hair. "Zoe was here."

Chapter Twenty-Six

Zoe huddled on the couch in the living room. The image of Jacob, beaten and bloody, played in a continuous loop in her head. Hugging her knees, she rocked back and forth.

He's dead. He's dead he's dead.

Tim had only been out of prison for a few weeks. He'd already killed Jacob. She was next.

The temperature had dropped. The cold and shock had chilled her to the marrow, but she didn't dare build a fire. Someone would see the smoke. Rain beat a relentless rhythm on the roof. If the bridge washed out, she'd be safe for a while. There was no way she'd get down the driveway in the van, let alone make it all the way to the main road until the storm passed and the roads dried out.

She was stuck—trapped.

Jacob had refused to leave town. He'd always said it was pointless. Tim had vowed revenge—that he would track them down like a wolf following a wounded elk.

How long would it take him to find her?

The only person who'd known her escape plan had been Clarice, and she was dead. Zoe's getaway vehicle was registered in her name too. Harold might be able to guess she would go to the cabin, but he didn't know for sure. Because of the podcast, Tim would go looking for her in Scarlet Falls first. But when he learned she wasn't there, he would have come to Summerton and found Jacob. She would have to leave this area as soon as the storm passed.

Would Tim go to Harold? Would he kill him?

Tears welled in her eyes, and sorrow closed her throat.

She couldn't bear it if Harold died because of her.

Clarice and Harold had been so good to her. Harold wouldn't give her up intentionally. He'd die before he helped Tim find her. But Tim could be persuasive. He knew how to inflict pain—and he reveled in it. Even if Harold didn't give her up, he might have tax records or the deed for the cabin at the house. If Tim learned about the cabin, he'd come here directly.

Jacob's face flashed in her mind again, her imagination superimposing Harold's face behind the blood and bruises. She wanted to check on him, but visiting or calling him was too risky for both of them. Tim could be watching Harold, waiting for Zoe to make contact.

Zoe reached for the bottle of whiskey she'd found in the cupboard and poured a small amount into a tumbler. She couldn't afford to get drunk. She had to be coherent—to be aware—to listen.

Tim would never stop until he killed her.

She wiped a tear from her cheek. She hadn't seen Jacob in many years, but their bond could never be broken. The trauma they'd endured together connected them for life. His was over now. Would she follow him to an early grave?

Glass shattered downstairs. Zoe froze. A scuffling sound floated up the stairway.

The bear?

Tim?

She'd have a better chance with the bear.

She rose to her feet and wiped her damp palms on her thighs. She was dressed to run in warm hiking pants and thick socks. She eased her feet into her hiking boots and laced them. Her backpack and parka waited by the door. If she had to go, she'd have to escape on foot. She put on the jacket now, just in case. The van would never make it down the driveway. Where could she even go? The storm would make foot travel miserable and dangerous. With the temperature dropping and the rain pouring, she'd have hypothermia in no time. She could head up to the ski resort. No one would be there. It wouldn't open for months yet.

She strained to listen through the roar of the storm. Thunder boomed. Lightning flashed, brightening the interior of the cabin for a second, like a strobe light. Maybe she'd just heard branches falling or brushing up against the house.

Something scratched. Her heart sprinted, echoing in her ears.

No.

That was inside the house.

Glancing around, she picked up the only handy weapon, a fireplace poker. Panic knotted her belly. She walked to the top of the stairs and stared into the darkness. Her whole body trembled from her toes to her face. She should have left a light on downstairs. But that would have given away her location. She drew the poker over one shoulder like a baseball bat.

Lightning flashed again.

And she saw him. In the fraction of a second of illumination, she registered his tall, burly shape. A black parka, the hood up. Giant shit-kicker work boots. Had he always been that big? Was her imagination enlarging him, or had he beefed up in prison? She'd never met anyone as frightening as Tim Brown.

Evan had been scary as fuck too, but he was dead. Everyone could be killed. Tim wasn't some sort of supervillain.

She tightened her hands on the poker as the cabin went dark again. She heard his boots on the steps. She counted, *one, two, three.* He wasn't rushing, nor was he trying to sneak up on her. He was taking his sweet time.

Four, five . . .

There were, what? Twelve steps?

Six, seven, eight.

Lightning pulsed.

He was right there. Just a few steps away and already almost as tall as her. In the brief staccato of light, she saw him lower his hood.

And smile.

Like a predator staring at its dinner. No, animals didn't kill for the enjoyment of it.

But Tim did.

Her insides turned to water. Her fear became palpable, radiating from her like a sour odor. She was sure he could smell it.

He stopped an arm's reach away.

Terror paralyzed her. Her feet locked in place. Her hands still clenched around the handle of the poker, but she couldn't muster the courage to swing it.

She couldn't summon the guts to run either. She would just stand like a deer in the road, waiting to be mowed down by a fast-moving pickup.

"Hello, Zoe. I told you you'd pay for what you did."

Zoe broke from her fear trance, turned, and ran. He was right behind her. She spun and swung the poker. It connected with his shoulder but didn't even slow him down.

He yanked it out of her hands and tossed it aside. "You can't fight me. You know it. Just lay down and take what's coming. That's what you should have done thirty years ago." He stepped between Zoe and the back door, cutting off her exit. She glanced longingly at her backpack, still waiting for her. She'd have to run without it.

Then she turned and sprinted out the glass door onto the deck. The storm slapped her in the face. Wind whipped her hair around her head. She backed to the railing and looked over her shoulder. The drop was significant, at least twenty feet to the ground. The grade was still steep enough that she'd tumble all the way to the road. If she climbed over, hung from the base, and dropped, the fall would be five and a half feet less. She'd have to risk it.

She'd jump to her death before she ever allowed Tim to torture her. She wouldn't let him have the satisfaction, and she knew he would enjoy every minute. He wouldn't just kill her.

Zoe climbed over the railing and stood, facing him, balancing on her toes on the edge of the deck. One step backward was all it would take. His shadow appeared in the doorway. Rain poured over her head. Water ran into her eyes. Lightning split the sky.

She had no time to dangle from the base of the railing.

Dead end for Zoe.

Or maybe just dead.

A flicker of brightness gleamed on something metal in his hand.

A knife.

Chapter Twenty-Seven

Olivia's heart stumbled as she stared at the bloody blond hair. Her gaze went to the body, then swept the room. "So where is Zoe?"

Was she here after Jacob died? Or while he was being killed?

Is she still alive?

Lincoln glanced around. "We've checked the whole place. She's not here."

Olivia's own kidnapping flashed through her mind like a slideshow on fast-forward. Memories pelted her. Being gagged. Bound. Held underground. The dampness. The cold. Her asthma flaring. Her lungs tightened. She wheezed.

"Hold on," Lincoln said. "Let's get out of here."

"We can't go!" Olivia gasped. "We need to find Zoe."

"In a minute." Lincoln guided her through the house and out the front door onto the covered front stoop. "Did you bring your inhaler?"

"Yes." She fished it out of her pocket and puffed. The medicine instantly eased her breathing. "Better. Thank you."

"Do your breathing exercises. I'll be right back. I want to check something." Lincoln went back inside.

She listened to the dog barking and waited for what felt like an hour but was probably ten minutes.

Lincoln reappeared. "His wrists were slashed."

"Slashed?"

Lincoln nodded. "Both of them. Vertically."

"He didn't do it himself."

"No."

"Wouldn't it be more expedient to slit his throat?" Olivia asked.

"Maybe expedient wasn't his goal. Maybe he wanted to drag it out."

"Harold said Tim wants revenge." Olivia shuddered. "Either Zoe found Jacob like this and ran or Tim has her."

Lincoln frowned. "Why would he take her when he could just kill her here and be done with it?" He shook his head. "I think she found Jacob like this and left."

"So we try the cabin?"

"Let's do it."

Olivia jerked a thumb at the house behind her. "Do we report the death?"

"Nothing can hurt him now." Lincoln headed for the SUV.

Olivia flipped up her hood and ran for the passenger side. In the vehicle, she shook off the hood. Water dripped from her jacket. "Feels wrong to leave him."

Lincoln turned on the heater. "If we call it in, the cops will want us to stay here and wait for them."

"And we need to find Zoe."

"Yes." Lincoln headed up the mountain. "We'll call after we find Zoe. We need to report the dog too. It has shelter tonight, but someone will need to take charge of it." He paused. "We'll make an anonymous call asking for a wellness check." Lincoln used an app to disguise the number of his phone and called the local police. He ended the call a minute later, turned, and stared at the house. "They said they don't have the manpower to send anyone out here unless it's a life-or-death emergency."

"We can't leave the dog here, not in this weather," Olivia said.

"I agree." He opened the door again. "I'll be right back."

He ran around to the rear yard and came back with a shape tucked under his arm. Sliding behind the wheel, he handed the shivering, bony lump of fur across the console.

Olivia tucked the mud-covered dog inside her jacket. "This is the terror that was barking at us?"

"He did try to bite me. Good thing my boots are thick. I think he was just scared, but now he seems to understand I'm OK." Lincoln shifted into gear and drove away. "We'll deal with the legal fallout of dog thievery afterward."

"No one will fault us for taking him under these conditions."

They passed a sign for Hidden Cavern, which offered guided tours of the local caves. The sign boasted a half mile of underground walking trails with seventy steps. Olivia shuddered. She'd pass on exploring any caves.

At the entrance to Hidden Mountain Estates, they followed the GPS onto a dirt-and-gravel road that had not been graded in a long time. It was more mud than gravel. The SUV slipped in and out of ruts. The road appeared to have been cut into the mountain, with a steep incline on one side and a drop-off on the other.

Olivia gripped the armrest and held her breath as the vehicle slid sideways toward a deep ravine.

Lincoln maneuvered the vehicle back to the center of the road.

Water lapped over the edge of a small bridge. Branches brushed the sides of the vehicle. He made a turn and stopped the SUV on the side of the road. Rain sluiced across the windshield. The wipers swept back and forth in a frantic arc. "It's right up there." He pointed to a steep driveway. "Do we want to go quietly on foot? Or attempt to drive up?"

"Where is the SUV safest?" Olivia asked. "We won't get off this mountain without it."

Lincoln nodded. "On foot it is." He parked at the base of the driveway. Lincoln was wearing a rain jacket, but Olivia zippered her waterproof shell over her puffy jacket.

Olivia was well aware that the ascent was steep and the mud deep, but the longer they waited, the worse conditions would become. Lincoln stuffed his pockets with equipment. Olivia watched a flashlight and extra ammunition disappear. She grabbed her own flashlight, tugged on a knit hat and gloves, then flipped up her hood. "Let's go."

She opened her gym bag, dug out a sweatshirt, and bunched it as an impromptu dog bed. The little dog curled up immediately. When Olivia slid out of the SUV, the dog made no attempt to follow her.

The rain found its way into her waterproof layer in seconds. Water dripped down her neck. She trudged behind Lincoln. It seemed to take forever to climb fifty feet. The mud sucked at their boots. Her foot slipped and she went down on her knees. She pulled a foot under her, then slipped again, sliding on her side a few feet. A glance over her shoulder told her they'd climbed more than fifty feet. The path was rocky and rutted. Tumbling down it would hurt. She reached for anything to stop her descent, scrambling for purchase with her hands and the toes of her boots.

"Liv!" Lincoln shouted, scrambling toward her.

The sole of her boot finally caught in a rut. She breathed, sweat mixing with the rain running down her spine. "I'm OK." She'd slid about fifteen feet. She dug in and hauled herself back up to his level. He grabbed her hand and helped her up the last few feet.

Their eyes met, his grim. "Maybe we should go back to town."

"No. We've come this far." She eyed the remaining driveway. "We're almost at the top. It'll take ten minutes to check the house. If Zoe isn't there, then we'll head back. If she is, we take her with us." If Zoe wasn't at the cabin, Olivia had no idea where to look for her. "We have to find her before Tim does. He's going to kill her next."

Lincoln nodded toward the cabin. "Let's do it."

They trudged up the muddy hill without any further incident. At the top, Olivia stopped and stared at the cabin. Unlike many of the vacation homes in the area, this one hadn't been refurbished. It was old and rustic. The cabin was dark.

"Looks empty," Lincoln said in her ear.

She leaned close to him. "Do we risk using a flashlight?"

Lightning zigzagged across the sky. In the flicker of light, Olivia saw boot prints in the mud. She pointed just as the night went dark again.

But Lincoln nodded as if he'd seen them. He mouthed, "Someone's here."

"Too big to be Zoe's," Olivia mouthed back.

Footprints would wash away quickly in this rain. They must be recent.

The garage door was closed, and there were no windows on it to see inside. They walked around to the back of the cabin. Another burst of lightning illuminated the back door. It stood ajar, the lock broken. Lincoln drew his gun and eased through the opening. Olivia followed him inside. Voices floated from somewhere else in the cabin. Olivia and Lincoln shared a look. Zoe was probably here. But so was someone else.

Tim?

They crept through a mudroom to a flight of stairs leading upward.

Above them, boots thudded on the wood floor.

The cold, the damp, and the fear tightened her lungs until every breath felt shallower than the last. But she didn't dare fish out her inhaler.

Lincoln motioned for her to stay low and behind him. Olivia didn't need to be told twice. She crouched and followed him up the stairs. He paused before his head poked above the last step.

A woman screamed.

Zoe!

Chapter Twenty-Eight

A female scream wailed over the storm. The panic and desperation in it pulled at Sharp's soul. Olivia lunged for the landing, but he caught her arm and held her back. He was the only one armed. He knew it was pointless to ask her to stay behind, but she was sensible enough that she'd allow him to go first.

He led with his handgun, stepping softly but swiftly onto the landing. He took in the scene in a quick visual sweep. Empty living room and kitchen combo. Glass doors opened onto a deck. A large man stood in the doorway, his back to Sharp. He could see no weapon, but that didn't mean the man, presumably Tim Brown, didn't have one.

Where's Zoe?

He couldn't just shoot a man in the back. He took three steps toward the large shadow, then raised his handgun and shouted, "Freeze!" Out of more than two decades of habit, he almost said *police* but choked that off at the last second.

The man whirled to face him. He was a big, big dude. Sharp recognized his face from the articles on the Brown case. Tim Brown. Wait. Was that a knife?

"Who the fuck are you?" Tim called.

"A guy with a gun," Lincoln answered. "Where is she?"

"Help!" Zoe's shout sounded from outside the door. Tim's bulk blocked Sharp's view of her.

"Drop the knife and step away from the door." Sharp squinted. He needed light. He needed a better view of Zoe. He couldn't shoot Tim for fear of hitting her.

Sharp moved left to see Zoe on the wrong side of the deck railing, barely holding on while the storm lashed at her.

The deck lights turned on. In Sharp's peripheral vision, he could see Olivia at the wall, her hand poised over a switch. *As if she could read his mind.*

"Fuck you." Tim took a step in the other direction, toward Zoe. He raised the knife and slashed it at her. With no room to move, Zoe barely evaded the strike. Sharp couldn't let Tim try again. Now that he could see both of them, Sharp pulled the trigger. Tim flinched. Was he hit? Or just reacting to the noise? Sharp hoped the bullet went right through Tim's rotten heart. But he didn't drop. If he was hit, the shot must have struck him in a less vital area.

"Come on, Tim," Sharp shouted over the wind. "You don't have to die tonight."

Tim glanced back. "My life is ruined. I don't care if I die. As long as I take this bitch with me."

Before Sharp could react, Tim rushed forward and hopped over the railing. As he jumped off the deck, he grabbed Zoe by the arm and pulled her with him. Branches crashed, and bodies tumbled.

No!

Sharp rushed onto the deck. Grabbing the railing with both hands, he stared down the slope. But all he saw was rain and forest. Zoe and Tim had disappeared into the darkness.

Chapter Twenty-Nine

Zoe hit the steep ground feetfirst. Something snapped. Pain slammed through her ankle and exploded through her leg from foot to hip. But she had no time to register the injury or agony. She pinwheeled down the slope, slamming into tree trunks and rocks, sliding on the wet earth. She tried to tuck her arms and legs close to her body, but it was impossible to control her descent in any way. She was at the mercy of gravity. Something sliced her face.

She tumbled into thicker underbrush. Branches snagged at her limbs and slowed her progress. She reached out for a tree root. Her fingers closed on it. Momentum carried her past, but she hung on. Pain ripped through her hand as her body weight tore at her grasp, her skin tearing. Blood made her grip slick. Her weight hit her outstretched arm, pulling at her shoulder. She flung a second hand upward and caught the root. Her body finally came to a stop. She propped a boot on a slick rock, bracing herself and enabling her to release her two-handed grip on the protruding tree root.

With her momentum halted, she wouldn't fall any farther if she stayed down. She pressed her body into the earth and panted. Her right leg was on fire. Tiny pinpricks danced in front of her eyes, even when they were closed. She couldn't see in the dark, but she knew her ankle was broken. Maybe it was best she couldn't see it. She had to keep moving. At this point, all she could hope was that the break was not an open fracture because she couldn't stay here.

Had she really seen Sharp in the cabin, or had that been her imagination? Her brain replayed the split-second interaction. Most of her view had been blocked by Tim, but she'd seen someone who looked like Sharp.

It must have been real. Why else would Tim have jumped off the deck? If Sharp was in the cabin, that meant he was looking for her. Was Olivia with him? Zoe wasn't sure if rainwater or tears were blurring her vision, but she blinked to clear her eyes.

Rain slicked her hair. If she hadn't been wearing tactical hiking clothes and a waterproof jacket, she'd be soaked to the skin. Still, she shivered. The temperature had dropped at least ten degrees. If Tim didn't kill her, hypothermia would. But the roar of the downpour was probably the only thing keeping Tim from hearing her breathless panting.

A bolt of fear shot through her.

Where is Tim?

He had to be close by. They'd started at the same place. Looking up, she couldn't see the cabin through the trees. How far had she rolled down the slope? Maybe seventy-five feet? It had felt like a mile, but she hadn't tumbled all the way to the road. The driveway was only about a hundred feet long, so she couldn't have tumbled farther than that. Where did he stop?

She didn't bother to consider whether he'd died in the fall.

Only the good die young.

Evil seemed to provide protection. She had no doubt he'd survived. That bastard would be as hard to kill as Michael Myers.

Be quiet, or he'll find you in a second.

She tried to control her breathing. Memories of him grabbing her and pulling her off the deck replayed over and over. Panic and pain were driving her toward hyperventilating. If she panicked, she'd die. He would find her, and he would kill her.

But how could she get away? Fuck him. She hadn't survived all these years to surrender now. She refused to make killing her easy. No. If she died, she'd go down fighting.

Which meant she couldn't stay in the first place he'd look for her.

She needed to move. She breathed and assessed her injures. She ached everywhere, but other than the broken ankle, the rest of her body felt intact. If Sharp and possibly Olivia were at the cabin, then Zoe had to get to them. They must have a vehicle, one that had made it up the mountain. They could get her down.

Carefully, slowly, she eased onto her belly, then pushed up onto one knee. If she had two good legs, scrambling up the slope would have been difficult, but possible. With a broken ankle, it was going to be a nightmare. She took one crawling step upward. The pain that sliced through her ankle blinded her. The woods spiraled. She stopped, wheezing and trembling. On her hands and knees, she vomited into the mud.

When her stomach was empty, she dry-heaved a few more times, then rolled back to the muddy ground. There was no way she could climb-crawl up seventy-five feet at this incline. She wasn't even sure she could go down. Maybe she could slip on the wet ground? She rolled onto her good side and let herself slide a couple of inches. The pain blasted her again but didn't threaten to make her pass out. She maneuvered around a small tree, making sure to not allow her broken ankle to touch anything. Once clear, she used tree roots and rocks as handholds and slipped a few inches at a time. As needed, she stopped to navigate around trees and rocks.

She paused to catch her breath. The effort of her slow descent was staggering. Rain poured over her head and invaded her jacket. Her shirt beneath was fleece, so it wouldn't hold water. But the moisture on her skin would still accelerate hypothermia.

As she reached for another handhold, something cracked nearby.

Zoe froze, her heart slamming in her chest like an animal that wanted out of a cage.

Something crunched in the underbrush.

Zoe stared into the gloom. Panic-sweat gathered under her layers.

Tim?

She couldn't run. What were her other options? She only had one legitimate chance.

Hide!

She crawled, the hairs on the back of her neck rising, fear churning in her belly. Her hands shook as she dragged herself away from the noise.

It kept coming. *Shuffle. Shuffle. Scrape.*

Zoe pulled herself on the ground. Her useless leg dragged. In the darkness, her ankle struck something hard. She curled on her side and jammed her fist in her mouth to stop herself from screaming.

A twig snapped.

Chapter Thirty

"We have to get her!" Olivia rushed onto the deck to stand next to Lincoln.

"I know." He fished a flashlight out of his pocket and shone it downward, illuminating the driving rain and not much else.

Olivia spotted a broken tree branch. "There! She must have fallen that way."

"Or Tim Brown did." Lincoln switched off the light. "I'll go down and see if I can track her."

"Tim is also down there."

"I know." He hurried through the house.

She stayed right behind him. "He had a knife."

"Yes, and I have a gun."

Olivia pulled her multi-tool from her pocket. "I'm not unarmed." The blade wasn't long, but it was sharp.

"Did you hit him with that shot?" Olivia asked.

"I don't know," Lincoln said as they crossed the room. "I thought so, but it didn't seem to slow him down."

Retracing their steps, they jogged down the stairs to the lower level and exited through the back door.

Lincoln touched her arm and spoke in a low voice. "Stay close."

She nodded. Unfolding the knife blade, she held it at her side, pointy end down in case she fell. They crept through the woods. The downward slope made the descent treacherous. Olivia hoped the raging of the storm covered the sounds of their footsteps.

Tim had to be injured, right? Even if Lincoln's shot had missed him, he'd jumped off a two-story deck and tumbled down a steep slope.

Zoe was likely also hurt.

Olivia banished her grim thoughts and focused on the trail. Between the darkness and the rain, visibility was limited. She could barely see her own feet. She wanted to turn on her flashlight, but that wasn't possible. The light would make them a target. She pushed forward, tripped on a rock, and fell to one knee.

Lincoln paused, turned, and helped her up. She pulled the knife from the mud, where it had landed tip-down. He leaned toward her ear. "I know you want to move faster, but one of us taking a tumble won't help Zoe. We could be all that stands between Zoe and death—either from Tim or exposure."

Olivia nodded. She rubbed her bruised kneecap and followed in his footsteps. They rounded the house and skirted the driveway. A grunt in the shadows of the trees stopped them. Lightning flashed.

There was nothing there. Olivia blinked hard to clear her eyes. Still nothing.

Lincoln headed toward the trees. He stopped at a skinny, broken evergreen branch.

Olivia touched the break. The foliage dripped with rainwater. "It's fresh. They fell through here." She peered over the edge but couldn't see much. "I don't see how we climb down there without a flashlight."

"We don't." Lincoln traded his handgun for the flashlight in his pocket, then switched it on. "If we break our necks, we're no good to Zoe."

Even with the flashlight, the visibility was dismal. Lincoln kept the beam on the ground, looking for broken underbrush and branches. The slope was about forty-five degrees, and they needed handholds as they worked their way down.

But were they following Zoe?

Or Tim?

They couldn't be that far apart. They had both fallen from approximately the same location.

Olivia was fit, but the dampness aggravated her asthma. She was out of breath three-quarters of the way down the slope. Lincoln stopped to wait for her as she pulled her inhaler out of her jacket pocket and used it. She'd barely zippered it back into her jacket when something snapped. Lincoln whirled, the beam of his light arcing across the darkness. Olivia held her breath, prepared to see Tim Brown geared up like Rambo. But nothing emerged. They waited, straining their ears to listen for sounds of movement over the storm. Maybe the wind had broken a branch.

"Help," someone called out.

Olivia froze. She knew that voice. "Zoe?"

"I'm here."

Olivia followed the sound. Lincoln pulled aside the bough of a square pine. Zoe lay curled in the mud at the base of the tree. Her eyes were closed.

Olivia dropped to her knees beside her friend. She yanked off her gloves and pressed two fingers to Zoe's throat. A weak pulse thrummed against her fingertips. Olivia exhaled hard in relief.

Zoe opened her eyes. Fear widened them, then recognition dawned. "You found me."

"We've got you." Olivia took her hands. Zoe's fingers were ice cold.

Lincoln crouched, scanning Zoe. "What hurts?"

"Pretty sure my ankle is broken." Zoe moaned. "I was crawling away, but I heard something and decided to hide. I'm not outrunning anyone like this."

Lincoln shone the beam of light on her leg. "I don't see any blood, but ankles aren't supposed to bend that way. Our vehicle is parked on the road. Let's get to it, and then we can assess you better."

"OK," Zoe said in a weak voice.

Olivia took the flashlight. "Can you sit up?"

Zoe pushed to a sitting position, stretching one leg in front of her. "I can't put any weight on this leg."

"Then don't." Lincoln stooped and took her arm. Zoe helped as best as she could, pushing with her good leg as Lincoln dragged her to her feet.

Her face went white, and she sagged against him for a minute, breathing in short pants. In a few seconds, she lifted her head. "Let's get out of here."

Before Tim finds us was implied.

Olivia went in front, holding the flashlight, finding the flattest places to step. They took the final twenty-five feet one step at a time. They emerged from the trees and stepped down onto the gravel road. Olivia wanted to kiss the flat earth. The SUV sat at the end of the driveway, less than thirty feet away.

Lincoln turned toward it.

A shadow stepped out from behind a tree and swung a large branch. Lincoln must have sensed or seen the attack in his peripheral vision because he dropped Zoe, turned his upper body, and took the impact on the back of his shoulder instead of across his head. The force sent him to his knees.

Zoe screamed, "No!"

Tim stood over Lincoln and raised the branch again, preparing to deliver a fatal blow.

No! Olivia looked around. She had to protect Lincoln. She had a four-inch knife blade in her pocket. In order to incapacitate Tim with it, she'd have to be precise, which wouldn't be easy. A shoulder blade or rib could deflect a stab. He was a large, strong man who'd spent the last thirty years in prison. He knew how to fight.

Desperate, she searched for an alternative weapon. She picked up a rock the size of a bowling ball. If she hit him hard enough, she could knock him unconscious or at least stun him. Surprise was her best bet. This would only work once. She raised the rock over her head and brought it down on the back of Tim's head. His legs folded like a cheap snack tray. He dropped the branch and went down on both knees, groaning. His hands went to his head and cupped it as if that would contain the pain.

Olivia front-kicked him away from Lincoln. Standing between Tim and Lincoln, she pulled her knife from her pocket, opened the blade, and faced Tim. She held the blade close to her thigh and angled her body to keep it out of sight. If he saw it, he would take it from her. She would not let him kill Lincoln or Zoe while they were down. Zoe lay still, curled in a fetal position, moaning softly. Lincoln was trying to pull himself to his feet using a tree, but he seemed stunned.

Tim rose to his feet but looked wobbly. "I'm going to kill you for that."

"Like you hadn't intended to do that anyway." Olivia tested the weight of the knife. She was small, and Tim was huge. She could never overpower him or even fight him on equal terms. No, she had to be sneaky.

She had to fight dirty.

Tim pulled his own knife from his pocket. A flash of lightning glittered on the blade, which was twice the size of Olivia's. Sweat and rainwater soaked her back, and her hands shook from the surge of adrenaline. Her knife handle felt slippery and small in her grip.

He waggled his knife in the air. "I don't even need this. I could kill you with my bare hands and enjoy doing it." He took two steps forward, then lunged, flicking out with the knife point. Olivia evaded the attack by ducking under his arm. Still crouching, she slashed at the back of his ankle and sliced his Achilles tendon.

"Fuck." He went down, instinctively covering the wound with one hand. "Now I'm going to make you pay before I kill you. You'll be sorry." He straightened, brandishing his big blade again. "I'm going to cut off your ears first, then work my way down your body. You'll die in pieces. By the time I'm done, they'll need a bucket for your remains."

Fear gripped Olivia's insides for a few seconds. Her entire being trembled as she held her ground. Then she deliberately backed a few feet down the road, leading him away from Lincoln and Zoe, giving them whatever time she could. If she lured Tim away, maybe they could get to the SUV. Tim wouldn't be able to move at full speed, not with his tendon cut.

She hoped.

"Come here, bitch." Tim staggered after her, half dragging his wounded leg. Had she not cut the tendon completely? It wasn't like she'd had practice. Even wounded, he managed to keep pace with her, maintaining the same distance between them. "Get what's coming to you."

Surely, he wouldn't be able to run. Olivia turned to flee. She stopped before she started. A huge black shape emerged from the roadside thicket. A bear! The cold that swept through Olivia went far deeper than the rain and wind could reach. It chilled her soul. This was an apex predator. It could eat her, and it was standing a dozen feet away, blocking her path. The underbrush rustled near it and a tiny black lump the size of a golden retriever ambled out.

A cub.

The chill in her bones turned to ice.

Olivia didn't move. If the bear thought she was a threat, it might attack. Not many things were more aggressive than a literal mama bear.

Behind her, the sound of mud sucking at a shoe made her glance over her shoulder. Tim staggered closer, dragging his wounded leg. Olivia's heart stumbled. She couldn't go forward but she had to get away from Tim. She stepped sideways, trying to put as much distance between her and both threats—though frankly, Tim scared her more than the bear.

Sure, it could eat her, but it wouldn't torture her for kicks first.

"What the fuck?" Tim stopped short.

The bear chuffed, then stood up on its hind legs and bellowed. The roar vibrated Olivia's bones.

Tim faced the bear. "Jesus Christ."

Olivia had done a piece about black bears early in her career. Posturing could chase them away. They weren't known to be aggressive.

Except when they had cubs.

Tim held out his knife, shaking it at the bear. "Don't fucking come at me."

The bear roared, then charged him. It swiped a paw. Tim staggered backward. A scream ripped from his mouth. The bear lunged forward. Tim stumbled back and almost went down on his wounded leg. Lightning flashed, and Olivia could see rivers of blood running down his chest. He fell backward, scrambling like a crab while the bear pursued. The bear continued to push him across the road.

On the opposite side, the bear charged again, another swat landing on the side of his head, splitting open his face like a ripe watermelon. The blood flowed faster than the rain could wash it off. Olivia couldn't look away. Her feet were riveted to the muddy gravel road.

Tim lurched to his feet and swayed. His feet caught on a rock. His arms flailed. His shredded face emitted a scream as he teetered, arms windmilling, body tipping. He fell backward into the gorge below. Fear rooted Olivia in place, though she realized she should have gotten away while the bear was engaged with Tim. She'd missed her opportunity, and now she was faced with a raging, protective mother bear. But she'd been mesmerized. Her pulse hammered in her ears. Lightning flashed, and thunder cracked. Olivia flinched but kept her feet rooted in place.

If she ran, the bear would chase her, and she could not outrun it. Climbing a tree was pointless. Black bears were excellent climbers. She had no bear spray, and no weapon that was in any way practical against a bear. She breathed shallowly and waited for the bear to decide. The ball was in its court.

The wind gusted. The bear gave the air a final deep sniff, then dropped to all fours.

Olivia focused on a tree a few feet away from the bear, in case direct eye contact could be perceived as a challenge.

Think nonthreatening thoughts.

The bear turned and lumbered away. Three cubs burst from the thicket and followed in her tracks. They ran into the woods, accelerating up the slope effortlessly. Olivia stared until they disappeared into the forest. Relief made her lightheaded.

Get your shit together. Just because the bear knocked Tim off a cliff doesn't mean you're out of the woods—literally—yet.

Zoe needed a hospital, and she didn't know how badly Lincoln was hurt. The storm continued to rage. If the roads weren't impassable, they soon would be.

She crossed the road and looked over the edge of the ravine, just to make sure Tim hadn't landed on a handy ledge. He hadn't. She could only see the first twenty feet or so, but the gorge looked deep. Could Tim have survived a fall from a deck, a tumble down a steep slope, a bullet wound, a bear attack, a knife wound to the Achilles tendon, and a fall into a gorge?

It was unlikely unless he was a comic book villain, but Olivia couldn't exactly climb down to make sure.

"Liv!" Lincoln's voice spun her around.

She ran toward him, splashing through a mud puddle. He wrapped his arms around her, and she rested her head on his chest for a minute. His heart thudded against her cheek, solid proof that he was alive. They had to go—but she needed this moment. He grounded her. She lifted her head and cupped his cheek. "You're all right?"

He nodded. "He must have hit a nerve or something. I was stunned for a few minutes. All good now."

"I'm sure you'll be black and blue."

"I'll never be happier to live to see my bruises." He put her at arm's length. "What happened? Where's Tim?"

Olivia nodded toward the gorge. "He fell. I'll tell you all about it while we drive out of here."

Zoe was pale and only semiconscious as they half carried her to the vehicle. The dog barked as they approached but behaved as they loaded Zoe into the back seat, stretching her leg with the broken ankle on the seat next to her. "I'd prefer to elevate her ankle, but it's just not possible."

"No. Road conditions are not good. We have to move. Make sure her seat belt is fastened." Lincoln brought an emergency blanket from the cargo area, and Olivia tucked it around her friend's shoulders. They were all wearing waterproof jackets, but the relentless rain had infiltrated their outer layers. Olivia pressed a hand to Zoe's forehead. Her friend felt clammy.

"Let's go." Lincoln slid behind the wheel.

Olivia got into the passenger seat, putting the dog on her lap and wrapping him in the sweatshirt. She brought in so much rainwater with her that it puddled on the seat. Didn't matter. Her ass was cold and wet anyway. She spotted seat heaters and turned them on. At least her butt would be warm. Not dry, but warm. She'd take what she could get.

Lincoln started the engine. "We'll have heat in a few minutes."

Turning the SUV around felt precarious now that Olivia knew how deep the ravine was on the south side of the road. But Lincoln safely navigated the one-eighty and headed back down the mountain. They approached the narrow bridge. On the other side, a cop car approached the bridge, lights swirling. Water lapped across the wooden slats. Lincoln slowed, then brought the vehicle to a halt. "I'm going to get out and see how deep that water is." He stepped out and walked to the edge. Olivia watched him through the windshield. The wipers arced frantically but couldn't keep up with the continuous downpour. Lincoln walked onto the bridge. The water barely covered his ankles.

He returned to the vehicle and slammed the door. "It's not that deep. The SUV has good clearance. We'll be OK."

He eased the SUV into gear. Keeping the speed slow and steady, he drove onto the bridge. They didn't speak. The only sounds were the rush of the rain and the rumbling of the tires on the wood. A sudden roar brought Olivia's head around to the passenger window. Her breath locked in her throat as she recognized the wall of water headed for them. "Flash flood, Lincoln, hurry!"

He punched the gas pedal, but four inches of water did not make for great traction. The wheels spun. The vehicle fishtailed. "Hold on."

The water hit the SUV broadside and pushed it sideways. They slammed into the side of the bridge. The guardrails held for the first few seconds. The SUV inched forward, and Olivia thought maybe they'd be OK. Then everything shifted and the world went upside down.

Chapter Thirty-One

Nicki hated to be left behind. She might have pretended Harold needed babysitting, but Nicki knew the truth. Aunt Liv didn't want to be responsible for putting her in danger.

She understood, but that didn't mean she had to like it.

"Rummy!" Harold fanned his cards on the kitchen table with a delighted flourish. At his elbow, a small glass of whiskey sat on ice.

"You shouldn't be drinking. What if you have a concussion?"

Harold wagged a finger at her. "I'm old enough to do exactly as I please. You're welcome to a glass if you like, if you're old enough, that is."

"I am, but no thanks. One of us has to keep a clear head." She checked her phone again. Nothing from Aunt Liv or Sharp. Worry knotted her gut. *They're smart. They'll be OK.*

Harold got up to splash another finger of the Macallan into his glass. "You're sure?" He lifted the bottle and gave it a little wiggle.

"Positive." Nicki swept the cards into a pile and began shuffling them. "If you get drunk enough, maybe I'll beat you."

"There isn't enough whiskey."

"Aren't you cocky?" she quipped.

"I am." Swelling made his grin lopsided, but she was happy to see him smile. "How about food? I have a dozen casseroles in the freezer.

Women usually outlive men, so the ratio of widows to widowers is approximately fifty to one. Someone has brought me dinner every week since Clarice died." He sat back down gingerly, as if his bones hurt.

"Any of them datable?" Nicki asked.

"I've already had the love of my life." He sipped. "Can't compete with that." He said it in a matter-of-fact tone.

"Do they have to compete?"

He looked up but said nothing.

Nicki continued. "I mean, I get that you loved your wife with your whole heart."

"That I did."

"But does that mean you have to be alone forever? What about companionship? Maybe there's a widow out there who loved her husband but also doesn't want to be alone forever."

He shrugged. "Not interested."

"Do you think Clarice would be fine with you just giving up on life?"

"She'd understand." Harold snorted. "If I were twenty years younger, I'd probably think differently, but that just isn't where I am in my life anymore."

Nicki's phone vibrated. She snatched it up, hoping for a text from Aunt Liv. Instead, a weather alert banner popped up. Another flash flood warning. They'd been coming in all day. Her phone began alarming, a loud, pulsing emergency alert. Nicki read the text. "Oh, shit. The bridge washed out. The town is being evacuated." How would they get out of town? "Do you have a vehicle?"

"This house will be fine. We're not in a flood zone," Harold said.

"The bridge washed out," Nicki repeated, in case he hadn't understood.

"It's happened before." Harold stood, his face transformed by purpose. "We will be fine. In fact, this is one of the only safe spots in town. Anyone who can't make it out will need somewhere to go. We'd better get ready."

"Ready for what?"

"Company." He walked to a door and opened it to reveal a walk-in pantry the size of Nicki's living room. He jerked a thumb over his shoulder. "Would you go down to the basement and grab the crate of emergency supplies? It's on the shelves under the stairs." He pulled candles and matches off a shelf. "There's a crank radio, flashlights, and batteries. After that, we'll start moving the water and food upstairs. The basement might take on water. Thanks to Clarice's emergency planning, we have plenty of food on hand."

Nicki spent the next twenty minutes moving gallons of water and crates of canned goods.

"I'm putting out the word that we're here." He bent over a laptop. "We need to fill all the bathtubs with water so toilets can be manually flushed if necessary. I have a generator, but if the pump should be struck by lightning, we could lose water."

Nicki followed orders, filling tubs and sinks and putting clean linens on beds. Bedding was stored in every closet in zippered bags labeled in a woman's handwriting. Clarice had been super organized. By the time Nicki finished and jogged down the stairs, Harold was opening the door to a cold and wet family with an equally cold and wet border collie that smelled like sheep.

She went out onto the porch. The rain was still coming down in sheets. The solid gray sky indicated the storm was not letting up anytime soon. A minivan was driving up the hill toward the house. On the other side of the hill, the river had overflowed onto the street. A couple paddled toward them in a kayak. Nicki turned to scan the town. "The whole valley is flooded. I hope everyone got out in time."

But Nicki knew many hadn't had time. Much of the town—including the main roads—was underwater. She scanned the closest blocks and saw people waiting for rescue on the roofs of houses mostly underwater. Her chest tightened, and she placed a hand over her aching heart. She couldn't imagine driving in these conditions.

Where were Aunt Liv and Sharp?

Chapter Thirty-Two

Olivia's world tumbled. The seat belt yanked her hard into the headrest. She held the dog against her chest in a death grip. Disoriented, she pressed back into it until the vehicle stabilized. It felt as if they were floating. Water sluiced off the cracked windshield. They were in the river. The SUV bobbed. Water was halfway up the doors already.

They had to get out of the vehicle before it sank. Panic clouded her brain and choked off her air. She couldn't breathe. She gasped and wheezed.

"Liv?" Lincoln said.

She couldn't answer. Couldn't force a word out of her throat. Fear was an ever-tightening noose, cutting off her voice and her air.

"Breathe," he said. "I need you. Zoe needs you. I think my collarbone is broken."

Lincoln was hurt! The dog barked.

Olivia held her breath, then let it out slowly until her vision cleared. She turned to him. His face was white, and she could see the effort he was putting into remaining calm.

"Stay calm," he said through clenched teeth.

She forced an answer out. "Too late." She clenched her hands into fists, driving her nails into her palms and using the small pain to center her. Cold water rose onto her feet. "The car is filling up!"

"I know. Are you hurt?" he asked.

She looked down but saw just a few lacerations, no obvious serious injuries. "I don't think so."

"I can't see Zoe," he said. "Is she OK?"

Olivia scanned him. He was turned at an odd angle, hanging awkwardly from the seat belt. She looked over the seat. Zoe wasn't conscious. The only thing holding her up was the seat belt. Olivia tried to unclip her own belt, but the latch was stuck. Panic and cold made her fingers numb.

"If you don't have your tool in your pocket, there's one in the glove compartment," Lincoln said, his voice strained now. "Hurry."

She felt disconnected, the situation surreal. They were going to die. She was sure of it. She felt her pockets and was almost surprised to find the multi-tool in one. She had no memory of pocketing it. She pulled it out. Her hands shook so hard that it took three tries to cut her own belt. Lincoln released his strap. He slumped in the seat, pain tightening his features. "We're not going to be able to open the doors. The water is too high."

Water sloshed over Olivia's knees. Claustrophobia threatened to paralyze her.

"Olivia!" Lincoln shouted. "I need you." The dog barked to echo his urgency.

Right.

She set the dog on his lap, crawled over the seat, and cut Zoe's belt. OK. They were all free, now what? "How do we get out?" She pressed the window button, but nothing happened.

"The windows are all cracked. Try to kick out the glass."

But the water was already halfway up the windshield. The water inside was catching up. Cold waves lapped over her thighs. She leaned back and stomped both feet on her window. Nothing happened.

She looked up. The sunroof was also cracked, and it already had a hole it in. She pulled a big metal flashlight from the glove compartment and used it to clear the glass. The water had risen to her ribs. Her legs were going numb. She trembled with cold and fear.

"Good job." Lincoln held the dog out of the water. "Don't worry about me. I can pull myself out. See if you can get Zoe out through the sunroof."

Olivia floated over the back seat. Without the seat belt holding her in place, Zoe slumped down, her face disappearing under the water. Olivia hauled her back up.

"I'll hold her up. You get out and pull her onto the roof." Lincoln set the dog on the dashboard, extended his good arm over the seat, and grabbed Zoe's jacket collar. He kept Zoe's head above the surface while Olivia went out the sunroof. On the top of the vehicle, she saw that they weren't far from the shore. But the floodwaters raged, and the current was swift. The river was sweeping them along at a frantic pace.

Olivia grabbed Zoe by the arms and pulled. When her friend's shoulders were clear, she hauled her onto the roof from under the armpits. Zoe cried out. Her eyes opened.

Olivia wasted no time explaining. "Hold on." She put Zoe's hands on the edges of the sunroof. "I have to go back in."

She reached in to grab Lincoln, but he shoved the dog at her. She put it next to Zoe and turned back to the sunroof. The vehicle was almost entirely full of water. There was no air bubble left, and Lincoln was still in there. Visions of being trapped underground—and suffocating—nearly paralyzed her.

You can't freeze! He'll die.

Olivia did the hardest thing she'd ever done in her life—she put her head and shoulders through the sunroof. Lincoln was free and floating toward her. She guided him out onto the roof just as the vehicle sank. Their heads broke the surface, and they sputtered. She didn't have time to celebrate not being dead. They had no time to recover. The bank wasn't far away, but the current was swift. They could still drown.

"I'm OK. Help Zoe." Lincoln leaned back and half floated and half backstroked with one arm. Barely keeping his head above the surface, he held one arm close to his chest. The dog was practically perched on his face and seemed to be clutching his injured shoulder.

Zoe couldn't tread water or swim with her injuries. Olivia's boots made swimming difficult. A muddy wave crashed over their heads. She swallowed a mouthful of nasty water. Zoe floundered. Leaning back, Olivia towed Zoe by the collar while her friend used her hands to help them along. Thankfully, the riverbank wasn't far away, and they managed to paddle diagonally across the current to the shore.

When Olivia's feet hit solid ground, she wanted to cry. She hauled Zoe into knee-deep water. Next to her, on his hands and knees, Lincoln spit mud. The dog ran onto the shore and shook itself.

They'd only been swept a quarter-mile downstream, though it had seemed farther. Olivia saw the red and white swirl of an emergency light approaching. The cop on the other side of the bridge must have seen them get washed into the river.

They were going to survive.

Now that they were safe, her entire body began to tremble. Her stomach churned with river water and the drop of adrenaline. She paused to gasp for air, her lungs heaving. On his knees beside her, Lincoln put a hand on her back, as if to help her.

Gasping for air, she didn't try to speak, but forced her body to move.

They dragged themselves onto the weedy ground and flopped onto their backs. Rainwater pummeled her face, but Olivia didn't care. She reached across the wet earth and took Lincoln's hand. His fingers were as cold as hers, but she felt the squeeze of his fingers and returned his silent *I love you*.

Chapter Thirty-Three

Olivia sat in a chair next to Zoe's hospital bed. She was still shivering despite the hot shower and clean scrubs the ER staff had provided her and Lincoln. His arm was immobilized in a sling that he'd need to wear for the next six weeks until his collarbone fracture healed. Next to her, he held the dog on his lap. Everyone who came into the room said the dog couldn't be there, but they were so short-staffed that no one followed up.

The break to Zoe's ankle was clean. As soon as an orthopedist was available, she would be sedated and the break set. They'd given her painkillers in her IV, and her eyes were droopy.

"Jacob and I were more than boyfriend and girlfriend. We were best friends. We were the same. Outcasts. The children of criminals. Jacob had it worse because his father and uncle Tim had dragged him into a burglary when he was sixteen. He had a juvenile record. At least my record was clean." She cleared her throat and took a sip of water from the plastic cup by the bed.

Olivia said nothing. She'd let Zoe get the story out in her own time. The water was receding, but it would be a while before the roads to Harold's house were passable. She'd called Nicki and was relieved that she was fine. There was no rush.

Zoe continued. "In the spring of my senior year, I was seventeen. Jacob had just turned eighteen. I stopped to pick him up. He didn't have a car and Harold let me borrow his. Jacob wasn't ready. I waited in the car. Evan and Tim were scary, so I never went inside. The car was old, and the air-conditioning was broken. So I had the windows down and the radio on. I didn't hear Evan sneak up to the car. It was dumb. But I was just a kid." She breathed. "He pulled me out the window. He'd been drinking. I could smell it on his breath. He forced me into the garage and closed the door."

Olivia could feel where the story was headed, and it made her sick.

"I knew he was going to rape me. I could see it in his eyes. He ripped my shirt. I was frozen at first. Paralyzed with fear. I couldn't even scream. He was twice my size, and I knew he'd already killed two people. I'd been in the house after the fatal burglary. I'd seen the stolen property and heard them discussing the two men they'd killed. So I had no illusions. Evan was going to rape me. Then he'd probably kill me. He pushed me to the floor onto a camp mattress and started to unfasten his pants. I wanted to throw up. I tried to crawl away. I can still hear him laughing at me. He was enjoying my fear, reveling in it. That was the point for him. He liked hurting people, but he also liked the power other people's fear gave him."

Olivia was transfixed. No wonder Zoe had never shared this story.

Zoe drank a little more water. "The garage was full of discarded tools. As I tried to get away, I belly-crawled over an awl. I didn't know what it was then. To me, it looked like a screwdriver with a pointed end. It didn't matter. I grabbed it, and when he came at me again, I stabbed him in the neck. The blood—" She shuddered. "It looked like I bathed in it."

She took a few seconds to regroup. "I screamed, and Jacob came down. He just stared. We didn't know what to do. The camp mattress had soaked up all of the blood. None had leaked onto the floor. We wanted to call the police, but we knew we couldn't. Jacob had a juvenile record. The police hated his family. We thought he'd be blamed for his father's death. So I backed Harold's car to the garage door. We rolled Evan up in the mattress and put him in the trunk. Then I drove out to Sparrow Lake. Jacob followed me in his father's car. We didn't even know he still had some stolen jewelry in the trunk. We put him behind the wheel, wedged his foot on the gas pedal, and released the parking brake. The car went into the lake and sank." Tears overflowed her eyes and ran down her cheeks.

Olivia handed her a tissue.

Zoe wiped her face and blew her nose. "It was me. I killed Evan Brown."

"In self-defense," Olivia said. "You could have gone to the police."

"Maybe. But at the time, Jacob's fear made sense. We were young and dumb." She sniffed. "We agreed that we could never speak of that night. When Tim came home the next day, he kept asking Jacob where his dad was. Jacob said he didn't know. Evan went out and didn't come back. Tim was suspicious. Some of the stolen jewelry was missing. He accused Jacob of taking it. He punched him a few times, but Jacob managed to get out of the house. That's when we decided that Tim was too dangerous. He was going to kill Jacob eventually. I made the call to the police saying that I'd seen a pile of jewelry at the Brown house, and that I'd heard Tim and Evan talking about someone they'd killed. These things were true. Jacob made sure the right jewelry was there for the cops to find when they came with their search warrant. I was a minor, so my name was kept out of the newspaper. But my statement is what put Tim away. In the courtroom, he mouthed, 'I will kill you.' The prosecutor promised me he'd never get out of prison. But he was wrong."

Olivia touched Zoe's hand. "I'm so sorry you had to go through that."

Zoe squeezed Olivia's fingers. "Me too. Both Tim and Evan were terrible people. They'd both beaten Jacob since he was tiny. They were violent, cruel men. And yet, Jacob was still upset that Evan was dead."

"Did he blame you?" Olivia asked.

"Oh, God, no. He knew exactly what kind of man his father was, but Evan and Tim were his only family. So, with Evan gone and Tim in jail, Jacob was all alone."

"What happened to his mother?" Olivia asked.

"He didn't remember her. She died when he was a baby, and he didn't dare ask about her, not that he ever willingly spoke to his father. Jacob was like a ghost in his house, always trying to exist but not attract any attention to himself. Attention usually took the form of a fist." She frowned. "You'll let me know when they find Tim's body, right? I need to know. I spent my whole adult life fearing him. I want it to be over."

"Of course. You'll be the first to know," Olivia promised.

"What will you tell the police?" Lincoln stroked the dog's head.

"Everything. I'm done running. I'm done hiding. I'll face whatever penalty they throw at me." Zoe looked resigned. "There will probably be consequences for dumping the body and covering up the crime."

"I know a great defense lawyer," Lincoln said.

"Morgan Dane?" Zoe asked.

"She's the best," Olivia added.

Zoe nodded. "I'm going to need the best."

"You seem . . . I don't know. OK," Olivia said.

"Having it all out in the open is a relief," Zoe said. "The secret was a substantial burden to carry, and I'm tired."

"Who sent you the *Run* text?" Lincoln asked.

"Jacob," Zoe said, her voice groggy. "I don't know why. When I went to talk to him, he was already dead. I assume he knew his uncle had been released. We were both supposed to be notified, but I didn't get anything. Maybe he did."

"Was Tim the creeper who called in to your show Saturday night?" Olivia asked.

Zoe shrugged. "I think so. I also had two strange DMs on social media."

"CRYUNCLE25 and SPARROW25?" Olivia asked. "Assuming the *uncle* referred to Tim being Jacob's uncle and the *25* was his sentence."

"That's what I thought. Sparrow is the name of the lake. It can't be a coincidence." Zoe tilted her head. "You dug deep to find me." Her eyes misted. "Thank you. You're a good friend."

"Nicki was the one who found those. But yeah. I knew you would never run out on your show. Did you mean to run out on Dylan?"

Zoe grimaced. "I'll also need a divorce lawyer. He's been cheating." She looked like she was going to cry again.

"I'm sorry," Olivia said.

"It's OK. It's not your fault. I married him."

Lincoln cleared his throat. "I have some bad news for you." He told her what he'd found in Dylan's gym locker. Then Olivia filled her in on Nicki's experience.

"Oh, my God." Zoe stared at Lincoln. "How could I not have known?"

Lincoln cocked his head. "Have you ever had any missing time?"

Zoe's mouth gaped. "Do you think he drugged *me*?"

Lincoln shrugged. "I have no idea. Dylan had GHB and a lot of women's underwear in his locker. He was in the bar when Nicki was drugged."

"What do I do about it?" Zoe's face flashed with anger. "How do I stop him?"

"You don't," Lincoln said. "In fact, is there somewhere else you can stay for a few days?"

"I was thinking about asking Harold if I can hang out with him for a while," Zoe said. "His house was a refuge for me once. Maybe it can be again."

"I'm sure he'd be fine with that." Olivia smiled. She thought Harold would be more than fine with it.

"You leave Dylan to me." The corner of Lincoln's mouth curled up. "I have a plan."

Chapter Thirty-Four

Two nights later, Olivia and Lincoln sat in the living room. Olivia nursed a glass of red wine. Lincoln, taking over-the-counter painkillers for his broken collarbone, drank tea. Across the room, Nicki had her face buried in her latest dragon romantasy book. She seemed in no rush to go back to her apartment.

Lincoln's cell phone buzzed. "It's the cops from Summerton." He answered the call and mostly listened, occasionally making noises of agreement. When he lowered the phone five minutes later, he made a strange face. "So, they found Tim's body."

Olivia exhaled. "That's a relief. I didn't see how he could have survived that fall, but he seemed invincible that night." She understood why Zoe had feared him so drastically. She pictured him stalking her in the rain and shuddered. He'd been terrifying. "I have to call Zoe."

"The police already notified her, but I'm sure she'd appreciate a call from you." Lincoln nodded. "No one has to worry about Tim anymore. His remains had been predated upon. They had to run a rapid DNA test."

"Oh." Olivia didn't know if she wanted the details.

Nicki lifted her head. "Predated? What does that mean, like hunted?"

"Not quite." Lincoln paused, then said simply, "The bear ate him."

"Huh." Nicki cocked her head for a few seconds, then said, "That seems karmic." Then she raised her book again.

Olivia took an extra-large sip of her wine.

The doorbell rang. The dog burst into an earsplitting chorus of barking and rushed for the door. Lincoln went to the door, nudging the yapping dog away with a toe.

Lance and Morgan walked in. The dog barked and growled.

"Good job, buddy. I'm scared." Lance laughed. "He's just a puppy."

"Yeah," Lincoln said. "We thought he was a chihuahua, but once we washed all the mud off him and brushed out the mats, we discovered he's just a skinny puppy. The vet said he's about three or four months old."

Morgan crouched and held out a hand. "I think he's very fierce."

The puppy seemed to approve. He sniffed her hand and sidled up for a scratch.

"He weighs like, ten pounds," Lance said.

"Eleven," Olivia corrected. "I took him to the vet today. They think he's some kind of border collie mix."

"You're keeping him?" Lance asked.

"We haven't made a decision yet, but Jacob has no relatives." Olivia shrugged. "The shelter is already full of dogs, and he's underweight."

Nicki lowered her book. "They're keeping him." She sat up straighter and focused on Lance and Morgan. "What happened?"

Lincoln led them into the living room, and they all sat.

"It was beautiful." Lance rubbed his hands together. "We followed Dylan from his apartment to the SportsCar, that little bar on Twelfth Street. Morgan went in and sat at the bar. Two eye bats was all it took to lure him in. He bought her a glass of wine, and she pretended to drink it. He was already hammered, so he didn't notice. When he went to the restroom, Morgan used one of those drink test strips, and it was positive."

Morgan frowned. "I never saw him put it in my glass. He was very slick."

Lance wrapped an arm around her. "I was at the other end of the bar, watching. I didn't see it either. But I viewed the security tapes in slow motion, and it's there. On video. The guy's a magician, but the camera doesn't lie."

"And?" Olivia asked.

"And he's going to jail." Lance's voice was almost gleeful. "The cops found the panties and powder in his gym locker." He coughed. "I might have suggested they look there."

"Fantastic!" Lincoln said. "Well done, you two."

Morgan smiled. "It felt good." Years ago, she'd been a prosecutor. "The police cleared Cody. He had nothing to do with drugging Nicki. It was all Dylan."

Nicki, who hadn't spoken a word, said, "Cody's still an asshole for leaving, but at least he's not a criminal. But why would Dylan drug me? He was hitting on someone else that night."

"Impulse," Lance said. "I talked to the detective who interviewed him. Dylan had been drinking that night, and he was angry that Zoe had left. He was also pissed off that you dumped him as a client. He took it as a rejection of sorts. He saw you across the bar. He had the GHB in his pocket. He gave it to you instead of the woman he'd been chatting up. Basically, he was baked and ragey."

"Zoe will be relieved that Dylan is in jail." Olivia had been in touch with her. Zoe would be back to Scarlet Falls to pack up her things. She and her podcast would move in with Harold for a while. They both seemed excited.

After Morgan and Lance left, Olivia turned to Nicki. "How do you feel about Dylan? He drugged you."

"Mad. Also happy he was arrested," Nicki said. "I wonder how long he's been drugging women?"

"A long time," Lincoln said.

Nicki nodded. "I think I'll be ready to go home tomorrow."

"You're welcome to stay with us for as long as you want," Olivia said.

"I know." Nicki gave her a one-arm hug. "And I appreciate it, but I'm going to pack my stuff." She tucked her book under her arm and headed down the hall.

Lincoln moved closer to Olivia on the couch. "Are you OK with her leaving tomorrow?"

"She's an adult, and I respect her decision."

He leaned over and gave her a kiss. "You know, you told her she could stay with *us*, not you."

"Did I?" Olivia hadn't realized. "You pretty much live here."

"Is that OK with you?" Lincoln asked. "Or am I overstaying my welcome?"

Olivia took a small sip of her wine. "For a while, I was worried that I only wanted you here because I was afraid to be alone, and you do make me feel safer. But I realize now that I want you here because I enjoy your company. The security is just a bonus." She kissed him. "I love having you here, and I love you."

Chapter Thirty-Five

Nicki opened her refrigerator and assessed the contents. It wasn't pretty. Olivia had driven her home and checked her whole apartment before leaving. With Dylan in jail, Nicki felt safe again, though she appreciated her aunt's thoroughness. But she hadn't thought to ask her to stop at the supermarket. She grabbed a grocery bag and headed for the door. A walk to the local store would do her good.

The sky was cold and bright, a true northeastern autumn day as she strolled two blocks to Brown's Market and grabbed fruit, milk, and a box of Frosted Flakes. She'd enjoyed staying with Aunt Liv, but it was nice to be on her own again. As much as she loved her family, she needed alone time to recharge. She detoured to the café for a Frappuccino and a breakfast sandwich. Joining the line, she eyed the guy in front of her. He was a little older than her, with short dark-brown hair and eyes the color of milk chocolate.

He stepped up to the counter and ordered a breakfast sandwich and coffee. The sound of his voice gave Nicki goose bumps. Her ears buzzed, and her vision swam. In her head she heard him say her name. *I need you to open your eyes.*

“Are you OK?” He’d turned to face her.

His words brought her back. She blinked. Her eyes focused. “Yeah, I’m fine. Thanks.” Stepping out of line, she scanned his face. “I know you.”

“You do.” His smile made her toes curl. “Let me buy you brunch.”

Chapter Thirty-Six

Late Thursday afternoon, Olivia tapped "Enter" and continued typing.

Lincoln walked into her office. "You've been typing all day. Do you still want to go to your parents' house? If you're working, we can skip it."

"No way." She ended her sentence. "It's family dinner night, and my nephew has challenged me to a backgammon game."

"Will you let him win?"

"Hell no. That's not healthy." Also, the Cruz family was ridiculously competitive. She closed her laptop, rose, and rounded her desk to plant a kiss on his lips.

He kissed her back. "You look happy."

"I am. I wrote an entire outline and the first chapter." Olivia was giddy. She hadn't been able to write in years. But the words had poured out of her all day. She'd typed so fast, her hands ached.

"I didn't know you'd decided on a case." Lincoln rubbed her arm. "Have you even been doing research?"

"I'm going to write about my own case."

"A memoir?" He looked surprised.

"Yes. I don't know why I didn't think of it before. I've always written to purge my demons." And this was one hell of a demon.

"Wow. Not what I expected." His hand slid down her arm to take her hand.

"I know it's weird, but it's my process," Olivia said. Zoe had fired Wendy and put the podcast on hold while Zoe sorted her legal issues. Olivia would write her own story, then do the interview later to promote her book. "I'm just taking things one step at a time." Considering she'd outlined the whole thing in a day, she'd finish the book in record time. She could feel it. "For once, I'm not writing on a deadline. I'm writing for me." She grabbed her jacket and purse. "Has Chewy been out?"

"Yes, and I locked him in his crate."

The border collie pup had earned his name both by being shaggy and by eating everything he could reach. Olivia spotted a ball of fur tumbleweeding down the hallway. She stooped to scoop it up and toss it in the trash. "I need to vacuum."

"Once a day is enough. Don't you think?" Lincoln asked.

"I don't know. He's pretty messy." Which was making her twitchy. So far today, she'd cleaned up fur, mud—he loved mud—an entire box of shredded tissues, and the stuffing from a destroyed throw pillow. She eyed the furball, wagging his tail from the dog crate. "He looks so innocent."

"Looks can be deceiving."

She paused by the garage door. She looked back at Lincoln, her heart warming, and realized that she didn't want him to go back to his own place. She no longer cared about feeling independent. After almost dying together, the label felt hollow and pointless. Why had she thought it was a bad thing that she slept better with him at her side? She no longer wanted to waste a moment of her life—no—of *their* life. "Since we're raising a puppy together, maybe it's time you officially moved in."

Lincoln spun her around by the shoulder. "You're ready?"

"So ready." Careful of his sling, she looped her arms around his neck.

"Even if that means Chewy and the accompanying puppy messes come with me?"

"Yes."

He wrapped his good arm around her waist. "Maybe we could skip family dinner."

"No way." Olivia laughed. "I've been challenged. If I don't show, I'll forfeit."

Lincoln rolled his eyes. "Would that be the end of the world?"

"I have a reputation to maintain."

He opened the door for her. "Rain check?"

She looked up at him, her gaze radiating heat. "Definitely rain check. I suggest a strong cup of my mother's coffee after dinner."

He was still laughing as they left the house. His sense of humor was as sexy as the rest of him. And he was more than just a boyfriend. They'd officially entered a new, more permanent phase in their relationship. They were committed, and it felt wonderful.

Definitely a rain check.

Acknowledgments

Special thanks to all my writer friends: Rayna Vause, Kendra Elliot, Leanne Sparks, Toni Anderson, Amy Gamet, and Loreth Anne White. Writing is a solitary business. I'm grateful for my virtual support system. Cheers, ladies! I love you all. As always, credit goes to my agent, Jill Marsal, for her continued unwavering support and solid career advice. My continued thanks to the entire team at Montlake, especially my acquiring editor, Anh Schluep; my developmental editor, Charlotte Herscher; and the copyeditors and proofreaders who all love Bree and her crew. As far as teams go, I am lucky to have the best.

About the Author

Photo © 2016 Jared Gruenwald Photography

Melinda Leigh is the #1 Amazon Charts and #1 *Wall Street Journal* bestselling author of *Echo Road*, the She Can series, the Midnight series, the Scarlet Falls series, the Morgan Dane series, the Bree Taggert series, the Olivia Cruz series, and numerous short stories, as well as the Rogue series novellas and the Widow's Island series novellas. Melinda has garnered numerous writing awards, earned two RITA nominations, and been an International Thriller Award nominee for Best First Novel. She also holds a second-degree black belt in Kenpo karate and has taught women's self-defense. Melinda lives in a messy house with her family and a small herd of rescue pets. For more information, visit www.melindaleigh.com.